Reader Praise for George Byron Wright's Novels

Praise for *Tillamook 1952*

"George Wright captures the attention of his readers on page one of *Tillamook 1952*. What's more, he keeps their attention until the final page is turned. This tale of personal redemption and intrigue tells of the trials faced when long dead emotions are brought back to life. Readers of *Tillamook 1952* will not be disappointed by this well crafted work of mystery and heart. I know I couldn't put it down."

> — Vinnie Kinsella, Adjunct Editing Instructor, Portland State University Publishing Program

"As with his first novel, *Baker City 1948*, George Byron Wright once again has taken a devastating historical event and expertly woven a tale of intrigue around it. *Tillamook 1952* is about one man's blazing search for the truth - in his hometown, in his class-conscious family, and deep within his own hardened heart. You won't be disappointed with this story. "

> — Jody Seay, award-winning author and host of the TV program, Back Page

"In *Tillamook 1952* George Wright tells a compelling tale of the searing scars left on our psyches and our souls when we dehumanize others be it the enemy in war or the disfigured in our daily midst. On the surface a young man embarks on a search to understand the circumstances of his uncle's death but his real quest is to free his soul from his inability to love, a legacy from his own war-scarred father. Wright tells the story with great narrative skill and careful attention to historical detail and place."

> — Barbara J. Scot, New York Times Notable Author of *A Prairie Reunion* and *The Violet Shyness of Their Eyes: Notes from Nepal*

Praise for *Baker City 1948*

"...the best [novel] I've read in a very long time. I like Wright's simplicity of style...I was able to envision each character clearly because the descriptive words were so aptly chosen. I truly loved this book and can't wait for the next one."
— Sandra Burlingame, Portland, Oregon

"I 'inhaled' *Baker City 1948!* [Wright] really captured the... matter-of-fact way a bright child observes and comments on things in the adult world. It was really terrific. The ending...was almost Steinbeck-like in its emotional effect."
— Leigh Evans, Lake Oswego, Oregon

"Through [Wright's] wonderful work...I once more returned to my youth...thank you so much for an enjoyable trip through my boyhood memories even though nothing so serious as a murder ever occurred...I REALLY liked the ending!"
— Richard Van Osdol, Salem, Oregon

"[Wright] captured the late-forties small town flavor of peoples' attitudes. The story had a *To Kill a Mockingbird* flavor to it... it's refreshing to see someone stand up for compassion."
— Paco Mitchell, Santa Fe, New Mexico

"I was so compelled to read...I just had the hardest time putting [the book] down. Wright is an amazing author! I couldn't help but feel like I was actually there."
— Cindy Hillard, Long Beach, Washington

Roseburg 1959
a novel

Books by George Byron Wright

FICTION

THE OREGON TRIO

   BAKER CITY 1948

   TILLAMOOK 1952

   ROSEBURG 1959

NONFICTION

THE NOT-FOR-PROFIT CEO:
A Survivor's Manual

BEYOND NOMINATING:
A Guide to Gaining and Sustaining
Successful Not-For-Profit Boards

Roseburg 1959
a novel

George Byron Wright

C3 Publications
Portland, Oregon
www.c3publication.com

Roseburg 1959, a novel
Copyright ©2007 by George Byron Wright.
All rights reserved.

C3 Publications
3495 NW Thurman Street
Portland, OR 97210-1283
www.c3publications.com

First Edition

Library of Congress Catalogue Number: 2007927031
ISBN10: 0-9632655-4-7
ISBN13: 978-0-9632655-4-8

CatalogingReferences: Roseburg 1959
1. Oregon-Fiction 2. Roseburg, OR-Fiction 3. Period 1959-Fiction
4. Explosions Oregon-Fiction 5. Philanthropy-Fiction 6. I. Title

Book and cover designs by Dennis Stovall, Red Sunsets, Inc.

Cover photos courtesy of Douglas County Museum of Natural &
Cultural History, Roseburg, Oregon. Interior photo of a car being
lifted courtesy of Oregon Historical Society, Portland, Oregon.
All other interior photos courtesy of Douglas County Museum of
Natural & Cultural History.

PUBLISHER'S NOTE
This manuscript is a work of fiction, but was partly inspired by
actual events. Certain liberties have been taken with regard to
names, dates, events, places and organizations. The plot is a product
of the author's imagination and characters portrayed bear absolutely
no resemblance whatever to the persons who were actually involved
in the revised true events used in this story.

Printed in the United States of America.

"As if in slow motion the sky lit up like it was the middle of the day and a large mushroom cloud proceeded to rise from the area. I never heard or felt the sounds that went with the explosion, I only saw and felt that this was very, very serious."

Wanda Nicholas, *Roseburg News-Review*
"The Blast" supplement, August 6, 1999

Dedicated
To the People of Roseburg who lived
through the Blast, August 7, 1959, and
persevered, and to the fourteen who died:

Bonnie Jean Berg, 19
OCCUPATION UNKNOWN

Harry Carmichael, 70
MONARCH CIGAR STORE EMPLOYEE

Don DeSues, 32
POLICE OFFICER

Richard Knight, 20
GAS STATION ATTENDANT

Lela Kuykendall, 41
WIFE OF BICYCLE SHOP OWNER ALVIN KUYKENDALL

Virginia Kuykendall, 3
DAUGHTER OF LELA AND ALVIN KUYKENDALL

Martin Lust, 42
COCA-COLA BOTTLING PLANT PARTNER

Eva McDonald, 60
WIFE OF ROLLIN MCDONALD

Roy McFarland, 44
ASSISTANT FIRE CHIEF

Jimmy Siles, 15
SON OF MR. AND MRS. FRED SILES

Dennis Tandy, 17
MILLWORKER

Wayne Townsend, 35
OCCUPATION UNKNOWN

William Unrath, 46
OWNER OF COCA-COLA BOTTLING PLANT

Rufus Wiggins, Jr., 29
LOGGER

Acknowledgements

First and foremost, I want to acknowledge the people of Roseburg, Oregon who on August 7, 1959 endured a cataclysmic explosion and fire at the heart of their town. I lived in Roseburg in1950–52 and so was not surprised when the town's strength of character and resolve rose to the occasion. A mere nine days after the blast, The Oregonian reported, "The city…is determined to build a new Roseburg rather than merely restore what was destroyed." These were people who set about the formidable task of reclaiming their town with can-do determination and grit and succeeded.

Many people responded generously when I asked them to assist me when I was writing this novel. Special thanks go to several persons who grew up in Roseburg and shared their remembrances of the blast: Dee Crooch, Salem, Oregon, was 18 and home from Willamette University for the summer working for the family business, Kier-Crooch Plumbing Company whose store was destroyed in the blast. Patty Nevue, Monmouth, Oregon, was age seven that year; her father was manager of Millers Department Store, which like many downtowns stores suffered broken windows and damaged merchandise. Linda (Lemos) Ornelas, Portland, Oregon, whose father was a sawyer for Roseburg Lumber Company, was 10 years old and recalled that the broken windows on downtown streets seemed as pretty glitter to her.

I so appreciated Alice Parker, Roseburg, Oregon, who served for 30 years on the Roseburg Parks Commission and was a long time Audubon volunteer. Her historical perspective and memory helped me sort out the condition of the Roseburg's Duck Pond park in 1959. I owe thanks to Ron Edwards, Parks Superintendent, City of Roseburg, and a true steward of the Roseburg's parks, who led me to Alice Parker and her bank of historical knowledge.

When I called Bill Leming, who had been Myrtle Creek's Fire Chief for 27 years, he knew exactly which La France fire truck his department had sent to assist with the fire in Roseburg—after 48 years, he still knew every detail and specification of that apparatus.

The Douglas County Museum of Natural & Cultural History archives of the blast are amazing and extensive. I want to single out museum curator, Jena Mitchell, for her assistance and in particular for scouring the photo files to locate most of the pictures featured in this book.

The Douglas County Public Library's archives of newspaper microfilm, city directories and other records of the blast were vital to establishing and confirming the footprint and demographics of Roseburg in 1959.

The Roseburg *News-Review's* comprehensive retrospective publications of the blast were invaluable, in particular the 35th Anniversary edition "The Blast" August 7, 1994 and the 40th special edition of August 6, 1999.

When I needed to pin down details about community services affected by the blast, I turned to, Daniel Michaelis Hill's thesis "Community News Media In Disaster: A Study of the Roseburg, Oregon Fire-Explosion Disaster" for the School of Journalism, University of Oregon, June 1960. His work was invaluable.

Thanks to my brother-in-law, Cameron Emmott, M.D., Hillsborough, California, for consulting on certain reproductive issues of importance to the protagonist and his wife.

The Oregon Historical Society was most responsive in providing access to its photo archives of the Roseburg blast; its photographic services department was equally helpful.

Once again special thanks go to Dennis Stovall, Director of Ooligan Press and Coordinator of the Publishing Program at Portland State University for his kind support and for using his considerable talents to create the design and format of this novel. Likewise, thanks to Vinnie Kinsella, PSU editing instructor, and his graduate editing class of spring 2007 for critiquing this novel as a class project; a great and valuable experience. Thanks also to Karen Brattain for her superb services as my copy editor.

As always, my wife Betsy for her many readings of the manuscript in its various stages and for giving me her loving support.

George Byron Wright
Portland, Oregon
August 2007

Our Motto

*To ignite human potential when all
that is lacking is a humble flame.*

**Emiline and Jonah Kaswell Armbruster Foundation
Founded May 8, 1952
Roseburg, Oregon**

PROLOGUE

Before the last floating piece of glass hit the ground in the early morning hours, Roseburg was a flash point broadcast around the world. Headlines from Los Angeles to Okinawa shouted that on August 7, 1959, in a place called Roseburg, Oregon, there had been a horrific explosion; people were dead, the town mangled. Within days, Movietone newsreels confirmed those headlines across the nation. The town that had been a town since 1852 was on its knees but unbowed. Now, instead of being known for having the largest reserve of uncut timber in the U.S. and for having the most logging employment of any county in America, Roseburg was the town that blew up. Fifty-eight percent of Douglas County's residents worked in the woods and in the mills, but the visiting curious only saw the ugly hole in the ground. On the way back to where they came from, they dodged hurtling log trucks as numerous as taxis in New York City, but they just talked of the pungency of death and destruction. Roseburg was now famous for being maimed.

The powder truck had driven innocently into town on Thursday night and parked on Pine Street in front of Gerretsen Building & Supply. Signs on all sides of its aluminum body spelled out **EXPLOSIVES** in five-inch-high letters. The bright red van carried a cocktail of dynamite and a blasting agent made up of ammonium nitrate pellets, ground walnut shells, and diesel oil; ten thousand pounds in all. But it was late; the danger-ous cargo would be delivered to the powder magazine outside of town the next morning. The driver of the truck went to the Umpqua Hotel and to bed. While he slept fitfully, the Gerretsen building caught fire, the sirens screamed, the heat grew, and his red truck exploded.

In the days following, Roseburg became the subject of offi-cial study and public preoccupation. Curiosity seekers flooded in by car, planes flew over, and the streets were crowded with those wanting to see the disaster firsthand.

With the ceaseless sound of circling aircraft overhead, an entourage soon arrived from the state capital led by Oregon's young governor in his summer-weight suit. A delegation con-sisting of the mayor, the police chief, the commander of the Na-tional Guard, and the news media trailed along with the man. They climbed over debris, inhaled the foul air, and stood above the bomb crater. They looked in, pursed their lips, and shook their heads, then said, *My oh my*. The governor encouraged people to support Roseburg's recovery. He was sincere, and ev-eryone was photographed.

1

Ross Bagby stood at the patio window of the big Cape Cod on Reservoir Avenue, his body warm and moist, wearing only red and white boxer shorts. In the quiet darkness, he had been given a start by the sudden wailing of sirens downtown and was looking with alarm down the hill into a symmetrical pattern of streetlights wavering in the humid night air. He unstuck his wide bare feet from the hardwood floor of the dining room, inched forward, and looked for something out of the ordinary. But the emergency, whatever it was, didn't make itself immediately evident and slipped away as he sipped from his tumbler of bourbon.

Ross's sleeplessness this night was due partly to being driven from his bed by the heat, but mostly he rose once again to brood over his dissatisfaction with life. *At thirty-six*, he mused, *a third of my life can be chalked up to perseverance.* The question he asked himself on similar night prowls was always the same: *What the hell am I doing here?*

He raised the glass in silent toast to that question. The bite of the whiskey had barely reached the back of his throat when the town exploded. It was 1:14 A.M. It was Friday, August 7, 1959. Roseburg, Oregon just had its guts blown to pieces.

Ross heard the enormous thud, saw the ball of fire rise and rise, and felt the shudder roll out like thunder underground, up the hill, up his legs into his groin. The ice cubes bumped around in the tumbler, and a crack sizzled from corner to corner of the big window, bottom to top, as if by a spiritual glass cutter. He stood dumbstruck in the dream, waiting for it to fade—it didn't. Instead, a mushroom cloud rose as the illuminated night sky fell back to earth and burned there. Glittering specks of glass floated down, more and more of them, reflecting the fire in their descent. The streetlights had gone out in a blink. There was another sound behind and above him that didn't fall away; it was Maybelle shrieking. He stood at the window stupefied, holding his drink and staring mouth open as she stumbled down the stairs hollering, "Oh my god! Oh my god! Ross where are you? My god, what was that? The windows…the windows exploded. There's glass everywhere."

She inched forward in the dark and stood beside her husband; he in his boxer shorts and she in her yellow nightie. Seeing the eerie glow from the fire, she held a hand up to her mouth and moaned some more. Her dark brown hair hung over her face like seaweed and hid the astonishment written there. She reached out and clutched Ross's arm.

"What has happened? Good lord in heaven." She raised a foot and looked at it. "I think I've cut myself."

"I don't know," Ross said, swallowed the last of the bourbon, and squatted down to look at her foot. "Just a scratch."

Maybelle pushed her hair back with both hands and looked at her husband. "What are you doing down here drinking in the dark?"

"An explosion," he said. "Something really big. Maybe it's the propane tanks. All I can think."

"Propane tanks?" She looked puzzled.

"Down by the train station," he said. "Liquid gas tanks. The big white ones, three or four of them. You've seen them."

She tilted her head forward and squinted. "Don't know what you're talking about, don't recall any tanks like that. Oh," she moaned again. "Mother of mercy."

"Could be them, I suppose," he went on.

"Look at that," she said in a whimper. "Do you think people were hurt…or killed?"

"Likely," he said. "It was big, whatever it was. Look at our window."

"Oh my," she said, her voice calming. "And there's glass all over upstairs. We'll have to get Mr. Salter to come out."

Just then the big pane shuddered, and the topmost section flexed out and slashed down shattering into shards and splinters.

"Damn," Ross blurted and pulled Maybelle back, turning to shield her. He looked out through the new opening. "Fire's getting bigger. God, look at that. I'm going to call the police." He came back tiptoeing gingerly and shaking his head. "Line's dead. I'm going down there, see what's what."

"Ross," Maybelle protested, "you're doing no such thing. And leave me here all alone?"

"You'll be all right," he said. "People could be hurt down there."

She stood in the frame of the open front door, wailing her angry fear after him when he left. Ted Smith, his neighbor, was coming out at the same time, wearing slippers and Levi's with his pajama top tucked into them. Ross had lurched into a pair of chinos and a tee shirt and loafers with no socks. He yelled to his neighbor to go with him and they sped off in his Chrysler, grunting their disbelief and sharing guesswork. They talked excitedly as they sped down the hill into the orange-lit darkness. Ross parked at Cass Avenue and Main Street, a couple of blocks from the fire, and they half-ran the rest of the way toward the edge of the chaos. The sights and sounds were eerie. Instead of a cacophony, there was the stomach-turning sound of the fire eating its way through buildings like a monstrous creature. A couple of blocks away stood the back-lit forms of men with hoses, some firefighters, some men who happened along or who threw themselves into the fray. In the distance, sirens wailed the intentions of other machines and other men yet to arrive.

Ross and Ted Smith held up at Cass Avenue and Rose Street, sweating, their mouths agape in amazement. Glass and bits of concrete crunched and popped beneath their feet as they moved forward, and debris drifted down, floating ash and charred splinters of wood. People were running away from and toward the conflagration. A sobbing woman ran past them in her nightgown, barefooted, her face speckled with blood where glass fragments must have cut her. A national guardsman, a rifle slung over his shoulder, had already been posted at Stephens Street; he stopped them. Ross recognized the young man as a grocery clerk from McKay's Market.

"What is it, Jim? What happened?" Ross shouted.

The man leaned forward in a uniform that hung on his bony frame like a borrowed suit and raised his voice shrilly over the noise. "Truck load of dynamite, Mr. Bagby. Blew up down at Gerretsen's Building Supply. All I know."

There was a rending of agonized timbers and a roar as a roof or a wall gave way somewhere in the center of the firestorm. The men cringed and fell back, rolled their shoulders in and ducked. Then they looked up at one another, grimaced, and shook their heads.

"Jesus!" Ted hollered, veins standing out on his neck. "Damnable mess. People dead and hurt in there?"

The national guardsman looked over his shoulder. "Yeah. Heard there are. Dead and hurt. Don't know how many. It's terrible, that's for sure."

"Anything we can do, Jim?" asked Ross, leaning close to the guardsman's ear. "I mean, shouldn't we…geez, look at that!"

Flames roared up like a Roman candle from someplace in the core of the fire. They all looked at the sight bug eyed and the young man swore. "Damn! I don't know about going down there. Just got here myself. All I know is they told me to watch this here corner and not let folks in 'cause it's so dangerous. They're trying to hold the line on the fires. Guess I can't let you go down there." His helmet slipped forward when he shook his head; he shoved it back up.

"The propane tanks," said Ted, "what about them?"

The soldier's eyes widened. "Wow, didn't think of that."

"Hope to hell someone does," Ted shouted. "They blow, be living hell."

When three boys came riding up on their bikes, the guardsman moved over to cut them off and send them away.

Ross looked back up Cass Avenue at the Pacific Building. He spent most days there in the southwest corner office on the third floor. The Roman brick was red orange now in the light from the fire. Every window opening was startled and vacant. An air conditioner teetered on a window ledge; splintered sashes sagged, clutching teeth of serrated glass. The California-Pacific neon sign had been ripped from its supports above the sidewalk. One end had dropped down, and the glass tubes that spelled out *Tank Gas Service* were shattered. Ross thought again of the propane tanks down by the tracks and shuddered.

"Think I'm going to see if I can get in back there," Ross said to Ted Smith.

"Where?"

"My office building," Ross gestured.

Ted looked toward the fire. "What difference does it make?" He turned back, his face moist; flecks of soot dotted his forehead. "What you got up there? Some papers? Electricity's out. Best you can do is fall down the stairs and bust your ass."

"Suppose you're right," said Ross.

"Yeah, what can you do in the dark, anyhow?" said his neighbor.

"Maybe we ought to help out down there." Ross stared into the fire again.

Ted waved an arm and shouted over the din. "You heard the National Guard kid. They don't want a bunch of amateurs wandering around down there, getting in the way and all."

Ross looked toward the blaze and wiped something out of an eye. "Maybe I'll go down anyway, see if I can do something. Maybe someone's house is burning."

"Suit yourself," said Ted. "I'm going to walk up the block a ways see if I can get a better look from Washington Avenue."

Ross watched him go then turned back to the fire. He was thinking about getting past the guardsman when a hand gripped his shoulder. He thought it was Ted coming back, but it was Maybelle's uncle. Neville Armbruster's reddish face looked even more florid as the flames danced in the lenses of his rimless eyeglasses and on his high gleaming forehead. He looked past Ross's shoulder and blinked at the destruction, his jaw muscles working.

"Damnation!" Neville spoke at the top of his voice. "What the hell happened? You know?"

Ross tipped his head toward the chaos. "Gerretsen's, truckload of dynamite blew."

Neville just stared. "Knew it was big. Hell of a thing. This is bad, real bad."

"Yeah," Ross said, "was thinking I ought to help with the fire. Hold a hose or something. But the National Guard won't let anyone go down there."

Neville shook his head. "Yeah, they need men that know what they're doing in there. Besides, we've got us another problem."

"What? May's okay, isn't she?" Ross asked.

"Yeah, just whimpering," Neville said. "Nelda's with her. Had a hell of a time getting across the river. But Nelda, she was worried about Maybelle. No, it's the Colonel."

"What?" Ross searched Neville's face.

"A mess, that's what," groused Neville. "He's been hurt. He's alive but unconscious."

"What…where? In the explosion?" Ross asked.

"No time to talk. Come on." Neville started off. "My car's up a block."

An old Studebaker slowed, and the driver yelled something about tanks blowing and drove off, leaving a blue haze in his wake. Neville's dark blue Cadillac already had a layer of ash on it. They jumped in, and he accelerated away driving south on Jackson.

"Where is he?" Ross leaned over in the seat and dumped something sharp out of a loafer.

"Apartment over on Mosher," Neville said.

"Neville," said Ross, "what the hell is going on? Was he hurt in the explosion?"

"Yes," Neville answered while swiveling his head, watching for errant traffic.

"Has somebody called an ambulance?" Ross plied.

Neville gripped the steering wheel and turned right onto Mosher Avenue. He didn't answer.

"Neville?"

"No, they're all tied up."

"What's going on?" Ross pressed again.

Neville slowed, looking at addresses. "He was with a woman."

Ross wiped a hand across his damp forehead and leaned fully against the seat back thankful for the tepid air that stroked his face from the open window. Colonel Gordon Butler McKenzie caught with another woman. Ross thought, *My, my,* and folded his arms. Mister imitation war hero turned into a figurehead director of the Emeline and Jonah K. Armbruster Foundation caught with his zipper down—again. Ross looked over at the grim-faced bulk of Neville Armbruster. The idea of the president and CEO of Armbruster Lumber driving smoke-filled streets to clean up after his friend and local lothario forged gave Ross a sense of satisfaction.

Neville made a U-turn and pulled up hard against the curb on Mosher in front of a tired building obligingly called the Ponderosa Arms. The funnels of light from the car's headlights shown on two women who were standing in the yard next to a big blue spruce; a blanket-covered form lay on the ground next to them.

"Jesus, this is bad," Neville said. He killed the lights and the engine and swung his big body out of the car slowly. He looked around like he was being watched, hitched up on his belt, and walked over. Ross danced along behind him then stopped and dumped something sharp from a loafer again. The two women watched as Neville kneeled down over the motionless form and lifted the sickly-green blanket. The women were speechless pillars. Neville raised an arm and held it at the wrist for a moment then let it down and pulled the blanket back up to just below the chin of the square, tanned face.

"Tell me," Neville said to the women.

The younger of the two, thin, blonde, pretty in a sad way, maybe in her late twenties but hard to tell in the dark, dropped her arms and sighed.

"He was just here visiting, Mr. Armbruster," she said. "He was just—"

"Stop!" Neville held up a hand. "I know why he was here. That's why I'm here. I want to know what happened to him. How did he get this way, and where is he hurt?"

The young woman looked over at her companion, who seemed old enough to be her mother but probably wasn't. She sniffed.

"Well," she said, "we heard them sirens, you know, guess it was a fire. Couldn't really tell 'cause we was in bed." She laughed at that then stopped, eyes wide. "I mean, what I mean is…"

The older woman raised a hand to her throat and shook her head.

"Know what you mean. Go on," said Neville.

"Well, anyway," she said, "Gordie…I mean, Colonel McKenzie went to the window. After a bit he went out to see what was going on. Before he left I said that it probably wasn't nothing and for him to come on back to…oh I don't mean…"

Neville put his hands on his hips and looked down. "Forget that. How was he hurt? We've got to get the man help. Now damn it, just tell me!"

The young woman flinched and said, "All I know is that he got into his clothes real quick like and went out. I stayed in bed." She looked down at the still form on the ground. "He wasn't gone more'n a minute before there was this big boom. It shook the place good, and that window up there, I'm on the second floor, it crashed in. I…I ran out still in my nightie and found Gor—the Colonel on the ground. Right where he is now. I couldn't get him to wake up. I kept saying his name, but he didn't come 'round. Then I found this place on the side of his head, the bloody spot. Think he got hit by something."

Neville knelt down, felt for the wound, and drew back his fingers; there was blood on them. He wiped his hand on a handkerchief and checked the pulse again. He stood and looked over at Ross. "Well, we've got to get him to medical help."

"You want me to try and call an ambulance?" The young woman was eager to help.

"Don't know if I can. Think the phones went dead after I called you."

"No!" Neville said loudly. "No, like I told you when you called, I'll take care of it. By the way, how did you know to call me?"

"He talked about things," she said. Her voice was shaky. "About people he knows, like you. You're Mr. Armbruster, ain't you?"

Neville nodded.

"Anyway, you was the first person I could think of. The line was busy for a long time before—"

"All right, all right, Miss…?"

"Oh, I'm Mona…Johnson. Pleased to meet you. I work at Lucy's Beauty Shop over on Harvard." She looked toward the older woman. "And this here's Beatrice. She's the apartment manager."

Neville tipped his head toward the manager. "Ma'am," he said. "Okay, Miss Johnson, you said? Fine. Now listen. We're taking Colonel McKenzie to the hospital." He looked over at Ross. "And we'd like to keep this a private matter. You understand?"

"Don't you worry," she said, bobbing her head. "Not a word from me, not one."

"Good, appreciate that." Neville reached into his pocket and pulled out some folded bills and put them into her hand and closed her fingers around them. "Just a little something for your trouble."

"Oh, you don't have to do that." She shook her head.

"I know, but I want to," Neville said. "Lucy's Beauty Shop, you say?"

She smiled, showing teeth; an incisor was missing. "Yeah, over on Harvard Avenue."

"Fine," Neville said. "I'm sure my wife and her friends would like to come by. Remember, not a word now."

Mona Johnson nodded, smiling a scrunched smile, and watched as Ross and Neville carefully hefted the unconscious man and aimed him through the back door of the Cadillac and laid him crosswise on the wide back seat. Beneath the ivory pale of the interior light, they tucked the pathetic green blanket around the Colonel as if he were a sleeping child. Ross looked into the expressionless face of the man he worked for and answered to every day, looked at the angular features and golf-tanned skin, and felt no pity.

2

Neville one-handed the big car and swung it away from the curb in a wide arc. He drove back the way they had come, leaping across several intersections. Neither man bothered to look again at the two women standing slack-jawed in front of the Ponderosa Arms. Above the town, the sky was angered with the fire, and more sirens cleaved the air as engines from outlying towns began to converge, un-muffled and bellowing. Neville slammed on the brakes at Stephens Street to avoid hitting a fire engine racing from the south, its warning lights agitating and siren warbling like a scream under water. The driver of the red American La France pumper, the pride of the boys from the Myrtle Creek Fire Department, laid on his horn, slung out an angry, get-out-of-the-way arm, and thundered by, trailing black exhaust and adrenaline ready to pump 750 gallons a minute on the firestorm.

"Damn," Neville said. "What a fucking disaster. Is he all right back there?"

Ross turned. Gordon McKenzie had slid onto the floor. Ross shouted for Neville to wait and got out to push and pull the sack of meal back up onto the seat. He checked for a pulse; the wrist was lifeless, but the heartbeat was that of an innocent man. Neville looked back once more then continued on across Main Street to Kane Street and drove north around the core of ruination. More people were venturing out now walking, running. Frantic, astonished, stunned, they wore the crinkled masks of people in a nightmare. Neville drove like a man who might be willing to take a life or two to save one, honking the tuned Caddy horns with quick punches and weaving by and around the startled and the angry. People shrank back as the car sped by, and Ross could hear voices raised in alarm, some spouting curse words.

"Can we get over the bridge now, do you think? You going to Mercy or Community?" Ross asked.

"Neither," Neville answered.

Ross hung on to the door armrest as Neville raced the residential streets in a desperate slalom. He jogged onto Fowler and broke out left onto Diamond Lake Boulevard, tires singing their tenuous grip on the pavement.

"What do you mean?" Ross said.

"We're going to the VA Hospital," Neville answered.

"The VA?"

Right onto Stephens. The sound of the four-barrel carburetor sucking air rose up as Neville floored the accelerator and the big car romped forward. They faced a stream of cars coming at them, people drawn to the flame—the Cadillac's headlights exposed wide eyes and gaping mouths. Ross knew how they felt, curious and fearful, certain they would see something horrible but unable to resist looking.

"It's all set up out there," said Neville, driving one-fisted. "They're expecting us. The Colonel was never in town tonight. He wasn't hurt in the explosion. There was an accident, an automobile accident."

"What the hell is this?"

"Just listen." Neville checked the rearview mirror. " It's his regular poker night at the country club. Every Thursday. Same group. Like I say, regular."

"But he wasn't at the club tonight," Ross corrected.

Neville looked over. "How thick are you? He was there, got it?"

Ross didn't speak.

"Okay," Neville continued. "So on the way home, the Colonel lost control of his car. We're bringing him in because all other emergency vehicles are tied up with the explosion and fire."

"I see," said Ross.

"I hope the hell you do," Neville said.

Ross turned silent and stared straight ahead. He had an urge to laugh, thinking of the Colonel shacked up at the Ponderosa Arms sharing bodily fluids with a hairdresser who could likely pop her chewing gum in several octaves during an orgasm.

"So you going to send Nelda there, really?" Ross asked.

"The hell you talking about?" Neville said.

"Lucy's Beauty Shop?" Ross teased.

"Don't be an ass."

"But you promised."

Neville cleared his throat and spit out the window, ignoring the sarcasm. "Lorna or Mona, whatever, Johnson will be curling hair in Tijuana this time next week if I have my way. Gordon is a jerk when it comes to his prick."

"How's Germaine?" Ross asked, thinking of the Colonel's wife.

Neville grunted. "Waiting at our place. Didn't want to come."

"What? Think she'd be in a state."

"You'd think so," Neville said. "They had dinner with us. Germaine stayed to visit while Gordon went to his *supposed* poker game. When he didn't show by midnight, we put her up in the guest room. Not the first time."

"So she's just waiting at your place," Ross said. "Unbelievable."

Neville snorted. "Yeah waiting and drinking my best Scotch. Hell, Germaine's used to this. Like I said, not the first time Gordon's been off the reservation. Just the first time he's ever got blown out of the saddle." He smiled at his own humor.

Ross chuckled reluctantly, but what was really coursing through his head were thoughts of, *What now? Where do I fit in, with his eminence out of commission?* Reviving the debate he was having with himself just before the world blew up. What can you do when your life doesn't work out? Not like you thought it would, like you imagined after casting your lot with the girl you met beneath the Willis Hall tower clock—1943, spring, Carleton College campus, Northfield, Minnesota. The one who took you in with her slow hazel eyes, her smile, and that elegant face with the high-boned cheeks and you knew you would do your life with her.

So Ross Upton Bagby, with the light brown hair and wide shoulders, the blue-eyed boy from North Platte, Nebraska, graduated with his degree in finance and came west. He came west because Maybelle Knox Armbruster had to return to the hundred valleys of the Umpqua in southwest Oregon, where her grandfather's lumber dynasty made her royalty. Royalty always came home to marry, and she did, with the blush of her college years on her cheeks and a Midwest accountant in tow.

Ross came from the prairies of the Great Plains to a place where huge stands of Douglas fir straddled the Umpqua River and reached from the Cascades to the Pacific Ocean. Where a handful of men with guts and vision, had gambled on tall trees and their own resoluteness. The losers, and there were many, were not even a footnote. The winners claimed the timbered West. And before those other Oregon lumber barons, Kenneth W. Ford and Ralph L. Smith, there was Jonah Kaswell Armbruster.

It was beneath the canopy of a pervading Armbruster influence that Ross had married the granddaughter of Jonah Armbruster. The twelve years since had slipped away with so little to show for them.

Ross shuddered at the thought and looked out over the pool-table-sized hood of the Cadillac. He wondered about the slippage, about being absorbed, losing his own dreams—whatever they had been—and ending up not liking himself much. After six months he knew that a bookkeeper from North Platte could never compete with local mythology, so he slowly blended, eased into a numbing go-along existence. He resisted at first; he truly did. He set up shop keeping books for the likes of Monte Coe Well Drilling and a handful of even smaller enterprises: Fircrest Cleaners, Rex's Rexall Drug, and Hub Laundromat; all but the well-drilling outfit were two-hour-a-month clients. He rented a small office downtown, plunked down a new ten-key Remington adding machine, and began.

Of his clients, Monte Coe, water witch and driller, was his favorite. They made an interesting pair and liked each other from the start. Maybelle wasn't impressed by Ross's collection of clients, like Coe, who worked out of a former gas station surrounded by a collection of greasy uncouth drilling equipment. Ross liked the work and the man and sitting out front after work with the crew beneath the former gas pump canopy, having a cold beer at day's end. But Maybelle's belittling wore him down. When she looked him in the eye one day and said there was a position for him at the Armbruster Foundation, he caved in and said goodbye to Monte Coe and the cleaners and the drug store and the other clients he'd gathered. It had been easy somehow to say yes to the woman he slept with—the one with the slow hazel eyes, the one who was so much an Armbruster that she gave her parents' name second place and her married name no place. He let that happen, with no resistance.

The Cadillac wallowed onto Garden Valley Boulevard, rousing Ross from his reverie. He turned to check on the Colonel. The swaddled figure remained serene. Neville drove up the long drive to the VA compound of red brick buildings and wound around behind the hospital building to a rear entrance and parked beside an ambulance. People injured from the blast were being brought in, as the town hospitals were overwhelmed. Neville motioned for Ross to stay put; he went inside. Moments later two men in white jackets came out pushing a gurney. Without saying a word, they lifted the Colonel out and rolled him away, green blanket and all. Neville spoke quietly with one of the men at the door; the man nodded, and they pushed the Colonel inside.

Neville came back to the car and sat behind the wheel. "Well," he said, letting a deep breath out. "They've got him now. Out of our hands."

"Aren't you going to find out how he is?" Ross asked.

"We'll find out tomorrow," Neville said. "He's alive. Heart's beating strong. The rest is up to the doctors. Like I said, it's all arranged. Anyway, what can we do except sit in a waiting room and stare at the walls while our wives are stewing at your house?"

"If you say so," Ross said.

"I say so." Neville draped his forearms over the steering wheel and rolled his neck. "What a night. Armageddon right here in my own town and what am I doing? Driving the back roads to protect our reputation because one of us dipped his wick with a bubble-brained hairdresser." He breathed deep and let it out. "Now let's go face the music. "

Ross hung his arm out the window and breathed in air that didn't smell like burned socks.

3

When the men came in wearing "the-deed-is-done" expressions, Maybelle and Nelda Armbruster were sitting at the kitchen table by candlelight. They popped up as if on springs. In the flickering light, their faces were a matched set of corrugated foreheads and darting eyes. They stood in their robes and wanted to know everything. Ross looked at May. Their eyes met and he toyed with a smile, but she lowered her eyelids and looked instead to her uncle. Neville deflected the women's anxiousness by walking to the back of the house. Everyone followed him as if on leashes; they stood in a clump, in the dark, and stared out through the patio window's missing upper half at the surrealistic sight of their town burning. The sound of sirens reached up to them as more engines rumbled in from elsewhere. They debated about whether the firefighters would be able to keep the fire from getting bigger.

"They won't hold it," Neville said, his voice framing inevitability. "Looks like it'll break south and those neighborhoods will be torched."

"They'll stop it," Ross disagreed. "They're knocking it down. Look how much lower the flames are on the outside edge."

"Oh, Ross," said Maybelle. "It's still burning, like Neville said."

"For crying out loud, Neville," said Nelda. "Tell us about Gordon." She looked at her husband and cinched up the belt of the pink satin robe she had donned in haste. Her face looked erased without makeup. "Is he okay? Where is he?"

Neville flicked something off his slacks and somehow managed to make the rest of them look unwashed by comparison. Ross thought the man might be on his way to a country club patio party. Neville was overweight and unfit, but he knew how to dress and make appearances—even at a firestorm.

"Took him to the VA," Neville said and glanced at Ross.

"How is he, really?" Nelda asked, facing her husband.

"The VA? Why the VA?" Maybelle asked.

"He's a veteran," Neville said. "Besides, heard Mercy took some damage and Community's full."

"So tell us what happened," Nelda insisted. "The Colonel, what happened to him?"

"He was having his nails done," Ross said.

"Damn it, Ross!" Neville heaved a sigh. "He was with someone…a woman. When everything blew up."

"What?" Maybelle looked from face to face, her eyes spread open. "Not again. That bastard! Germaine know?"

Nelda looked at her husband. "Well, she knows something happened to Gordon. She was with us when we heard the explosion. The sound had barely died, the boom you know, when the phone rang. Was some woman asking for Neville. Who was it this time?"

Neville slapped the air. "Some beautician."

Maybelle closed her eyes. "Where is she? Germaine?" she asked.

"Our place," said Nelda. "She was staying the night.

"Your place?" Maybelle said.

"Don't get me started," Nelda said. "It was the Colonel's night out, is all I'll say. Anyway, Germaine decided to wait there until we knew Gordon's condition. And we better be going, Neville. She'll want to go out and see him."

"So," Maybelle said, holding them there, "how *is* the Colonel? Will he live? And if he does, will his recovery be painful? I hope so, the cheating SOB."

Neville went over to his niece and put an arm around her shoulders. "Come on now, May." He squeezed her. "Gordon has a head wound. Evidently something from the explosion hit him. Don't know what. But his pulse was strong when we left him at the hospital."

"Of course he wasn't really there, Mazie," Ross said. "With the woman, I mean. You see, he was playing cards out at the country club with his cronies." He could feel Neville stiffen next to him, but he went on anyway. "On the way home he had an accident. Ran his car off the road into a… You never told me, Neville. Was it a tree or a telephone pole? Or don't you know yet?"

A house can empty in a hurry. Ross took his sudden isolation in stride, poured himself another bourbon, and was drawn again to look down into the burning blocks in the town. He went out onto the patio, stood with his feet planted wide and watched the flames diminish under siege from the firefighters. He watched until the whiskey was gone; then he went to the basement and showered in the metal box stall next to the laundry tub and the washer and dryer. The water was tepid due to the power being off, but the needles pecking away at the stink and sweat still felt good—he was clean but not rid of the ordeal. He took most of his showers down there; it was his space. He felt the best there. It was also where he kept his set of weights. Lifting was a practice he had begun in college, and a three years after his marriage he ordered a set of barbells and dumbbells from the York Barbell Company. The day they arrived, Maybelle watched him unpack the black iron and chided that he wasn't exactly a ninety-pound weakling and poked his belly.

He put the weights in the basement with no declaration and began to lift most days. Eventually his body began to take on proportion and size again, and even some definition, beneath the layer of softness he still couldn't seem to lose. Maybelle looked at him one night as he stood naked in their bedroom and called him brutish. For a while, he didn't expose himself to her, always wearing pajamas or a robe. But when daytime temperatures had lingered near one hundred degrees over the past week, the act of sleeping had been reduced to wearing only his shorts and lying spread eagle on damp sheets.

Maybelle had stared at him one night and mumbled something about sleeping with an ox. Angered, he had dropped to the floor and done fifty pushups.

She had reared up on an elbow. "What are you doing?"

"Pushups," he had said. "It's what all we brutes do before retiring."

Now he smiled, remembering her groan and her muttering. He opened the door to a storage closet and looked at himself in the full-length mirror he had hung there. His naked body was not displeasing to him. His chest and shoulders were coming along, pectorals and deltoids more defined. He flexed his arms and admired his growing biceps. He toweled his thinning brown hair and studied his nose that was too big, compliments of his departed mother. His face was just ordinary, except for the dimple on his chin that Maybelle had said was cute on their first date, but didn't mention anymore. At six feet, he was a couple of inches taller than Colonel McKenzie, but he knew he lacked the man's lean face—the chiseled look people admired. He smiled and thought, *But I have good teeth.*

When he went up to bed, Maybelle was lying on her back breathing heavily. He spread himself out atop the sheets and fell into a sluggish humid slumber. Neither of them slept soundly, how could they?

Some time in the night, the firefighters conquered the flames. A young fire department lieutenant suddenly found himself in command after his chief had suffered a heart attack and the assistant chief was killed instantly by the blast. He issued an order to hold a fire line at Stephens Street and Cass Avenue shortly before two o'clock that morning. The young firefighter committed every available piece of fire fighting apparatus he had. The gamble worked, and the fire was brought under control two hours later.

The town woke to a smoldering stench and a hole in the ground, a crater fifty-two feet in diameter and twenty feet deep where the two-and-a-half-ton Ford van owned by the Pacific Powder Company of Tenino, Washington, had exploded—vaporized. Nine were known dead, but others were missing, and many were injured, well over one hundred. The blast and the fire had destroyed twelve square blocks at the town's core.

After a fitful sleep of but a couple of hours, Ross awoke to find Maybelle lying beside him eyes wide open, staring at nothing. He got up and splashed cold water on his face and wet down his bed-snarled hair. He had a headache that pounded out painfully through his temples. Maybelle was still lying on her back when he came back into the bedroom.

"Was it a dream?" she asked.

He pulled a short-sleeved shirt from the closet and put it on. "No. It happened."

"Where are you going?" She scooted up in bed, drew her legs up, and hugged her knees. "I mean where is there to go?" She spoke as a child might.

"Power is back on, so I thought I'd have some toast and coffee then go downtown, see if I can get into the office." He stepped into clean chino pants, sat down, and pulled on a pair of lace-up boots figuring he would be walking through ash and debris. "After that, I'll go out to the hospital and check on Gordon. You want to go with me?" he asked.

She watched him lace his boots and blinked. "No. Absolutely not. I couldn't."

"Okay," he said. "I'll be going, then. You want toast and coffee?"

She nodded.

"I'll leave it on the counter."

‎———————————————————————————

Ross drove his green and white Chrysler Imperial down the hill, parked on Kane Street, and walked the rest of the way. At Jackson, two national guardsmen stopped him then made out a pass so he could go inside the perimeter that had been established to prevent looting and protect people from danger. It was already hot, and the town reeked of wet smoldering ash and death. Several more bodies had been found under cars and collapsed walls. People were wandering and staring and murmuring and shaking their heads. Men who had been to the war in Europe, made comparisons to the bombed-out cities they had wandered and fought through. Exhausted policemen, firefighters, shop owners, and others who were just there continued to search for the missing. On one street, a phalanx of men heaved against a burned Dodge and tipped it up to see if the body of a missing policeman was beneath it. Later, part of a body and buttons and scraps of uniform were found nearer the blast site. One man paused to pick up what he thought was a glove and was staggered when he discovered it was a hand.

Ross stood on the opposite side of Cass Street with his hands in his pockets and studied the wounded Pacific office building, the place where he spent much or most of every day. When he crossed over, glass and debris crunched beneath his boots. He peered into the dark, windowless chambers of the storefronts. Two men were standing in the savings and loan office, hands on their hips, just looking and turning in circles—at a loss for what to do. A moose head hung unperturbed on the wall in the insurance office and stared the same glass-eyed indifference it had the day before. The Broiler restaurant had open seating but not by design. Ross walked through the grit and pebbled glass, each step grinding and popping, and entered the lobby; he jumped when a voice called his name out of the gloom.

"Hey there, Mr. Bagby, some mess, huh?"

It was Charlie Beamus, the elevator operator. Beamus was a retired logger, or more accurately he was a crippled-up logger who could open and close the elevator doors and the expansion gate, advance the rheostat, and take the car up and down. That creaky elevator was his world.

"Charlie," said Ross. "Elevator working?"

"Nope. No power down here yet. Besides, Mr. Brown came down and threw off the switch at the main box. Said he'd wait until power's been restored to turn it back on. He's afraid there might be raw wires and such dangling somewheres, you know."

"I see," Ross said. "So what are you doing here?"

Beamus moved a toothpick from one side of his mouth to the other and grunted. "Couldn't stay away. Then when Mr. Brown come down, he asked me to stay on and, you know, keep an eye on things. Guess there's been some looting going on. Damned idiots. I catch any jackass trying that he'll be peeing out his navel."

Ross laughed. "You folks suffer any damage?"

"Nah. The wife and me, we live clean out the other side of Winchester. Heard it, though, and saw the fire, sky all lit up like it was."

"Okay if I go up?" Ross asked.

"Oh yeah," Beamus said. "Kinda dark, though, watch your step."

Ross felt his way up the dark stairwell to the third floor. Most of the inner glass panels, waffle-patterned panes you couldn't see through, were intact. On the second floor he heard the muffled voices of people stirring about in the land surveyor's office. The frosted glass window in the door of the Emeline and Jonah K. Armbruster Foundation office had survived. Ross used his key and stepped into the two-office suite. Calling it a suite was a misnomer. The Colonel had a large carpeted office with a resplendent desk and executive chair and sofa and bookcases; Ross had the small outer office with a surplus desk and steno chair from the lumber company.

The exterior windows were all broken out. The venetian blinds were in a tangled heap; bits and pieces and hunks of glass were spread out like an ironic jigsaw puzzle. Papers that had been on Ross's desk were scattered. His telephone, the pen and pencil set with the clock, and the framed picture of Maybelle had all been swept from his desk. Ross's favorite photograph of Jonah Armbruster hung catawampus on the wall, the picture of a lanky young woodbuck wearing high-top laced boots, holding a double-bitted axe in one hand with the tip of one blade stuck in a log. Ross stepped over broken glass and straightened the frame. The Colonel's office looked about the same, with a shank of venetian blind hanging from one corner and a chunk of window glass lying on the mahogany desktop. There was a gash in the wood, but Ross doubted that the Colonel would care any time soon.

He stood in the office and looked out through a glassless window above the alley. The acrid smell of the fire's aftermath was in the room as it was everywhere else. The August heat only made the stench deeper; it made the town and its people more permeable, magnets of the odor. From the southwest corner he couldn't see the blast site, but he could see the rolling knob of a hillside above the town, Mount Nebo, Irish green in the spring, now brown and tan and dry. The South Umpqua River flowed sluggishly along beneath the Mount Nebo Ridge next to Highway 99, its green water like a length of string, limp and meandering. Elk Island, just a patch of earth, sat mid-stream with no apparent purpose except to mark the point where the town was separated east from west. Where the bridge connected both banks, the little island split the river. *The heat has baked the hills and valleys*, Ross thought, *and now we've burned the town.* He looked again at the disorder and damage around him and wondered anew what would be expected of him with the Colonel comatose.

Then again, what did it matter? After all, he didn't much like his job of propping up the pseudo war hero. Colonel McKenzie drew his heroic fame from a minor injury in Korea, actually a wrenched knee when his Jeep ran off the road. Then he came home with a limp and evolved into a local legend with the support of his boyhood friend, Neville Armbruster. After the Colonel made a suitable number of appearances in uniform, with much fanfare, Neville appointed him the first paid director of the Armbruster Foundation.

When Ross first showed up for work, the Colonel handed him the books, shook his hand, and did even less of his job than before. The day he let Maybelle persuade him to work at the Foundation, Ross had one last beer with Monte Coe and closed his office. Someone else had to scrape *Ross Bagby, Accountant* from the door glass; he couldn't do it. That first morning, Maybelle straightened his tie, picked something off of his suit coat, and managed a restrained smile. *It's a position, Ross. Finally you have a position.* She actually said that.

Ross looked down from the third floor of the Pacific Building into the alley. A man was hustling along looking over his shoulder; Ross recognized him as the owner of a jewelry store up on Jackson. *Probably thinking of looters*, he thought. With glass bits grinding beneath his feet, Ross wandered into the Colonel's office, looked about, and considered how the jeweler felt. Somebody might be back there, behind you, someone who could change things. Change your life.

He toyed with cleaning the office but decided to do it later when he knew what he didn't know now—like how long the Colonel would be in the hospital, for starters.

4

The sun stabbed into Ross's eyes when he emerged from the dark building lobby. He instinctively ducked from the flash then raised a flattened hand above his eyes and squinted down past the post office. Overhead the sound of a small aircraft buzzed; it seemed a continual sound now as the curious and the official flew above the carnage to gawk, to photograph and document. Ross considered walking down there, into the zone, into the nucleus of the detonation; in fact, he was drawn to it. But then he thought of the Colonel and expectations that must be met. A cluster of men were staring and pointing into the blackened rubble that had been the flour mill. He watched them from a distance for a short time then turned and walked toward his obligation.

He was trudging, arms swinging, mind elsewhere, when someone called out his name. He turned his head and saw a young woman waving at him from in front of the Snappy Service Café No. 5. It was a waitress, Jill somebody. He knew only that she was a pleasure to look at and to chat with. He raised an arm in return, waited for a dump truck to rumble past, and crossed over to her. The café was intact except for missing windows and a newspaper rack that was tilted back in shock. Errant bricks littered the sidewalk, and broken glass was scattered onto the café's booths and tabletops.

"Something, huh?" she said, looking into the darkened diner. "Just awful."

"Unbelievable," Ross said.

She turned, smiling, her shoulder-length light brown hair bouncing. "It's a mess now, but we'll open Monday."

"Really?" Ross said. "What about water and electricity?"

She shrugged, her blue eyes dancing. He had been on the receiving end of her smile and bright eyes almost daily; they were part of the diner's charm. The male customers all liked Jill; she was cute, perky, and could handle their sass and dish it out if she had to.

"Sam says they promised electricity'll be back on this morning some time," she said. "And we still got water. So you can count on us being open Monday. All we'll need to do is clean up the glass and get some plywood to cover the windows. Sam says there's not a pane of glass for a hundred miles around. Besides, I got to get back to work. Need the money."

"Any damage where you live?" Ross asked.

"Well yeah, some," she said. "My apartment, over on Brockway, has broken windows just like everybody. But nothing else. Geez it was terrible, like a bomb or something. What about you? You okay?"

Ross twisted his head a bit and hooked a thumb over his shoulder toward the hill. "We lost most of our windows, but we're okay too."

"Anybody you know hurt or anything...killed?" she asked, forehead wrinkled.

He thought of the Colonel lying face up. "In the blast?" he answered carefully. "No fortunately not. Say, I'd better be going, Jill. I'll be by for a cup of coffee for sure come Monday."

"Hey, I'm holding you to that, Mr. Bagby." She smiled, showing her teeth, and Ross thought of how seldom anyone he knew smiled like that.

Germaine McKenzie was the only person with the Colonel when Ross sidled cautiously into his room. She was sitting on a straight-back metal chair next to the bed, thumbing through a frayed copy of *Redbook*. Her husband lay immobile on his back beneath unruffled white sheets. His head was wrapped in a swath of gauze, his eyes were closed, he was motionless. Germaine closed the magazine and looked at Ross, placidly, almost disinterestedly. She was tall, had black hair, a long neck, and a strong face—not ravishing, but dramatic. Mostly she had an austere demeanor and, at the moment, she was a picture of endurance.

Ross said hello and edged over to stand beside her; he patted her on the shoulder. She didn't react. He stepped closer to the bed and looked down at the tanned, lean face, the face of a man who seemed merely napping. "What do they say? About his injury?"

Germaine laid the magazine on the table beside the bed. "A piece of metal from the explosion. They removed it without any difficulty. At least that's what the surgeon said."

"Serious?" Ross asked.

She took a tube of lipstick from her purse and twisted the tip out. "Seems to be, yes. How serious I don't know. They say he's in a coma." She held up a compact mirror and spread redness on her lips. Ross watched her and noticed the familiar smell of her, the tangy sweetness of her perfume.

He looked at the inanimate form again, a white loaf with someone's head attached.

"He could be that way for quite a while or wake up in the next ten minutes," she said. "Funny, he served in two wars, came home with a scratch, and gets a piece of shrapnel in his head in downtown Roseburg."

"I'm really sorry, Germaine."

"Aren't we all?" She sighed. "Thanks, by the way, for helping Neville get him out here."

"Of course."

She put everything back into her purse. "I understand he was in an automobile accident," she said matter-of-factly. "Do you happen to know the details? Where? When?"

Ross looked at the woman. "Germaine, I..."

"Don't be alarmed, Ross," she said. "I know. It's just that no one's gotten around to telling me the fairy tale. Do you know it?"

"Part of it. Hasn't Neville told you? It's his story."

"Haven't seen him since last night," she said. "Nelda brought me out, stayed quite a long time until I kicked her out. Neville hasn't been here. Assume he's busy putting the pieces in place. You know, making the story come out right."

"You seem pretty calm," Ross said.

"You get that way when you live with the Colonel." She sat up and brushed at her dress. "A man known for two things: chasing golf balls and chasing women. Other women."

"That may be," said Neville entering the room, "but is this the place to discuss it, Germaine?"

She drew herself up and lifted her chin higher. "What better place? Right here beside this slab of a man who—"

"Not now, Germaine," Neville said. He closed the door to the room and stepped over to the bed and looked down at the Colonel. "We have more important matters to deal with. I just talked with the doctor who's treating Gordon. It is his opinion that this coma may be fairly long term."

"That's not what he told me," Germaine said. "Not more than an hour ago he said Gordon could wake up at any time."

"They have reassessed the situation," Neville said. "The penetration of the piece of shrapnel was deeper and the injury more profound than was originally thought. They've re-examined the X-rays and gotten a couple more opinions."

"The bastard," said Germaine. "He's really screwed things up this time."

At that moment the door opened with a rush, bouncing against the rubber stop on the wall, and an oval man rolled into the room, breathing heavily through his nose, face flushed, eyes dancing behind Douglas MacArthur glasses. Wendell Kribs, feet planted on a moving deck, stared at the bed before looking at the trio of faces considering his arrival.

Kribs was called Senior Vice President at the Armbruster Lumber Company, reporting only to Neville. His was a title of unknown origin and vague duties, but wherever Neville Armbruster went, Wendell Kribs was right behind him. The two had grown up together, played sports at Roseburg High and both gone to Oregon State College. Jonah Armbruster put them to work in his mills while their college degrees were still warm. They bent their soft bodies, collecting calluses and experience until Jonah thought he saw men. The day Jonah stepped down and Neville stepped in, Kribs was crouching in his friend's shadow.

Now he stood open-mouthed and apologetic. "Sorry, Neville, Germaine. Meant to be here earlier, couldn't get across the bridge," he said. "Jesus, Mary, and Joseph. How is he? What happened?"

"Alive," said Neville. "In a coma." He paused. "Gordon had a car wreck."

Kribs stared open-mouthed for a bit. "Huh? A car wreck? Really?"

"Really," Neville said.

"Gee, I just assumed he was caught in the explosion," Kribs said. "Downtown."

Neville looked at his minion dead on. "No. He ran off the road on the way back from his weekly poker game at the country club," he said. "Billy Mohr towed the car to his storage lot this morning."

"Really?" Kribs fussed again. "I thought for sure that he'd… so what now?"

"We wait," said Germaine.

Kribs ran a hand over his head and patted his thin gray-blond hair. "A coma," he said, as if he were saying the name of a car. "When's he going to come out of it?"

Neville shrugged. "Could be a while."

"Like a couple of days?" Kribs plied.

"Longer," Neville offered.

"Longer? Jesus," Kribs said. "But he'll come out of it. He'll be okay."

Neville tipped his head to one side. "Wendell, we don't know."

Kribs stared at the Colonel, looked up at Neville then back then up again. "So...what now? About the Foundation? Sorry, Germaine, I don't mean it to come out like that."

"It's okay, Kribs," she said. "You're right. Things must go on. What about it, Neville? What are you going to do while His Honor here is sleeping it off?"

"Damn it, Germaine, don't talk like that," Neville said. "He's your husband, for god's sake." Neville shook his head, went over to the window and looked out over the Veteran's Hospital compound.

A nurse came in, seemed startled at the number of people in the room, and went over to her patient. She leaned over, her white cap sitting atop tightly permed hair like a starched tiara, lifted an arm, felt for a pulse then gently thumbed an eyelid open and peered into the expressionless orb. After a few motions to freshen the undisturbed bedcovers, she exited on silent white feet.

"Frankly," Ross said as soon as they were alone again, "I don't think there's any urgency about this. I mean, it's not as if we can't just go on handling affairs as we have—until his status is confirmed."

"What about what's happened?" Germaine asked. "This damned explosion. Won't the Foundation be asked to help, to fund emergency needs?"

Neville turned from the window. "The insurance companies will cover most of that."

"What about people who weren't covered?" Germaine asked. "Houses burned. Some will be without homes."

Neville raised a hand. "Enough of that for now. I'm more concerned about making sure we take care of this." He looked again at the Colonel's inert body.

"What difference would it make if people knew that Gordon was hurt in the blast and even that he was shacking up?" said Ross. "It's not as if he's a saint."

Germaine murmured.

"What?" Kribs said. "Thought you said—"

"Wendell, never mind," Neville said. "And it does matter, Ross, you ought to know that, understand that. It makes a difference in this town what Armbrusters do—and those close to us."

"You had the car wrecked," Ross said. "Right?"

"You're trying me, Ross," Neville said. "Drop it. By the way, I want everyone to be at Jonah's at two o'clock this afternoon. We'll sort things out then."

Neville patted Germaine on the shoulder and walked out of the room without looking at the Colonel—or Ross. Kribs nodded to Germaine and trotted after the man who brought him to every party.

5

After he left the hospital, Ross drove back to town and walked into the blast site. He saw the crater where the truck had been. Others stood around the rim with him peering in; still others would come to take their places. Everyone had to see the hole. The day was hot and the smell was putrid. Ross saw the fused mass of Coca-Cola bottles from the destroyed bottling plant and knew that the owner and another had died there. Over on Stephens Street, the cinder block walls of the Kier-Crooch Plumbing building had fallen outward and the roof caved in; one wall crushed four company trucks. Al's Bike Shop on Washington Avenue was ruined. The owner and his family had lived above the shop, now the mother and a daughter were dead from countless penetrations of glass, and the father lay twisted and broken in the hospital.

The sounds of reclamation were everywhere: metallic clinks, surging engines, whumps and thumps. From block to block, groups of men lifted and heaved and grunted, grimly looking for the worst. At a destroyed apartment house on Spruce Street a coroner's team, leaned, looked, and pointed into mounds of ash contained within the ribs of the concrete foundation; they spoke in clipped sentences of the three bodies they expected to find there. Trees stood naked and skeletal, and power lines drooped from poles like day-after crepe paper. At one point

Ross bent over, hands on his knees, and closed his eyes—but he couldn't block out the smell.

There were no intact windows; every pane in every building had been shocked out of its frame and pulverized. At the junior high school, empty window frames dangled out, hanging on invisible strings like marionettes. The streets glittered with broken glass sparkling in the sunlight. On Jackson Street the shops had startled openings, windows with no glass. Mannequins still fully clothed stood on display frozen in their elegant poses. Shoes, greeting cards, men's hats—all had been released from their aquariums. At Miller's Department store the windows were blown out, but crystal glassware sat dignified and untouched in the gift department.

Ross backtracked until the trees were green again. He found his car and slid behind the wheel, rolled the window down, and rested his arm on the sill. He sat in the humid air and processed what he had seen; then he drove home. Maybelle was having a bowl of vegetable and barley soup with soda crackers and iced tea. She offered Ross some; he waved her off and went to the basement and showered, hoping the hot water would push the images of devastation away, or at least fog them over. Afterward, he didn't see the comatose figure in the hospital bed as clearly, and the stench of the blast didn't cling to his nostrils like it had. But the images of the blast sight were the same.

Maybelle chided him about taking such a long shower. He ignored her, got some iced tea from the refrigerator, and told her about the meeting at Jonah's.

"Who says?" she asked.

"Neville."

She rinsed her soup bowl. "So what's it about, this meeting?"

"Control," he said.

Laurelwood was a tight enclave of people with money. It lay across the river from the blast site, on a bluff where the river regathers itself after flowing around Elk Island. It was a carefully contained assemblage of homes, outlined by the river on its north and east sides. Mercy Hospital stood on the southeast corner; the high school blocked the southwest. There was one way in and out—Madrone Street. Ross was pleased, when it came time to buy a house, that Maybelle and he were of the same mind for once—to be far away from the Armbruster coterie for they all lived in Laurelwood. But each time he drove in on Madrone past the pristine little Laurelwood Park and on to Riverside Drive, Ross found it a pleasing place to look at. In Laurelwood, snug and privileged, were Tudors, expansive ranch houses, Craftsman bungalows, Spanish revivals, and even a Cape Cod or two. Jonah and Mercy Armbruster's house sat on the outer curve of Riverside, a Colonial revival built in the thirties. Mercy often recalls that on the day they moved into that fine house, Jonah had insisted on hanging pictures showing himself in leaner times. He never wanted to forget that he had once been poor.

Jonah Kaswell Armbruster had been his own man since he was seventeen. At an age when Ross was sleepwalking through high school, Jonah had been a woodbuck in the northern California woods, feeding fuel into the firepot of a steam donkey at the Manuel Mill. The rangy youth had logged in the Sierra Nevada in 1886, felled virgin timber on the Oregon Coast in 1888, and come to Roseburg in 1891, looking for opportunity. He found it in one Cyrus Pickering who owned a portable sawmill but had an itch to mine for gold down off the China Ditch south of Roseburg.

Jonah had gone to work for Pickering after coming from the coast. Six months later he bought Pickering's little sawmill for one horse and $102.34—all of his savings. Later that year, Jonah borrowed $50 from his father and put it down on a permanent sawmill site at Tenmile, west of Roseburg. Jonah was twenty-two. Pickering lasted two months at gold mining and left the area broke. The sprawling Armbruster Lumber Company grew from that original payment of one horse and a little over a hundred dollars.

At two o'clock that afternoon, as decreed, the Armbruster assemblage gathered at Jonah and Mercy's big house. Jonah, now frail and a shrunken remnant of the man he had been, rolled about in his wheelchair and wondered what was going on.

"Why all you people here?" he kept asking until Mercy whispered to him. "Well all right then, but why didn't somebody tell me? Can't just barge in." Mercy patted him, and he sulked.

It was the same bunch that always *barged* in. Jonah and Mercy's house had somehow become the official meeting place for all things Armbruster. Mercy loved the idea, but Jonah had never gotten used to suddenly finding people, known and unknown, wandering about his house. To Jonah's further exasperation, he was often treated as though he were senile. Being ninety made him old, not feeble-minded, he would remind those who spoke slowly and loudly to him.

Ross watched Jonah with fond amusement. When the old man saw him looking, Ross winked; Jonah just smiled and shook his head.

After Neville had endured enough chitchat, he more or less ordered everyone into the dining room, where they sat around a huge oak table. Ross held a chair for Maybelle, sat beside her and across from Wendell Kribs and his wife, Bernice, a tight-skinned woman who wore too much makeup. Kribs nodded reluctantly; Ross mimicked a smile in return.

"All right, people," Neville said, rapping a knuckle on the tabletop. "Let's do this."

He leaned back and surveyed the faces turned in his direction. Nelda sat on his right, and Maybelle's mother and father,

Anna and John Knox, were on his left. The others sat where they always did, as if by seating chart. Mercy was moving about on the periphery setting out plates with slices of her anchor-weight chocolate Bundt cake.

"We'll make this short," Neville said. "As you know, the Colonel is lying unconscious in the hospital. First the good news," he said and looked at the opposite end of the table where Germaine sat. "The Colonel's vital signs are strong, and there is optimism that he will soon come out of this damnable coma. Right, Germaine?"

"So they say," she said and ran a forefinger around the edge of her open mouth to redistribute her lip color. "Yes," she added when Neville seemed to want more, "Gordon is doing as well as can be expected."

"Oh, Germaine, I'm so sorry." Anna Knox spoke with a quaver in her voice. "It's so sad. I'm just heartbroken for you…I can't believe it." When Anna began to cry, Maybelle reached out and patted her mother on the arm. Anna closed her eyes and squeezed out big tears that ran down her face. Side by side, mother and daughter bore no resemblance; Anna's fair skin, light brown hair, and smallness set her apart from her daughter.

Neville smiled tolerantly at his sister. "Yes, Germaine, our prayers are with you both," he said. "Now, let's move on. We all know what happened in town, so I won't say more except to note sadly that a number of lives have been lost along with major destruction of property. It will take months to turn things around. Fortunately, all Armbruster holdings are unscathed. The ship of state is intact. The only purpose for this meeting is to decide how to keep the Foundation operational while the Colonel is…is unavailable."

"Where's Emeline?" Jonah's voice suddenly erupted. "She's on the board."

Emeline Armbruster was Jonah's only sibling. He treasured his sister above all others. While he was crashing about in the woods, Emeline attended teachers' college in California and taught primary school until the day Jonah asked her to come run the office for the J. Armbruster Sawmill. They worked together, lived together, and built the business together. It caused a minor scandal when people learned they weren't man and wife; the treatment they received bordered on shunning until Jonah began to scout marriageable young women.

Soon thereafter, Jonah went forth to court Josephine Brownlee, the daughter of Hiram Brownlee, owner of the Douglas Hotel and Emporium. Mr. Brownlee soundly rejected Jonah's overtures, saying, *I would not sully my daughter's reputation by associating with you, sir.* Jonah flew into a rage. Emeline calmed her brother, told him not to mind—that they would never do business with Mr. Brownlee again.

Thus began Jonah's courtship of Mercy Gottcher, daughter of Randolph Gottcher, the Baptist minister, who had no compunction against the man who had one of the fastest-growing companies in the county. The reverend readily gave his blessing for the union, and on New Year's Eve, 1900, Mercy and Jonah were married in his church. Jonah was thirty; Mercy was nineteen. As soon as his worth allowed, Jonah built the Armbruster Hotel, ran Hiram Brownlee out of business, then sold off the property. Jonah was compassionate but never endured those who belittled him or his family.

"Why isn't Emeline here?" Jonah asked his son again.

Neville's tone was indulgent. "Dad, Emeline never comes to meetings."

"Did you call her?"

"Seemed no point."

"Should've called her." The old man thumped his forearms on the wheelchair armrests. "Next time you call her, Neville."

Neville hesitated then unveiled a smile. "Okay, Dad. She'll tell me not to bother, but I'll do it anyway."

"She's on the board," Jonah repeated.

Neville's eyelids fluttered, and his jaw muscles flexed. "All right. Now, with Gordon out for an indeterminate period, we need to assure that the business affairs of the Foundation go on smoothly."

Ross probed the piece of dense cake in front of him and hid his amusement over how off-handedly the affairs of the Armbruster Foundation were managed. It was no secret that Neville considered the Foundation nothing more than an Armbruster hobby. But Ross also knew that the man had a fixation on protocol and appearances. Anything with the name Armbruster on it had to retain a certain dignity, carry a badge of importance—from a railroad car of lumber with its green ALC emblem stamped on it, to the public image of the Armbruster Foundation. Regardless of what Neville actually thought of the Foundation, he knew it was held in high esteem in the community.

The Foundation existed because Jonah was a man who never forgot what it was like to be looking for your next meal and a place to bed down when you were wet and cold. He had been amazed at the accumulation of his wealth and not a little embarrassed by it.

He had also witnessed his children growing up living lives of privilege. And he knew that one day he would be old and no longer in control of his own company, his mind, or even his body. So he had planned it all out with Emeline and Mercy. The banker who helped Jonah set up the Foundation once told Ross that in the spring of 1952, the year the Foundation was formed, Jonah had looked at an accounting of his worth and shaken his head.

"Isn't decent to have all this," he told the banker. "Body's wearing out. I'm eighty-three. Could be I'll die before this year's out, and then what? Have my kids pissing all over themselves about who's going to get what they'll be practically handed? Damned if I will." He squinted at the banker. "So I've been looking into things. Going to set up one of those benevolent foundations. A lumberman I know up in Washington State has one, told me all about it, and I'm going to do it."

Ross remembered that the banker had leaned toward him and said, "Darned if the old man didn't take a big scoop out of his assets right then and there. Had all of the legal work done by some lawyer in Portland without a soul knowing. Set up a new tax-exempt corporation devoted to philanthropy. Had it printed out just how he wanted it named: *The Emeline and Jonah Kaswell Armbruster Foundation.* I tell you, Ross," the banker had said, "you don't move that many dollars in one lump every day. Never saw so many zeroes."

The Bundt cake was dry and the consistency of an exhumed mummy. Ross was slogging through another bite of it when his life changed.

"So," Neville said out of a quiet lull, "while we wait for the Colonel's condition to improve, I think it's best if Ross assumes the duties of director of the Foundation."

Ross felt a clump of compressed chocolate stop at the top of his throat. He swallowed hard twice before the mass agreed to move on down. His watering eyes were on Neville, and Neville was looking at him.

"Temporarily, of course," Neville added. "Just to keep things moving."

The sound from Kribs was like the squeal of a baby's rubber toy under a pillow. His face inflated and grew crimson and he coughed out the word *actually*.

"Actually, Neville," Kribs huffed. "I've been thinking of how I might be of assistance. And short-term, at least, I'm available to step in…fill in for the Colonel."

Neville moved his head side to side. "No," he said. "I need you right where you are, Wendell."

"But really," Kribs said, "I could, Neville, really. Besides, no need to have Ross here carry the whole load, now, is there?"

"Wendell, no," Neville insisted. "Let's face it, the Foundation doesn't take a genius to run it, now, does it?"

Ross felt Maybelle's hand grasp his thigh and squeeze, signaling him to just accept the slight. But Ross found Neville's assertion hilarious. He couldn't keep from chuckling; he held it in, but his upper body was moving in time with his internal mirth. When he looked at Neville, his smile turned into a wide grin, and once again Maybelle squeezed his leg.

Neville's eyelids lowered by half then rose. The president of Armbruster Lumber was in no mood for levity. "What I mean," he said slowly, "is that at the moment we're concerned with appearances. There will be a short article in today's paper about Gordon's...the Colonel's accident. When that happens, there may be questions about how the Armbruster Foundation will function. *Armbruster.* Got that? It's not just about the Foundation. It is about everything Armbruster. And everything Armbruster must be sound, strong, impervious. Our image, folks."

Neville called for a vote of the board, eyeballed people until he got *ayes* from every member of the board, and plopped an open palm on the table. "That makes it official, then."

Maybelle patted Ross on the thigh again but didn't look at him. He poked at a lump of cake with his fork and wasn't sure if he wanted to laugh or run screaming from the room and catch a ride out of town.

"More cake anyone?" Mercy was back with her silver serving spatula.

That was it. Ross choked out a laugh. Maybelle was staring at him as if he had something hanging from his nose, and every other face turned in his direction, unsmiling. In his gut he felt the gross convulsion of a guffaw that wanted out. He bent forward and breathed in, sounding like the sucking of a bathtub drain. He swabbed a napkin at the tears clouding his eyes and managed to quell another outburst with humming deep breaths. He drank from his water glass and set it down gently.

The room was silent. Jonah's was the only face smiling.

"I'm sorry," he said and held rein on another chuckle.

"Did I miss something?" Neville asked.

Ross looked toward Neville. "No, sorry. I will do my best during this interval." He looked at Germaine. "Until the Colonel is back with us. And may that be soon, Germaine."

She created a smile out of nothing.

"I'm sure you'll do fine, Ross," said Neville. "But really, all I need you to do is keep things going. No bursts of creativity, please. The director thing, the title and all, is so people will have a sense that the Foundation is still on track. You won't be representing us at the Chamber or on any of the committees or state commissions the Colonel is on." He saw Ross's expression. "No need to get you involved in those responsibilities short-term. As president of the board it will seem more natural if I attend those things. I'm on the Chamber board already...as you know."

Ross drove away from Laurelwood knowing.

6

Maybelle didn't speak in the car until they crossed the bridge onto Oak Avenue. The odor from the smoldering buildings and wet ash and incinerated vehicles drifted into the car's open windows. Maybelle snatched a handkerchief from her purse, held it to her nose, and waved her hand for Ross to speed up.

"People working," Ross said. "Need to be careful."

"Well, keep driving," she urged. "Ugh."

He braked at Pine Street behind an old pickup where a crew from the California-Oregon Power Company was moving a damaged power pole. Ross and Maybelle sat watching the scene as if it were a newsreel; neither spoke as they waited for a flagman to let them pass. She kept the handkerchief pressed against her nose until they were nearly home.

There was a flatbed Armbruster Lumber Company truck sitting in front of their house when they returned. Two men from the mill were putting sheets of plywood over the broken-out window openings. Ross knew that Neville had sent them. Maybelle thought it was so sweet of her uncle, glad that someone was actually doing something. Ross stood in the driveway, hands in his pockets, and watched the two wide-shouldered young men cover the upstairs dormer windows, feeling once again like a spectator of his own life.

When he tired of watching his work being done by others, he went in to tell Maybelle that he'd decided to go down to the

Foundation office. He found her in the kitchen getting some iced tea out of the refrigerator. He paused in the arched doorway from the dining room and watched her. The hair was shorter, but still dark brown, shiny and soft, and her finely shaped nose and long neck were the same; he loved the hollow at her throat and how her neck curved out onto her shoulders. In their newness, way back, there had been a stretch when they had been intoxicated with each other. They were juniors when they met at Carleton, when her hair was longer and she had smiled more. She had a killer smile—when it came from inside.

He had been outside Willis Hall talking with a young woman he was dating, the woman with whom he had even discussed a nebulous future: Carolyn Hansen. He remembered her clearly because they had enjoyed one another and were becoming more serious about their relationship. One moment he was saying something to Carolyn, smiling into her fair-skinned face, and then there was Maybelle, smiling over Carolyn's shoulder. He had stopped talking, and Maybelle moved right in and began an animated conversation with Carolyn about some class they both attended. Ross stood grinning and admiring this lush animal, her long elegant face, her high cheekbones and hazel eyes that radiated amusement. She apologized for her interruption, winked at Ross, and was gone. The next time he saw her was at *The Cave*, the college-owned pub beneath Evans Hall. They were part of an amorphous group of imbibers reveling because midterms were over. Ross caught her eye, raised a glass, and waved; she did the same and ended up joining him and Carolyn. He left with Maybelle and now often wondered whatever happened to Carolyn Hansen that night. Had he just abandoned her? He had.

He walked up behind Maybelle at the sink and put his arms around her and playfully cupped a breast in each hand. She set the pitcher of iced tea down with a clunk on the tile counter and pushed his hands away.

"Must you do that?" she said. "So predictable."

"You used to like it," he teased.

"No I didn't," she said.

Pressed up against her buttocks, he felt himself begin to rouse; so did she. She turned and stepped away and looked at him oddly for a moment before smiling. It wasn't a nice smile, not from inside, but it was familiar.

"Maybe if something ever came of it," she said.

"Meaning?"

"Mercy asked me again."

"Maybe if we did it more than once a month."

"You think that's it, Ross?"

He put a hand on the counter and leaned on a locked arm. "We've been over this. There's nothing wrong with either of us."

"As far as we know," she said. "That's what Doctor Jackson keeps saying: *As far as we know.*"

He sighed took a glass from the cupboard and filled it from the tap. He took a deep drink and said, "I suppose you're going to make the same suggestion."

"Why do you resist? Submit a sample," she said. "Get it tested, and we'll know for sure. You afraid? What is it, a masculinity thing?"

"What about you?" he asked.

"Ross," she chided, "I'm healthy, have a great lineage."

"So I give up a spurt of sperm," he said. "Somebody in a white coat will do a wiggler count and tell me if I'm a real guy or not. Is that what you want?"

She dropped her tone. "It's a start. Yes. Have to start someplace if we ever want children."

"There's the sixty-four dollar question," he said. "Have we decided?"

"Can't decide until we find out for sure if things are working," she said. "Can we?"

"Okay. If I do this and find out that I have a low count or whatever, then what?"

"Well, then we'll know, I guess."

"Then you'll whisper to Mercy that there will be no grandchildren from you, that Neville's the only side of the family where the men are potent," he said. "Too bad your fertile cousin Joyce and big Bob the stud live in Seattle with their munchkins. I can imagine the family grapevine announcement: *Isn't it too bad about Ross? Low sperm count, you know. Poor Maybelle.*"

She chewed on her lip.

"On the other hand, May," he said, "what if my sperm count could launch a thousand babies from a thousand women? Then what? Do you tell everyone you're married to super sperm? Or would you agree to a test of whatever kind they'd give you, count your eggs or whatever?"

Maybelle folded her arms but had nothing to say.

Ross took another long drink and set the glass down. "You know what? Do we even want to bring a child into this relationship?"

"Meaning what?" she asked.

"Mazie," he said, "what do we have to offer a child? Us? It takes more than a big house."

She picked the dishrag out of the sink and swabbed the counter quietly. "We could be parents if we tried, if you really tried."

"But you're married to the village idiot, aren't you?" he said. "I'd make great father material wouldn't I?"

"Don't be an ass," she said.

"Well," he laughed, "you heard it today. Anybody with a low IQ can run the Foundation, so Ross is just the guy."

"Neville didn't mean it that way," she said. "But I must say you sure played the buffoon."

"Why? Because I laughed? Jonah enjoyed it," he said.

"My grandfather is practically senile," she said.

"Damned if he is," Ross said. "That old man knows exactly what's going on."

"Going on about Aunt Emy like that. He's in another world half the time. I love him, but finding your outburst funny means nothing."

"Your granddad and Miss Emeline started this empire you enjoy. They started it with gumption and a handful of spit."

"Hey," she said, "don't lecture me about my family."

Ross finished his glass of water and walked to the kitchen doorway. The plywood sheeting covering the windows darkened the house. "Well, you're safe now—all boarded up. Uncle Neville saw to that. So I'm going down to the office and begin my low-intelligence cleanup. You know, work at that position I have, May, that *real* position you are so proud of."

Instead he drove out Jackson to Diamond Lake Boulevard and found Monte Coe tinkering on one of his drilling rigs with a gangly kid who bore a receding chin and an immense Adam's apple; Ross knew him as Ken Roy. Monte willingly handed the kid his socket wrench, wiped the grease from his baseball-mitt hands, and led Ross into the metal oven of the former Golden West filling station for a beer. He pried the caps off two cold ones; and they went out under the canopy, settled into a couple of derelict overstuffed armchairs, and looked out at the road through the space where two gas pumps used to sit.

"Damn, I'm glad you came along," said Monte.

"Good to see you too," Ross echoed.

"Hell, glad anybody came along. Dad-blamed machine." He held up a fist, brandishing three skinned knuckles. "How the hell are you, anyway? Ain't that some mess in town there? Jesus, like a war zone. Hey, you know that Shell Station, on Stephens right there at Oak? Next to the Coke plant? Well, buddy a mine was a neighbor of the kid working there that night. Richard Knight. Killed him like that." When he snapped a thumb and middle finger it sounded like a bone breaking. "He was holding a fire hose when that truck went up. Kaboom! Him and two other guys, just gone. Never knew. Kid was only twenty." He took a long pull on his bottle and sighed. "Damn shame."

"Uh-huh. Enough of that to go around," Ross said and looked out onto the highway as a truckload of logs roared by, coming down from up above Glide. The letters ALC were emblazoned in forest green on the truck cab's yellow door.

Monte stretched his legs out and wiped a dribble of beer off his chin. "Now, the hell you doing out here late on a Saturday afternoon, looking like you need to be burped? Your wife's time of the month?"

"Only place I know where I can get a free beer," Ross said. "Besides, I need a break from the stink and mess in town."

Monte emptied his bottle with one last chug. "I been in town, seen the ruination. That building you're in, it's right down close. Damaged much?"

"Windows blown out, air conditioner dumped in the alley, heck of a mess, but better off than a lot of others." Ross looked at the sweating bottle. "Our big news is that the director of the Foundation was hurt, Gordon McKenzie."

"You mean the Colonel," Monte said.

"The very same," Ross said. "He's lying in a bed at the VA."

"Caught in the explosion was he?" Monte asked.

Ross hesitated. "Well…"

"Hang on, sounds like this is worth at least a couple more beers," Monte said. "Don't move, right back." He came back with two more long-necked Pabsts, handed one to Ross, and dropped back into the chair. "Now, where was you?"

"Was about to say that the Colonel was in a car wreck," Ross said. "He's in a coma."

"Car wreck? Bullshit," Monte growled. "That may be true, but ain't why you're out here drinking my beer." Monte leaned forward. "I recall a night we was working late, pushing numbers and getting pie-eyed. You're nodding. We shot the shit until at least two in the morning. Ha! Remember, I told you about me and Janey Cunningham, in her daddy's tool shed? First screwing either of us had ever done. Didn't know a thing, but gad, we had fun. And you, what was that little gal's name?"

Ross snorted. "Donna. Donna Perkins. We wrestled around in her folk's basement one summer afternoon. Went down there because it was cool."

They laughed and tipped their bottles up.

"Yeah, I know stuff," Monte gloated. "You was stinko that night, told me plenty. Must be something, trying to swim in the Armbruster pond. Specially if you're not the biggest bug skimmin' the water." Monte chuckled and leaned back. "So tell me," he said and closed his eyes, "what it is. Why you're wasting my time. Tell me."

Ross sipped from the bottle and watched the traffic out on the highway some more then set the bottle down beside the chair and massaged his face. "I don't know…nothing important."

"Whatever. Makes me no never mind." Monte sat like a greasy Santa Claus, eyes still closed.

"They gave me the Colonel's job," Ross said finally. "Until he comes around, anyway."

"Sounds like a big deal," Monte said. "Worth another beer?"

"Was told it doesn't take a genius to run the Foundation. That worth a beer?"

"You bet," Monte said and shoved up out of his chair.

Ross took a long swallow from the next bottle and licked at the foam on his lips and swallowed back a burst of yeast.

"So you're temporary head cheese," Monte said, "but they told you it don't take a full load of marbles to do the job. You must feel special."

Ross raised the bottle and laughed around the lip before drinking. "I do."

"You came out here to brag or fart?"

"Fart. Definitely."

Monte rolled his head around on the back of the stained chair cushion, laid his hands on his stomach, and laced his fingers. "I'm all ears, 'cept for my big butt, of course."

"It's a lie," Ross said.

"You're not the head cheese?"

"The Colonel, he wasn't hurt in a car wreck." Ross raised his arms over his head, locked fingers, and stretched. "That's my fart."

"What the hell's going on?" Monte asked, raising his head.

"He was with a woman other than the one he's licensed to," Ross said. "Caught some shrapnel with his head in the blast, leaving others to clean up after him. Everyone keeps their mouths shut, and we hunker down until the Colonel rouses or passes."

Monte pulled a handkerchief out of his back pocket and blew his nose hard, swiped at his nostrils, and stuffed the foul rag back. "Okay, you've farted. Feel better?"

"Just needed to get inside my head," Ross said, "clear out the crap. Of course, you can't tell anyone about this."

"Now who the hell do I know to tell or who'd give a shit?" Monte stood and flexed his shoulders. "Get on out of here and go kick some Armbruster ass."

Ross thumped Monte Coe on a shoulder that felt like a bag of pig iron. "Thanks for the brews and for listening."

"I'll listen to you fart any old time if there's a beer in it." Monte waved and walked away, back to knuckle-busting with Ken Roy.

|||||||||||||||||||||||||||||||||||||||||||||||||||||||||||||||||||||||||||

Maybelle was on the phone with her mother when Ross walked in. She gave him a finger roll wave and kept talking, something about Germaine McKenzie deciding not to go see her husband again until he came out of his coma.

"Well, in a way I can't blame her," Maybelle said. "I mean, if Ross did that?" She winked at him.

He walked away before hearing what his punishment would be and went out onto the patio, sat on one of the chaise lounges and looked down the hill. A haze hung over the center of town, and there were dark plumes of smoke here and there where buildings were still smoldering. He could see the post office and the Pacific Building on Cass Avenue. Beyond that, a dozen or so blocks were leveled. There would be no bottles of Coca-Cola filled come Monday, no builders getting lumber from Gerretsen's, no curlicue cones from the Dairy Queen. He had a visual image of the Foundation office and the mopping up to be done, but mostly he thought about being the acting director under Neville's rules of procedure.

Maybelle came looking for him and said they would be having Salisbury steak. Dinner would be ready in about thirty minutes. He mumbled okay and continued to stare down into the ravaged center of the town and smell the odor that had already become expected. They ate outside on the patio table, chewing in silence. When their eyes met, both found something to look at beyond the other. The evening temperature held warm again. With most of the windows boarded up, their bedroom was close and uncomfortably muggy. They retired around ten o'clock and lay on the bed with no sheet over them, listening to the hum and occasional tick of the oscillating Montgomery Ward's fan and waiting for each pass of the mechanical breeze to bless their clammy bodies. Ross was drifting off when he felt her hand on his chest.

"Ooh, you're sticky," she said.

"Surprised?"

"No." She began running her fingers through his damp, matted chest hair.

Ross opened his eyes and stared up into the dark. He knew the signal, but he didn't know why. There was usually a certain rhythm, a preliminary playfulness before bedtime—signs that gave him permission. He reached up to where her hand was plying his chest hair and took hold of it. She stopped stroking and then rolled up on her side next to him. She wasn't wearing a nightgown.

"What's this?" he asked.

"What do you think?" Her voice was flirtatious, a rarely used tone.

"What is it, Arbor Day or something?" he asked.

She made a humming sound and pulled his hand over onto her. Her skin was moist. He could imagine what actual contact would feel like—a slithering glue-like engagement; still, he was becoming aroused. She brought her head in close and kissed him on the mouth, her breasts pushing against him; he responded in spite of his doubts. When it was over they both lay on their backs, flushed and glistening. He was rubbing at the wetness of his chest when she tossed a towel on him.

"You came prepared," he said, wiping his body.

"Girl has to think of these things."

He wiped his face and down his arms. "I get it," he said, drying his stomach.

"Get what?" she asked.

"A little incentive for the animal in your life. This is about getting me to offer up a sample of my fluids."

She kept wiping down her body and didn't respond.

"That's it, isn't it?"

"Well, why can't you?"

"Maybe I will," he said. "But not because you think I'll do it for a roll in the sheets."

He went into the bathroom and swabbed with a damp washcloth. Maybelle was lying with her back to him; she didn't react when he got back into bed.

On Sunday, Ross and Maybelle joined the Armbruster family at St. George Episcopal Church, as was their ritual. Sat in the same pew, the one directly behind Jonah and Mercy and Neville and Nelda, next to John and Anna. Ross and Maybelle didn't speak that morning. They didn't argue or act out either; it was just one of those times when it was best to let the matter of fertility wane in its own time. They dressed, had orange juice, toast, and coffee, and drove down the hill to do their weekly spiritual genuflection. Ross had one thing on his mind, and it wasn't his sperm. The sermon, predictably about surviving calamity, didn't make it past Ross's earwax because he was staring at the back of Neville's head and fantasizing what it would feel like to smack it with a hymnal.

7

When Ross came up from the basement after exercising that next morning, Maybelle was dressed to go out, sitting in front of the vanity fixing her hair, brushing and turning her head side to side. Over her left shoulder she told him with some formality that the chairman of Red Cross Disaster Relief had just called a meeting, so he would have to get his own breakfast. Maybelle served on the committee of volunteers responsible for collecting clothing, food, and other necessities in time of disaster; not surprisingly, an emergency call to arms had been given. Maybelle was a busy person with her civic and social obligations: the Red Cross, the United Fund board, some church committee on missions, and chair of the women's annual golf tournament at the country club. Being Jonah Armbruster's granddaughter put her name at the top of many lists. Ross was Mr. Maybelle Armbruster at most functions.

"They're releasing people from the hospital in droves," she said, looking at her reflection in the mirror. "Some of them don't have a stitch to their name or a pot of beans, for that matter." She spread lipstick on, wiped off the excess, then daubed some perfume behind each ear and in the hollow of her throat. "By the way," she said with Ross watching her, always fascinated by feminine embellishment, "I went through your closet and pulled out some clothes to donate. Mostly awful stuff you don't wear anymore. There, on the bed. Any of it you want to save, fine, but I think it's all eligible for the donation box. Besides, people are in need."

Ross sorted through the pile of pants and shirts and discovered what she found distasteful. He held up a pale green cotton shirt, a favorite of his. She screwed up her face.

"Oh, not that old thing, it's hideous. You need some new shirts, anyway." She looked at the petite gold watch on her wrist. "Now, help me get all of this into my car." She gave one more pat to her hair and gathered up her purse and a couple of blouses. Ross flopped along in his bathrobe and slippers, feeling conspicuous carrying the mounded armload of mostly his sacrificial garb, and stuffed the load into the back seat of her Olds 88. He held onto the green shirt in a moment of rebellion. In the wake of her exhaust, he wished he'd kept a pretty decent pair of slacks that had just been confiscated for being tatty.

He dressed sparingly for yet another excessively warm day, drove down the hill, parked two blocks away, and walked into the zone again. He showed his pass to the national guardsman on duty and proceeded on to the Snappy Service Café where a hand-lettered butcher-paper sign declared they were open.

The instant he stepped through the door, agreeable aromas overcame the biting odors from the street. The eatery was busy feeding workers, storeowners and others who made it past the sentries. Ross took the only empty stool at the counter and leaned on his elbows. Sam, the owner, a short, wiry man who never left his grill, waved at Ross. He was wielding an oversized spatula, plowing through a hump of hash browns, deftly flipping buttermilk cakes, and pressing down on curling strips of bacon. Eggs bubbled on the grill; the normalcy felt comfortable and satisfying.

Ross ducked his chin, snuck a look over his shoulder, and caught the eye of a couple of men he knew only in passing. He tipped his head. They responded in kind, but something was missing. Most of the café talk was murmured and low. Heads were down; there was none of the usual banter. Threads of conversation hung and floated like smoke; the mood was almost reverential. When the word *looters* spiked up from the talk, Ross looked down the counter to see who had said it. The jeweler he had seen in the alley behind the Pacific Building two days before was talking to a fellow retailer. The man sipped at his coffee and shook his head; there was disappointment on his face. He never expected such behavior in his town.

"Coffee there, Mr. Bagby?"

Ross looked up into the only happy face. "Hey, Jill. Sure need my caffeine."

"I told you we'd be open." She leaned over the counter, smelling of soap, and whispered, "We're the only café open downtown. No, we are. And we've been biz-ee, let me tell you."

"Place looks good." Ross looked around.

She slid the creamer and sugar jar toward him and watched him doctor his coffee.

"Let me tell you," she said, her eyes wide, "Sam and his wife. You know Ruth. Anyway, them and Blanche and me, we worked the whole darn weekend. There was glass, glass, and more glass. I mean itsy-bitsy pieces of glass. Everywhere. We must have swept the floor up by the windows a dozen times."

"And here you are," Ross said. "You did it."

"Yeah, we did, didn't we?" She titled her head and grinned. "You having breakfast or just coffee?"

"Breakfast. On my own this morning," he said. "Wife's at a Red Cross meeting, emergency clothing, food and what not."

"Geez, those poor people that lost their houses and all. Wouldn't that be terrible? No place to live, no clothes, and them that lost family…" She raised a hand to her mouth, and her eyes filled with tears. "I'm sorry," she said, plucked a napkin from the holder, and dabbed at her eyes.

Ross lifted his coffee mug.

She tried to laugh. "Look at me." She wiped her nose. "So you didn't want to eat your own cooking?"

"More like I wasn't in the mood to eat alone," he said. "Need to hear people."

She nodded and took his order for two eggs over easy, link sausage, and one pancake. When his food came, he ate without interruption, except for an attorney from his office building who stopped on his way out and asked how much damage the Foundation had suffered. They chatted aimlessly about the explosion until someone else buttonholed the man to share another sad story. Ross left Jill a nice tip then went back out into the brightness. The smell hit him again; more bodies had been found, but the town soldiered on.

—————————————————————

Ross found the door to the Foundation office ajar. He stepped in. Kribs was inside looking out a rear window. "Morning," Ross said, masking his displeasure at finding the man there.

"Not so bad," Kribs said, looking around. "Thought it'd be worse. Came down to see if I should send any help from the maintenance crew at the mill." He stood with his hands in his pockets, a white, open-collared short-sleeved shirt stretched out over his stomach. "But I figure you can handle this by yourself."

"Right," said Ross. "No need wasting your people's time."

"It's not a waste if I say it needs doing," Kribs said.

"I'm sure." Ross began straightening papers on his desk.

Kribs pushed up on the nosepiece of his metal-framed glasses, watched Ross being busy, and tapped a cigarette out of a pack of Old Gold. "The Colonel's the same," he said. "Called the hospital before I left home. No change." He lit the cigarette with a gold-plated Ronson and slipped the lighter back into his pocket.

"Not surprised," Ross said.

"Could go on for a while," Kribs lamented, "the coma. Sad, really sad."

"That it is." Ross went to the coat closet and pulled out a broom and dustpan. He moved a chair and coat tree into the middle of the room and started sweeping up broken glass.

Kribs stepped back when the broom came close to his shiny brown wingtips. He rested half a cheek of his behind on the edge of the desk and watched Ross make two trips to a trash bin in the hall before he stood up and cleared his throat.

"I better be getting on out to the mill," he said.

"Uh-huh. I'll have this cleaned up pretty good today," Ross said. "Be able to get back down to business in a day or so."

Kribs rubbed dust off the toe of one shoe onto his back pants leg. "About that," he said and tapped out another cigarette. "The business part?" He lit the cigarette and sucked in like he was drawing against a thick milk shake. "You are clear that this, being director, is a temporary thing." He exhaled smoke in a stream through pursed lips.

Ross stood silent and met Kribs's questioning look without reaction.

"What I mean is, this being *acting* director, it's just for show," Kribs said, grinning. "Hell, Neville is always so damned caught up in how things look. But I'm here to follow up. Make things clear." He tapped ashes into the wastebasket. "What I mean is, don't get to thinking that you're really in charge here. Course you and I know this isn't much of a job, not a lot to be in charge of, but since it carries the name of Armbruster, that makes it important."

"So," Ross interrupted, "Neville asked you to fill me in? On this low-class job that you wanted but didn't get?"

Kribs paused and knocked the ashes off his cigarette again with a practiced finger tap.

"No, this is just between you and me." His voice dropped an octave. "You see, Ross old boy, I spend most of my time covering Neville's backside, have since we were kids. Always will. He counts on it, doesn't want to know about all of it, but he counts on it. Know what I mean?"

"I get your meaning," Ross said, and reached out with the broom for another bit of broken glass.

"Good. Because we just want you to attend a few of the unimportant events, answer the phone, wear your eyeshade, keep the books, and set up board meetings—be our secretary. Got it?"

"There a point to this?" Ross asked as flatly as he could.

"Yeah, there's a point, and it's this: Don't for a minute think you're running things here. You get that idea and act on it and you'll be out of here like that." Kribs snapped his fingers.

"Just like that?" Ross smiled. "You have that kind of clout with the family?"

"What? You mean Maybelle? Let me tell you, Maybelle will not go up against her uncle.

Guarantee that. Family code." Kribs grinned. "Not even for her husband. No, you're way down the list. But you knew that already. Didn't you?"

"That's a good one," Ross said, "coming from someone whose only lot in life is following along in the shadow of Neville's backside."

Kribs took a step forward. "Look, mister, don't you get smart." He flicked his half-smoked cigarette onto the floor, drove a heel into it, and took two deep breaths. "Okay, if that's the way it's going to be, now we know where we stand."

Ross swept the cigarette butt into his small pile of dirt and glass bits. "Do we? Tell me just where we stand. I'd like to know."

"Simple. Just don't like you, Bagby. Haven't from the day you came to town trailing along after Maybelle."

"I can live with that. Saves me beer money," Ross said.

"What?"

"Yeah, I only buy beer for friends and people I respect."

Kribs stiffened, started toward the door, then paused. "This little conversation. Like I said, it's just between us. Never happened. Of course, that don't mean it isn't true. It is."

He raised a forefinger to emphasize his point and closed the door too hard on his way out.

Ross stood calmly, broom in hand, and wondered if his dear departed mother would say it was okay to think unkindly of someone after all. *Always be kind, Ross,* she would say. *You should never think unkindly of another human being.* She hadn't met Wendell Kribs.

He did the best he could to reclaim the office from the chaos, then around eleven o'clock gathered up the short stack of mail that had been accumulating on the Colonel's desk and sauntered up the street to the café. He slid into the only empty booth, planted his forearms on the table, mulled over his exchange with Kribs, and let the café sounds flow around him: the sound of men talking, dishes clinking, of Sam hollering "Order up!". The older waitress, Blanche, limped up, put a hand on the small of her back, grimaced, and sloshed Ross a cup of coffee. He smiled his thanks and began sorting through the mail: a few bills and a couple of funding requests. The Humane Society wanted $250 to repair some kennels. The mayor of Sutherlin to the north had written requesting an Armbruster scholarship for a young man from his town to attend college.

Ross sipped cooling coffee and reflected on being the temporary keeper of Jonah's curse, of his need to shed his riches to feel right about his life. From the curse came the motto: *To ignite human potential when all that is lacking is a humble flame. —Emeline and Jonah Kaswell Armbruster, 1952.* If nothing else about his predicament touched Ross, that maxim did. Maybe it was worth doing, this job, with that credo at his back.

There was an envelope hand-addressed to *Colonel Gordon McKenzie, Director* with the Foundation address filled out exactly. There was no return address. Ross opened it, but it wasn't an appeal. It began *Dear Gordon.* It was signed *Love, Mona.* In between, in short staccato sentences, the beautician managed to make a bad situation terrible. *We have to talk right quick. I saw the doctor last week.* Ross felt a chill. *Like I figured I'm PG. You're the one, Gordon. You won't talk on the phone so I'm writing. What do we do now? Call me. I mean it now.*

Ross read the childish hand twice more and folded the letter back into its envelope. There was a moment when he felt like laughing out loud, but right after that the moths of dread fluttered inside him and he imagined Neville's rage.

"Hello there." The voice tinkled down on him.

It was the young waitress. "Hey, Jill. Sure, warm 'er up." He raised his cup.

She topped it off then slid into the booth opposite him and set the Pyrex pot down between them. "You okay, Mr. Bagby?" She reached up and finger-combed an errant strand of hair. A gentle frown drew her eyebrows in.

"Why, I look sick or something?" He worked up a grin. "And call me Ross."

"No, *Ross.*" She said his name with emphasis and waggled her head. "You don't look sick."

"What then?"

"You had that far-off look," she said. "Course everybody's got the stares these days, you know, in shock sort of. It's like they're in a trance or something."

He nodded, fingered the envelope containing Mona Johnson's letter and knew he had to call Neville right away. He imagined the man's red face and bulging veins; he felt an eyelid twitch and came out of his fog. The waitress was still there, sitting on the edge of the seat across from him with one leg out in the aisle.

"You did it again. Went off somewheres," she said.

"I did, didn't I? Things on my mind."

"Yeah," she said. "Most everybody's zonked out right now. Dang explosion."

"Yeah." He jogged the envelopes. "Truth of it is a man I work with was hurt…in a car accident. He's in a coma."

"How awful. Wait, you mean that Colonel guy? Wasn't a car accident, was it? Not what I heard."

Another chill ran across Ross's shoulders. "What do you mean?"

"Heard he was hurt in the explosion," she said. "I mean, wasn't he?"

"No," Ross said. "No, he wrecked his car out by the country club."

She stared at him. "Really? I mean, I saw what it said in the paper and all, but I swear I heard different. That it was the blast that got him."

"Nope." Ross fiddled with the mail some more. "Ran his car off the road. Just coincidence."

"Guess you ought to know." She slid out of the booth. "Seems strange is all."

He nodded, looked up and saw her doubt. "Life's like that," he countered. He had an impulse to reach out and pat her on the arm—to comfort her, and to dislodge her doubt—but he didn't.

He was still thinking of her when he stepped outside into the sun, the heat, and the grit.

8

Ross returned to the office, sat at the wounded mahogany desk, opened Mona Johnson's letter, and pressed it out flat with his hand. He read it one more time then picked up the phone and dialed Neville at the mill.

"Ross." Neville's tone was that of finding an encyclopedia salesman on the line. "Everything all right down there?"

"Yeah fine," Ross said. "Got things pretty well cleaned up. Kribs was waiting when I got here this morning."

"That right?" Ross savored the wariness in Neville's voice.

"Uh-huh." Ross waited a moment. "Yeah, he got me squared away…about how things are going to be for now."

There was a pause. "That right? Squared away?" Someone came into Neville's office, and when he spoke the sound was muffled, so Ross knew he had his hand over the mouthpiece. "Sorry, secretary needed something. So you are squared away, you and Wendell?"

"Seems that way," Ross replied.

"Okay, good. That why you called?"

"Uh, no." Ross hesitated. "A letter came in the mail today for the Colonel, personal letter."

"Personal?" Neville's tone was cautious.

"That's right," Ross said. "From Mona Johnson."

"Who's…oh shit, the beautician," Neville said. "That's all been taken care of. But what's this letter?"

"I opened it, thinking it was Foundation business," Ross answered. "Didn't have her name or a return address on it, Neville."

"Never mind that," Neville said, "you're director…for now. Whatever comes into the office you take care of it. So you opened it?"

"Yeah. There's another problem," Ross said, "with this woman."

"What?" Neville's voice went up.

"Think we'd better meet in person, Neville," Ross cautioned. "Don't think we should discuss it over the phone."

He heard Neville inhale. "A problem? Damn, just what I need. Okay, let's do this over lunch. Country club at one thirty. I'll reserve the Armbruster Room."

When Ross arrived, Neville was already in the men's bar. Along with a martini, he was having a boisterous conversation with two men Ross thought looked familiar but whom he didn't know. Neville caught sight of him standing self-consciously in the doorway and raised an arm while he kept right on talking. The two men also looked his way but were unresponsive and continued to listen and swill. As soon as Neville's punch line was delivered, all three roared their pleasure. Neville motioned Ross in with a rolling arm wave.

"Hey, Ross," he said. "Meet a couple of rascals here. Fellas, this is Ross Bagby, Maybelle's husband. Maybe you've met. Ross, this one here is Randy Smythe, not Smith, Smythe. Owns Smythe Logging Supply. And here is Clemson Hardway, general manager, Douglas Diesel. See either one of them on the street, run the other way," Neville chided.

Ross watched the body language rebuttals, bobbing and jabbing and red-faced chuckling.

The one called Smythe swallowed the last of his martini and looked at Ross. "So, how's our Mazie? You treating her well?"

"Hey, he better be," Clemson Hardway butted in. "Otherwise, we'll ride him outa town. Right?"

"Well," Ross said, wishing to hell people would get off it, "today she's helping the Red Cross gather clothing and food."

The men's faces fell like they'd been told to go to bed early, and they took to shaking heads in unison. Neville gave his chums a wave and marched off with Ross following along. The Armbruster Room was a private room with a ceiling-to-floor window looking out on an enclosed patio. The room was finished in black walnut paneling, and on one wall was an inset of shelving filled with books likely never read. Neville had already ordered up two crab salads and bottles of beer on ice.

"Fresh," he said, gesturing at the salad. "Dungeness crab brought in from the coast. Love crab. You?"

"Sure," Ross said.

"Help yourself to a beer," Neville said. "Got the letter?"

Ross handed the envelope over and pulled a bottle of beer from an ice bucket. He pried the cap off, took a swallow, and waited for Neville's reaction.

"I'll be a son-of-a-bitch," Neville uttered in exasperation and leaned back. "Gordon, you twit. God, if he wasn't already unconscious, I swear I'd knock him cold." Neville looked at the letter again then waggled it like he was trying to dislodge something sticky from his fingers. "Jesus H. Christ. And now I've got to clean this up while he's sleeping."

Ross spread a cloth napkin across his lap, took a forkful of lettuce and crab, and washed it down with beer. Neville nibbled at his salad, stopping with each bite to hold his fork in mid-air and shake his head before shoving the fork into his mouth.

"Sort of changes things, doesn't it?" Ross said.

"Understatement," Neville grunted. "Had it all worked out, you know. I got Mona Johnson another beauty shop job in Redding. Friend of mine there lined it up. Found out she has family there. Figured on giving her a wad of cash, more than she's ever seen at once, and sending her on her way. Clean and neat.

But now!" He looked at the letter again and said, "Wonder how far along she is?"

"What?" Ross asked. "Oh, you mean her pregnancy?"

"Yeah, stop this thing now." Neville emptied his beer glass.

"Stop it?"

"See if she's willing to terminate the pregnancy." Neville pulled another beer out of the ice bucket and levered the cap off. "If she won't, this could drag out for years. Seen it happen. One of our mill supervisors had a fling long while back. Gal turns up preggers, had the baby, and the guy loses everything—wife, family. Cost him a fortune. Then the gal decides to give the baby up for adoption—would you believe it?

"Thing is, the woman could've been paid off to terminate the pregnancy and have a little traveling money. See what I'm saying here? Old Colonel zipper will be like our supervisor, who now will be working until he's eighty to cover his losses." He grabs the letter again. "What does this gal say? Yeah, right here. *What do we do now*? She's saying, *Tell me what to do.* Okay, it'll take a few more bucks, but this is doable. She sent that letter last week before the blast. Bet she and Gordon were arguing about it that night."

Ross finished off the crab while listening to Neville's analysis. He slouched in his chair, rotating an empty bottle in his hand, studying the man. "Sounds messy. What are you going to do? Anything you want from me?"

Neville stared across the table at him. "Let me think. Nah, keep you out of it. You see, Ross, let me explain something. This kind of thing, stupidity I'm talking here, ends up in my lap. That's the way it is when you're in charge of all the marbles." He took his glasses off, set them on the table, and rubbed the heel's of his hands in his eye sockets. "When you run a big company, there's an element out there that thinks they can shake you down for chump change. Threaten to sue ALC for everything from the smell of sawdust in the air to saying one of our trucks ran over their pet spaniel. Small stuff? I shunt that off to Kribs. He's my swamper. Leaves me free to handle the big stuff and the truly sleazy stuff. Like this. Sleazy is anything that can hurt us in the mid-section. Sleaze is not to leave the room. Get my meaning?"

"Believe so," Ross said.

"Sleaze never gets out on the street if I can help it," Neville said. "Mostly I do. Can't have it. And I won't."

Neville put his glasses back on. "So it's sleaze time, and yours truly is on tap." He held up the letter again. "I'm moving on this today, this afternoon. That's all you need to know. If anyone asks you about this Mona person, you don't know a thing. Nothing. Understand that? Damn, if I had a pair of tin snips I swear I'd cut the Colonel's Johnson off and feed it to the fish. Glad you caught this."

Ross followed Neville outside, pausing behind him whenever he stopped to chat or was collared by someone who sought access. It was like following an elected official, only with more power. They exited the air-conditioned coolness of the club and stood in the heat of the parking lot for a moment next to Neville's Cadillac while he administered one more admonishment for Ross to keep his mouth shut. Ross agreed and stood watching the big car with its sharp fins depart and felt a trickle of sweat run down the center of his chest.

||||||||||||||||||||||||||||||||||||||||||||||||||||||||||||||||||||||||

The first meeting of the Foundation board after Ross assumed his temporary directorship was scheduled without his input. Kribs called late in the afternoon on the second Friday after the blast. Ross snapped upright as if he would be scolded for sitting in the Colonel's chair. It was the first time he and Kribs had spoken since their tête-à-tête.

"Catch you in the middle of something important there, mister dye-wreck-tore?" Kribs mocked.

Ross drummed his fingers on the desktop. "Something I can do for you, Kribs?"

"Yeah, mister." There was an odd wet noise over the receiver, and Kribs went on.

"We're convening a meeting of the board for Monday morning, ten o'clock, Colonel's office."

Ross let the slight pass. "That right? Who is *we*?"

More of that noise trickled into Ross's ear.

"Neville and me thought we'd better get things squared away down there," Kribs said. "Business affairs and such."

"So the president is convening the board," Ross said. "Neville wants to meet, and he asked you to pass along the message."

Kribs made more of the wet sound. "That's right. Ten o'clock Monday morning like I said. Be ready."

"Not much notice," Ross said. "Be ready for what? What does Neville want on the agenda?"

"Agenda?" Kribs laughed and made more moist sounds. "Don't need a darn agenda. What do you think you got down there in that pee-box, a Fortune 500 company?"

"Let me ask you something, Kribs," Ross said.

"Yeah, what?"

"What are you chewing on? I'm getting a slobbery wet sound in my ear. Having a maple bar on your coffee break or something?"

"Hey," Kribs said, "you just be ready for your first board meeting. Can't be the ding-a-ling in the outer office this time. Board expects things."

Ross knew the Foundation board meetings as nothing more than aimless chinning sessions with the Colonel, Neville, and Kribs. He was never asked to sit in, so all he really heard was laughter through the closed door to the Colonel's office. It was usually just the three of them since Emeline Armbruster never attended—if she was ever notified—and John Knox came only when specifically asked. Ross *had* been the ding-a-ling in the outer office, sometimes invited in to give the group some financial information or to run up the street to the Snappy Service and bring back paper cups of coffee.

"I'll be ready," Ross said. "Is Emeline coming? And John, has he been notified?"

"John knows," Kribs said.

"Emeline?" Ross pressed.

"No idea," Kribs said.

"I'll let her know," Ross said.

"Waste a time," Kribs said, "but do what you want about Miss Emeline."

"Anything in particular that you'll want to address?" Ross asked.

"Could be. Just be prepared," Kribs said. "By the way, you told Neville about our little meeting, I understand."

"Just mentioned that you'd been by to give me a heads-up on how things will go until the Colonel's back," Ross said.

"Uh-huh." Kribs sniffed. "Be careful, wasn't just talking to hear myself, you know."

"Sounded like that." Ross was ready to end the conversation. "See you Monday."

"You just be ready," Kribs retorted "And mister dye-wreck-tore, make sure we have some maple bars to go with our coffee."

Ross hung up, went to the window with its newly installed glass, and looked down into the alley. *Maple bars. We'll see about that*, he thought.

9

On Saturdays Maybelle and Ross usually went to breakfast at the Waffle Shop, but Ross wasn't in the mood. All he could think about was Mona Johnson and Wendell Kribs—one was in trouble, the other was trouble. He rose early, let Maybelle sleep, dressed in silence, and went to the kitchen. He put the coffee pot on and pulled some eggs and sausage from the fridge. When Maybelle finally wandered in still in her nightgown, Ross was daubing up egg yolk with a slice of wheat toast. Her eyes were puffy, and she had wind-tunnel hair.

"Want me to fix you some breakfast?" he asked. "I didn't feel like going out. That okay?"

She shrugged and said no to breakfast, just coffee. They sat, quietly sharing the previous day's paper and the coffee—nothing else. The innocuous rattle of the paper seemed inordinately loud in the vacuum.

"So what's eating you?" Maybelle asked after a lengthy silence.

"What do you mean?"

"I may not be the most sensitive wife in town," she said, "but I can read a few signs. Something's gnawing at you."

Ross lowered the newspaper and looked into her face. "Neville's called a meeting of the Foundation board. Monday, ten o'clock."

"So you're nervous about it?"

"A little," he said, "but something's up. I can feel it."

"Like what?"

"I don't know."

"There must be something makes you think that," she said. "What?"

"Kribs, he's the one told me about the meeting."

"And?" Maybelle raised her eyebrows.

"He insinuated things."

"Like what?"

"I can't pin it down, but he kept telling me to be ready. Wouldn't tell me what to be ready for—just be prepared. Was the way he said it. Don't trust him."

Maybelle laughed. "Kribs has your number. And you're taking the bait. Just ignore him."

Ross pushed his chair back and stood up. "I'm going to the office for a little while. Take care of a few details," he said. "Maybe feed my paranoia."

"No," she said. "Wait. Ross? Don't...I was just kidding." She started to laugh. "I mean, it is funny you being taken in by Kribs, for heaven's sake. Ross..."

But he was gone. She came after him and stood at the open front door, her bare feet sticking out from beneath her nightgown. He turned the key in the ignition, grateful for the whine of the starter and the throb of the engine. He didn't look over at her before backing out of the driveway.

It was quiet downtown. The scorched odor was still there but the town was cleaner now, the streets were clear, and the pall had dissipated. Ross parked in the alley and took the stairs two at a time; the building echoed its weekend emptiness. He was glad to be alone. He sat at the mahogany desk and declared it to be his desk, not the Colonel's.

First he called the maiden sister. Miss Emeline Armbruster lived alone and had for fifty-nine years. She retired from the lumber company a very wealthy woman and tended her roses.

When Jonah decided to form the foundation, she helped him do it and consented to have her name listed on the corporation papers as a board member because, after all, she'd been the one who had planted charity in his heart.

Ross dialed her number about nine o'clock; she answered right away with a strong voice. "Yes, who is it?"

"It's Ross Bagby, Miss Emeline."

"Bag who?" she asked.

"Maybelle's husband," he said. "Ross Bagby."

"Yes, Ross," she acknowledged. "How are you? You filling in for the Colonel, I hear. How's that going?"

"Just getting started, Miss Emeline," he answered. "In fact, that's why I'm calling."

"That's a change." She laughed. "Must think I'm dead down there, never hear hide nor hair."

"Sorry, I didn't know," he said.

"Of course you didn't, Ross. Course you didn't. It's the boys," she said. "They don't see any need for an old lady to coddle. They'd be surprised. I could hold my own. Worked around loggers and their ilk for nigh on fifty years. Back when men didn't care if you were a woman or not, had to deal with them nose to nose."

"I'll bet," Ross said, smiling.

"Yes, well you didn't call about that," she said. "Something going on?"

"There's going to be a meeting of the Foundation board Monday morning at ten o'clock. Can you attend?" he asked.

"Now there's a funny thing," she said. "How often you figure that board meets, Ross? How often?"

"Oh, three or four times a year," he answered.

"Those rascals," she said. "I haven't been notified of any board meeting for, what? At least three years. Get some financial reports once in a while, but that's all. Are they voting on things at those meetings?"

"Guess so," he said, "I mean, yes, they vote on awarding grants and such."

"I see," she said. "So this meeting on Monday, what's so special that you'd keep me from my rose garden?"

"Well, as acting director," he said, "I just think every board member ought to be asked to attend these meetings."

"Hmmm. That all?"

"Well," he said, "this meeting will be about how things will be handled until the Colonel recovers."

"Well then, I'll be there," she said. "Now Ross, tell me, is there anything I need to know for this meeting? Anything you'd like to tell me?"

"What do you mean?" he asked.

"Look, son," she said, "I've been around the business world long enough to know that everybody has things on their mind, their own concerns. You have any of them?"

Ross laughed. "Mostly I just want to have this meeting go well."

"Now there's a bucket of warm spit if I ever heard one," she said. "What aren't you telling me? You aren't just inviting me for coffee and cookies. Now then, what's in the woodpile?"

"Miss Emeline, really…well, I just have the feeling that something's going to come up." He paused. "Something I'm not being told about."

"Like what?" she asked.

He breathed a small laugh. "Maybe I'm being too skeptical," he said, thinking of Maybelle's chiding, "but Wendell Kribs warned me about being prepared for something, but he wouldn't tell me what."

"Kribs, you say. That can't be good," she said. "Okay, Ross, I'll be there."

"I'd appreciate it," he said.

"By the way, Ross," Miss Emeline said, "since you're taking on this job, you ought to sit down with Jonah. Get his feelings about the Foundation. That would be a good thing for you to do. Give him a call. Before Monday, I'd say."

Ross hesitated. "All right, I will."

"Good, good," she said. "See you Monday."

She hung up, and he dialed Jonah.

Jonah was waiting for Ross the next day out on the flagstone patio at the back of the big house. He brightened when he saw Ross, who was surprised to find that Jonah was not in his wheelchair. He was sitting in a cushioned redwood chair wearing a pair of chinos and a crisp short-sleeved shirt, looking relaxed and alert. A pitcher of lemonade sat next to him on a round redwood table. He waved a thin arm, gesturing for Ross to sit beside him.

"Ross, come," he said. "Sit right there. Lemonade?"

"Sounds good," Ross said. "I'll pour."

"You better. I'm liable to spill it all over us," Jonah laughed.

Ross filled the tall glasses, ice cubes knocking about. "You're looking pretty spry today. Haven't seen you out of your chair for some time."

"Special occasion, don't you see?" Jonah said. "Not many visitors these days. When one comes, try to make a good impression. I look all right?"

Ross laughed. "No visitors. There's always a crowd around you."

Jonah took the glass from Ross's extended hand. "Mean the show-up gangs? Call 'em show-up gangs 'cause they just show up out of nowhere. Mostly mess up my day. But hellfire, them people they aren't visitors, just a crowd looking for a place to mill around. They think that using this house like a damn hotel ballroom is the same as a real visit. Tell you," Jonah said, "this getting old business is a pain if you want to know. You know how old I am, Ross? Ninety. Ninety goddamned years. Count 'em. You know what you are when you're ninety? A slab of rotting flesh with half your marbles, not a darn thing going on below the water line, a pittance of your man-child strength, can barely see or hear, no one gives a damn what you think, and you have no future. And every day you have to have to struggle to just get out of bed. So don't aim for it unless you're tougher'n aardvark jerky."

"Sounds pretty daunting, all right," Ross said. "You that tough?"

Jonah grinned and took a drink of lemonade. "Some days I am. Other days, weaker'n Mercy's coffee. Hit me on a bad day, and I look like a drooling cadaver, I swear. How I look today?"

"Ready to top a tree," Ross said.

"Like hell," Jonah laughed. "Could've once, though—and did a bunch of times. You know what it feels like to climb a big Doug fir, your body so strong and supple you have no fear, you top 'er and dance on the bit-off end? I done that, I tell you. More than once." He stopped talking and for a long moment was someplace else. "Just give me one more day of being nineteen working out there like it was. Just one day, then I'd be ready to check out with a smile on my face."

Ross was taken with a wave of fondness for the old man. He had never spent time with him alone before, had never had a real conversation. For some time, Jonah had just been the frail form in the wheelchair, usually in some corner with a blanket across his legs. People patted him on the shoulder in passing or leaned down too close and asked how he was, always speaking loudly.

"So you miss knocking around the woods, then?" Ross asked.

"Nothing like it," Jonah said. "You ever work in the timber, Ross?"

"I'm an accountant," Ross answered.

The old man's face sobered. "Oh. That's right. An accountant. Jesus, they made my life miserable at times. God almighty, they did. Them counters. Why'd you go and do a thing like that? Become an accountant?"

"Because I couldn't top trees," Ross said.

Jonah blinked. "Cause you couldn't…couldn't top trees?" He snickered. "That's good, couldn't top trees. Well, somebody's got to add up them numbers."

"Guess so," Ross said. "And you created a lot of numbers to be counted."

"Yeah, well, more to it than that," the old man said. "More lemonade? Help yourself and add some to my glass there. You know, I believe this is the first time you and me have just sat and palavered."

"It is."

Jonah studied Ross. "How long you been married to Maybelle now?"

"Twelve years."

"Can't be. And we've never had a sit-down before? In twelve years? Be damned. Why do you suppose that is?" Jonah asked.

"Guess I was always in a show-up crowd," Ross said.

"So what's the occasion, then? Usually when a body makes a special trip to see me these days it's 'cause they want something. You wanting something, Ross?"

"In a way, guess you could say that," Ross responded.

Jonah's face lost some of its verve, and Ross wondered how many times men with less than honor on their minds had tried to dupe Jonah Armbruster.

"It's about the Foundation," Ross said. "I'd like to know more about it. Like the motto…about igniting human potential. Where'd that come from?"

A smile played on Jonah's thin lips. "You know how that came about? Those exact words?" He edged up on his elbows. "Emeline. For years, from way back, she kept reminding me that we was lucky. It was terrible hard work in the beginning, but later on," his laugh was paper being wadded, "we couldn't hire enough men, expand the mill fast enough. I mean, the business became this monster, *our monster of success* I called it. Some days Emeline would show me our balance sheet, and we'd laugh so hard we couldn't breathe. Two kids. We was still just kids when it took off.

"We came from hard scrabble times. Just think, Ross, of going from eating rotten horse meat to having more money than you had a right to." He wagged a forefinger. "I was a hard-ass businessman, don't think I wasn't. But one day Emeline said *Enough, Jonah.* Just in those words. She was right. That was back in the thirties, middle of the Depression. But we was still making money. Couldn't walk down the street those days and not see the hurt. Emeline rode my butt, made me see it, made me look until her compassion took ahold.

"Damn," he chuckled, "near every day Emeline would say, *Jonah, we got to do this thing now.* Started out with food, then clothes. She found a way to see that people got this stuff without our name being on it. Pretty soon she was running a whole other operation, billing the mill for rent and house payments, warehousing foodstuffs and holding accounts with local department stores for clothing and so on. Went on like that until the war come along. Then times was good, lots of work for any able body willing to show up."

"Emeline, then," said Ross.

"Yep, she's been my spar tree since we was kids, kept me centered up, don't you know. I was the brawn, she was the brains. I was the hard-ass, she was the heart. I wouldn't have been a success without her. I knew how to make lumber, but Emeline, she knew how to make sure we made a profit and kept me on a leash on the business side."

"Tell me about the Foundation," Ross said.

Jonah swiped at the wispy strands of his hair. "What do you want to know, and why you wanting to know it?"

"Filling in for the Colonel. Guess you know."

"How's he doing, the Colonel?" Jonah asked.

"No change," Ross said. "Still in a coma."

Jonah shifted in the chair. "Knew a fella got hit in the head in the woods. Long while ago. Went into one of them comas. Unconscious he was, for a couple of years."

"He come around eventually?" asked Ross.

"Nope." Jonah shook his head. "Never left that bed. Died right there."

"Too bad."

"Yeah, well them woods is full of too-bads." Jonah looked off across the patio for a moment then said, "Now, where was we? Foundation, you want to know something. What is it?"

Ross dragged his chair over closer and sat down almost knee to knee with Jonah. "You see," Ross leaned forward, "the board has called a meeting for tomorrow morning. It'll be my first one since being appointed and…well, I want to be more knowledgeable about how and why you set up the Foundation."

"Horsefeathers," Jonah said.

"What?"

"That ain't what's going on."

Ross sat up and opened his mouth. Nothing came out.

Jonah wiped at his nose. "Emeline called me last night. Told me you'd invited her to the meeting. She liked that. Also said that there may be something going on had you worried. True?"

"Well maybe, but…"

"It's that brownnoser Kribs, isn't it? He's been following along in Neville's fart trail since he got out of diapers." Jonah shook his head again. "Can't understand Neville about that, never could. Man's a ferret. What's he up to, anyhow?"

"Honestly, I don't know," Ross said. "Maybe nothing. I just have a feeling, is all."

At that moment Mercy came out smiling and patted Jonah on top of his head. "You boys want more lemonade?"

"Hell no," said Jonah, "time for something stronger. How about a beer, Ross, cold beer? Bring us a couple of beers, woman."

Mercy slapped Jonah playfully on the shoulder and went back inside.

Jonah raised a forefinger. "I'd be on my toes tomorrow if I was you, Ross. Good Emeline's going be there. She doesn't trust that Kribs fella any more than I do."

"Tell me, Jonah, why'd you do it?" Ross asked. "What's your core passion for the Foundation?"

"What you after?" Jonah asked.

Ross leaned over again. "When I sit down with the board tomorrow, I want to be smarter than I am right now. Tell me why you started the Foundation, how you parceled out the money in the beginning, all of it."

The old man was squinting. When he stayed unresponsive, Ross said, "So, what was it? The real reason?"

Jonah tilted his head. "Possibility," he said, nodding. "That's the word, *possibility*. Just give me a bloody chance. That's been a burr in my bedroll since I was a kid. When we started talking serious about giving some money away, that was it. Was the only thing, had to be. You see, since I was seventeen, it clawed in me that if I could just get the sliver of a chance, I could do anything. Knew it. Then stand back, out of my way!" He slapped the chair arm with an open hand. "Figured it would be the same for lots of folks. Possibility, that's what it is."

"One more thing," Ross said. "How'd you run things? Where'd the money go?"

Mercy appeared with the beers and disappeared while they talked. Jonah picked up a bottle, wavered it around, poked it into his open mouth and sucked on it like a babe. And right then Ross saw the energy drain out of the old man's face.

"I'm not running things anymore, am I? Hell, don't run anything," Jonah said, unaware of the beer dribble on his chin. "I'm an ancient wreck. Some days don't even pee by myself. I'm irrelevant."

"Not as long as you have this goal, Jonah," Ross said. "Isn't that so? Tell me, what is it you want to hand down, to see perpetuated?"

Jonah sank back, his face ashen. "Sorry, Ross, I'm very tired now. That's the way it happens. Just drains away."

"Jonah." Ross reached out and gripped the arms of Jonah's chair. "Please, tell me." There were only sad, watery eyes.

As if on cue, Mercy had appeared with the wheelchair. Ross shoved his chair back and watched as she cupped a bony elbow in her hand and guided Jonah onto the sling seat. She expertly spun the chair around on its rubber wheels and started to push away.

Jonah raised a hand and Mercy turned his chair back. "Thank you for coming, Ross," he said. "Enjoyed it. What you want? Look at the records. The records and Emeline will give you what you're asking for."

Mercy smiled her sweet smile and pushed Jonah away. He slouched forward holding himself up by his spindly forearms. Ross stood alone in the sudden quiet for a bit then drove to the office.

10

It took considerable scrounging through a jumble of folders in a choked file cabinet to find the records from 1952 and 1953, well before Jonah and Miss Emeline had turned their mission over to caretakers and Colonel Gordon McKenzie became the handpicked figurehead. Ross sat hunched at the conference table and thumbed gingerly through each frayed manila folder page by page. A few requests for funds were typed out but most were written in hands both fine and indecipherable, often just addressed to *Mr. Jonah* or just *Armbruster*. In those first years, there were mostly plainspoken pleas for help: *I'm outa work have six kids*; *Our church's furnace gave out*; *I need five hundred bucks to make my invention work*. Most who wrote were unfamiliar with the true purpose of a foundation, but it looked as if every request had been respectfully considered—Jonah and Miss Emeline wrestling with every appeal, making decisions, joyous over saying yes, suffering with every rejection. They were the board then, just they and their lawyer, a man named Crenshaw. That had been the purest time, when every dollar was released lovingly, like an arrow, to the causes and people whom the brother and sister believed would surely thrive with some help—those were the *possibilities*. Ross felt certain that every solicitation had been saved and on most there were jottings by Jonah and Miss Emeline, each hand distinctive. *I like the sound of this. This boy's father worked for me, good man. Too cocky. This could work. Don't understand this at all! This made me cry.*

Ross read each request and became caught up in the stories and wondered what had happened to those people or that immediate crisis or those dreams so full of hope, all of those possibilities. He was drawn to the tortured hand of a letter written by one Henry Delay, who wrote, *I is good with my hands. I can make the Lord's wood into a thing of beauty by His grace. What I'm needing is about four hunerd dollars I figure to make my own business. That is what that electric saw and a router cost. Send the money right away.* What ever happened to Henry Delay? Did they send him the money? Ross read that letter over and again, and each time he had this fuzzy sensation spying on another man's dream.

Ross didn't sleep well that night. His imagination was alive with troubling, even terrible characters. He got up at five and stayed up. At six he left the house. Maybelle was still sleeping; he didn't wake her or even leave a note. Workmen were already lumbering about the ruins for yet another day of reclamation; a small plane flew over, circled around, and passed overhead again. But most of the town was not yet in motion when Ross parked in the alley and carried a new coffee maker up to the office. He had purchased the big percolator and supplies to outflank any attempt to make him an errand boy. The oatmeal raisin cookies were for Miss Emeline's taste—no maple bars. He deposited it all for later use and went to breakfast.

The Snappy Service was open and astir at six thirty. Ross stood just inside the doorway and looked around until he saw Jill joking with a couple of truck drivers at the counter. Soon enough she saw him watching and smiled in his direction. He popped her a wave, slipped into a vacant booth, and drummed his fingers until she came over.

"Ready for some Joe?" She raised the glass pot shoulder high.

"Sure."

She propped one hand on a hip and tipped the pot in a practiced motion. "I been wondering," she said, "about your friend, the Colonel? How's he doing?"

Ross poured sugar, stirred it in, and looked up; her eyebrows were arched in question. "Not well," he responded.

"But he's going to be all right?" she asked.

"No way of telling right now."

"Oh," she said, setting the pot on the table. "Too bad."

Ross took a swallow of coffee, expecting her to ask for his order. She didn't. "Yes, too bad," he repeated.

"So, the usual, pancakes, eggs, and bacon?" she asked.

"Think I'll have a Denver omelet this time," Ross said. "Why so curious about the Colonel?"

Jill scribbled his order on her pad. "A Denver, got it," she said then looked at Ross. "Oh, it's just that a friend of mine knows Gordon…I mean the Colonel, pretty well is all. Curiosity killed the cat." She laughed and danced away with his order.

Ross felt a feather flutter in his stomach when Jill used the Colonel's first name.

When she brought his omelet, they traded small talk and exchanged eye contact tinged with question. He ate the omelet quickly, didn't linger over refills, went back to the office, and focused instead on the board meeting. His uneasiness with the waitress would have to wait. He unpacked the shiny new percolator, hastily read the instructions, decided to bypass the breaking-in steps and made four trips to the restroom with a small flower vase to fill the urn; he hoped no flora residue would be detected. The device had just begun to hiccup and emit coffee aroma when Miss Emeline arrived. She marched into the office like a process server, her white hair shorter than Ross recalled, her lined face rosy pink and fair. She was tall, slender, and erect.

"Miss Emeline," Ross said. "Nice to see you, thank you for coming."

"I'm the first?" she said as an accusation.

"Indeed you are. Would you like a cup of coffee?"

She turned about, looking the place over, walked into the inner office, and appraised the room's trappings, assured and unflappable. She came back to where Ross waited and stood, hands clasped at her waist. She was wearing a short-sleeved floral blouse and gray skirt.

"Colonel has fancy tastes," she said.

Ross shrugged. "How about some coffee? Made it fresh."

She raised her chin at him; black, she told him. Good he'd forgotten cream. Male voices rolled down the hallway like a grumbling radiator; the door swung open only to have the threesome bunch up in the doorway upon facing Miss Emeline's sober examination. There was a vacuous moment before John Knox rallied, flashed his white teeth, stepped forward, and leaned into a warm respectful greeting. Neville managed an abbreviated version of the same; Kribs stumbled in, head bobbing. Miss Emeline accepted this deference with aplomb and stood fast until Neville extended an arm for her to precede him to the conference table. Chairs chattered on the floor, bodies bent, and there they all were. Kribs looked across at Miss Emeline.

"Well, Miss Emeline," he said, "I see our able dye-wrecktore got you a cup of coffee. Maybe we can hold off starting the meeting while he runs up the street and gets us all a cup. I could use one right about now."

Neville raised his head to speak, but Miss Emeline beat him to it.

"What do you mean?" she said. "Got mine right out of the pot in the other office."

"Yes, Kribs," Ross said, enjoying the man's confused expression, "we have our own coffee maker now. Help yourself. By the way, no maple bars. Miss Emeline thought cookies would be nice."

Kribs's face reddened.

"Wendell," Neville said, "get yourself some coffee so we can get going. While you're at it, get me one, okay?"

Ross thought Kribs was going to explode. By the time he had gotten coffee for him and Neville and made a return trip for cookies, his face was heatstroke red.

"I see we have an agenda," Neville said. "Good idea, Ross."

"I know you didn't want one, actually, hope it's okay," Ross said. "This being our first meeting since the Colonel's accident, I wanted to keep things focused."

"Didn't want an agenda?" Neville looked up. "Who said?"

Ross looked at Kribs who gurgled up coffee; some of it dribbled out. "Never needed agendas," Kribs laughed and palmed the wetness off his chin. "What's the point? Can do all we need to on the back of an envelope."

"You don't think the Foundation does important work then, Mr. Kribs?" Miss Emeline sat with her hands folded on the table, shoulders erect.

"Now, Emeline," Neville broke in, "of course Wendell knows that the Foundation is important to the community." He looked down at the agenda in front of him and squeezed his hands together.

"Another thing," she said. "I want to be notified of all meetings of the board. I am a member."

"Was our understanding, Miss Emeline, that you weren't interested in attending anymore," Kribs said. "Least that's what the Colonel told us."

"Horsefeathers," she said. "Never told anybody any such thing."

"We stand corrected," Neville said. "Guess Ross told you of the meeting this time. That's good, Ross, make sure Emeline is advised of all future meetings," he said. He nodded agreeably at Ross, but his eyes were burning cinders. "Now, let's move on here. Ross has put down three items, first one: Update on the Colonel. Simple. No change. Still in a deep coma, according to the doctors."

"You're saying he isn't likely to recover from this?" asked John.

"Never said that," Neville replied. "Heaven forbid we talk like that. To the outside world Colonel McKenzie is being treated, and we expect him to achieve a full recovery. That is how we must present this. I'm serious now."

"Even if it's not true?" said John.

Ross's father-in-law was also an Armbruster by marriage. John Knox was an attorney, a handsome man, lean and square-faced, with the only full head of hair at the table. He spoke with the self-assurance of a man who was not a feeder at the Armbruster trough. He was a principal in the law firm of Chapman, Hughes, and Knox. Until now, his service on the Foundation board had been sporadic.

"Is it true or not?" John repeated. "Is the man going to recover?"

"Hell, John," Neville said, "we know zippo. Since that's the case, we're putting the most positive light on the situation."

"You think he will survive this?" John asked, still pushing.

Neville looked at John and didn't speak for a long moment. "John, we don't know from a fart in the wind where this is going to end up. Excuse my French, Emeline."

"You're choirboys compared to the men I used to work with," she said.

"I'm sure," Neville responded. "Okay nuff said about the Colonel, on to item number two: Duties of the acting director."

Kribs grunted. "Easy, for now, keep the doors open, answer the phone, and wait for the board to make decisions." He looked around the table and shrugged. "Way I see it. Don't mess up until we know how it'll come out with the Colonel."

"Ridiculous," said John.

Kribs snapped a look at Neville; Neville shook his head almost imperceptibly, and Kribs slumped back.

"In my opinion," said John, "the Colonel's recovery seems

doubtful. Even if he survives, it's unlikely that he'll be able to work again."

"You don't know that," Kribs said.

John locked onto Kribs's face and spoke slowly. "I did a little research. Asked a physician friend of mine up at the medical school in Portland to look into studies on severe head trauma and comas. The prognosis wasn't rosy. It may be that the Colonel will go into a vegetative state, if he hasn't already."

"Come on," said Kribs, "we can't listen to this. You aren't qualified, John. You're just guessing."

John crimped his jaw muscles. "More than a guess, Kribs. There's a pattern to the signs, and a pretty strong presumption can be made for a negative outcome. All I'm saying is that we should make contingent plans in case the man is unable to return to his job."

"Okay, okay." Neville patted the air with his hands. "John has a point. Ross needs to know what his parameters of responsibility are."

"And authority," said John.

"Simple. Doesn't have any," Kribs responded.

"I can't work that way," Ross said. "Won't."

Kribs grinned. "Fine. Don't necessarily need you. We'll get somebody else."

"No you won't," said Miss Emeline. "Ross is our director during this time, and he will stay that way."

"Now, Emeline," Neville said. "You can't dictate that. Besides, we've already voted on Ross's being temporary director."

"Seems we need to vote again," she said. "To set things straight on authority and such. How about right now?"

"What good will that do?" Kribs held up his arms. "We're looking at a tie vote with you here."

"There's a provision to break such an impasse," said Miss Emeline. "Isn't there, Neville?"

"What's she talking about?" Kribs frowned.

"Jonah," Neville said. "He can break a tie if it's needed."

"Geez," Kribs blundered, "he can't even hear, let alone understand what's going on."

Neville closed his eyes and said, "Wendell, that a bag of mothballs between your ears? Sorry, Emeline."

"Should be," she said. "Where's the respect here? He's your father."

"You've made your point," Neville said.

"Not trying to make points," she responded. "Want this matter settled. Let's vote."

Kribs opened his mouth to speak but stopped when Neville glared at him.

Neville tapped his pencil on the paper in front of him. "Okay. Need a motion."

"I'll do it," John jumped in. "I move that Ross Bagby be retained as acting director of the Emeline and Jonah K. Armbruster Foundation until there is a final resolution in the status of the health of the current director, Colonel Gordon McKenzie, who is incapacitated. And further, that Mr. Bagby be given the same decision-making authority as the current director in his absence."

"Is there a second?" Neville asked.

"Second," said Miss Emeline, her face implacable.

"In favor. Opposed. Motion carries." Neville voted for the motion.

Kribs didn't vote. He started shaking his head. "Don't mean he's gonna be strutting around like he's the Colonel. Right?"

"We're moving on, Wendell," Neville said. "Next item: Grant requests. Short list. A fellow from Coos Bay wants to start a fund for cats abandoned by foreign ships docking there. Be damned. Wants five hundred. Buckhorn Boys' Ranch is asking for a thousand for a new kitchen. And the Humane Society, two-fifty for kennel repairs. That's it. Comments?"

"What about our local disaster?" said Miss Emeline. "What's being done?"

"No requests yet," Neville said. "That right, Ross?"

"My lord, man," Miss Emeline said, "you don't wait to be asked at a time like this. People are in need. I move that we give major gifts to the Red Cross and Salvation Army immediately."

The cat fund was denied, the boys' home and the Humane Society approved, and the Red Cross and Salvation Army were granted three thousand dollars apiece for services related to the blast.

That was the end of the agenda, but Neville didn't move to adjourn. Instead he folded his hands on the table and asked if there was any other business to come before the board. Ross saw him look in Kribs's direction as he spoke. Here it comes, he thought, whatever it is.

"Yes, Mr. President," Kribs cleared his throat and scooted up in his chair. "I have an item of new business."

Neville cleared his throat. "All right, Wendell, what is it?"

"Well," Kribs began, "I think there ought to be an audit of the Foundation's books at this time." When no one spoke, he looked around and pressed his point. "You know, have some accountant do a complete rundown of everything."

"We already have Dick Arthur do the books," said John. "Does a balance sheet every quarter. You said yourself this is not a very complicated operation, Kribs. What are you driving at?"

"I know, I know," Kribs answered. "But Dick's just a bookkeeper. I'm talking about a certified public accountant. It's just that since we're authorizing a new person to handle the funds, write checks and all...well, you know, start with a clean slate. In fact, Neville, I so move."

"You move what?" Neville held the yellow pencil between both hands, plying it with his thumbs as if he wanted to snap it in two.

"Uh, okay," Kribs began, "I move that we get a CPA to do an audit of the Foundation finances and report back within the next thirty days."

"Wait a minute," said Miss Emeline. "What's this all about? Just what's going on here?"

"There's a motion before the board, Emeline," said Neville. "Need a second before we can have discussion."

"For the sake of argument, I'll second," said John.

"Now can we talk?" Miss Emeline stared at her nephew.

"All right, Emeline," Neville said. "You have something to discuss?"

"I think something's funny here," she said. "I don't like the smell of—"

"Miss Emeline," Ross broke in, "it's all right. I welcome an audit. I do the internal books, and I know that our records will be found to be in good order." He smiled at her and saw the tension ease from her face. "In fact, it's the prudent thing for the board to do."

She nodded. "If you say so, Ross, I'll go along."

"I do," Ross said.

After a unanimous vote, Kribs turned his pink face in Ross's direction and let it be known that prior to the board meeting he had conferred with the firm of Smith and Squire about conducting the audit if the board approved it. In fact, a date had been set in advance, and Raymond Squire would be coming to the office the next day to collect the necessary records and begin the audit.

"Tomorrow?" said Ross. "That won't give me time to pull the records."

Kribs leaned on his elbows and looked across the table at Ross, smiling. "Don't worry about it. Ray Squire knows what he's doing. He'll find what he needs. Besides, better for you that way."

"Meaning?" Ross asked.

Neville slapped an open palm on the table. "I declare the meeting adjourned. Thanks everybody. Good meeting. Ross, can I see you alone for a moment before I go?"

Neville stood in the outer office pacing until the others had gone; then he faced Ross. "Your idea to get Emeline to attend?"

"You heard Jonah's insistence that she be included," said Ross.

"Yeah, and I heard you went over to see him yesterday, too. What you up to?" Neville probed. "Making nicey-nice with the ancients? You know, Ross, I need the Foundation to be inconspicuous. My focus is on matters bigger than you can imagine. No idea. You need to understand that I must do whatever it takes to preserve everything Armbruster."

Ross stared into Neville's insistent eyes. "Yes, but at what cost?" he asked.

Neville turned his head then looked back at Ross. "That is the deepest question, isn't it? There's always a cost. I just don't go there. Just move ahead, keep focused. And this," he swung his arm out, "is an incidental distraction. The Colonel and I, we had this understanding."

He stepped up close to Ross. "Goes like this. The Colonel, he had a title, a nice salary, and his only job was to keep the Armbruster name respected and the Foundation a quiet, admired presence. Give out a commendable amount in grants, show up for the check-handing photos, and that's it, Ross. Right now, the Foundation is a warm spot on the Armbruster image." He put a forefinger against Ross's chest. "That's what I want. Nothing more. No heroics. I don't want you to suddenly find your life's calling in beating the drum for Jonah and Emeline's *possibility* fetish. Noble maybe, but just a side road. And one more thing." He pushed harder with his finger. "Don't play games with the ancients. Their time at bat has passed. We keep them safe, take care of their declining health, and we'll go to their funerals and revere their memories.

"In a way, you're family," he said. "Maybelle brought you home, and so there we are. But you're not blood, and I will not accept you meddling in matters about my blood. You got that?"

Ross stepped away from the finger against his chest. "Yeah, I got it."

"Okay. One more thing," Neville said. "That motion at the board meeting? About your authority and all? Word of advice: we voted, but it was just window dressing." He looked at his wristwatch. "I have to go. Good meeting. Liked the agenda idea. The auditor will be here tomorrow."

In three thumping strides, Neville crossed to the door and was gone; the hallway echoed with his leaving. Ross stood in the vacuum and swallowed both anger and reproach.

11

They ate out on the patio that evening. Ross brought home his frustrations of the day along with some sirloin tips from Savoy Meats. He grilled the meat and brooded while Maybelle tossed a summer salad and cooked fresh ears of corn. It wasn't until they had both taken their first bites of medium-rare steak that either of them spoke, their first words since *hello* nearly an hour earlier. Maybelle reached for her glass of white wine, looked across the glass-topped table, and studied her husband for a quizzical moment.

"So how did it go?" she asked. "Your first board meeting."

Ross knifed through the sirloin; he didn't look up. "You want to know something? He calls them the ancients. Your uncle calls Jonah and Emeline the *ancients*." When she didn't respond, he raised his head. "That's abysmal."

"Don't get your water hot," she said. "Just a term of endearment."

"Endearment? Ha! Makes me wonder what he calls me behind my back."

"Don't be silly. He doesn't call you anything." She speared a cherry tomato and popped it into her mouth. "Neville's called them that since Emeline's eighty-fifth birthday. Just struck, him I guess. He's not being vicious, for crying out loud, Ross."

"Disrespectful," he said. "Maybe that's even worse."

"Family thing. Forget it," she said. "The board meeting, how'd it go?"

"Emeline came," he said.

"I heard," she said. "Mom called. "Guess Dad gave her a rundown."

Ross put his knife and fork down and picked up his bottle of beer. "Went okay. Your dad and Emeline were supportive. Kribs wants an audit."

"What's wrong with doing that?" she asked.

"Nothing, if it was coming from anyone else," he said. "But something doesn't feel right."

"The books are all right though, aren't they?"

"Yes, of course. I went along with the audit so I wouldn't look afraid of the idea."

"Are you?" She held a forkful of salad in midair. "Afraid of the idea?" When he didn't answer, she said, "Ross, is there something? What is it?"

"The Colonel, he handled some of the money in a way that... I didn't like it."

"How?" she asked. "In what way?"

"He, well, he liked to use cash in a certain way. I think it might look out of whack in an audit," he said. "Probably not, but it could. That's all I'm thinking."

"So what are you going to do?"

He buttered an ear of corn. "Nothing I can do now. Kribs has a CPA coming first thing tomorrow to get all of our records. Probably be over in a week or so."

"Tomorrow? That's quick," she said.

"That's what I don't like. Kribs had this all set up ahead of time," he said. "Before the board even voted to do it."

"Like you said, be over soon." She began clearing the plates. "Made the doctor's appointment yet?"

The accountant, Raymond Squire, arrived at the Foundation office right at ten the next morning, neatly attired in a seersucker suit, and methodically collected ledgers, check registers, cancelled checks, and file folders. A little after eleven, the CPA expressed his thanks and left Ross standing in a daze.

One week later, the audit was completed, and everything came apart. Neville called for an emergency meeting of the board two days later, on a Thursday morning. Raymond Squire was in attendance, along with every member of the board. Ross made coffee; no one complained that there were no cookies or maple bars. Neville thanked everyone for coming on short notice.

"We have a problem," he said, and looked from face to face.

Ross knew the problem; he guessed everyone knew the problem. His stomach had balled up as soon as Neville had called him two days earlier, and it had stayed that way. He had spent most of the time since trying to figure out how ten thousand dollars could be unaccounted for, of course, he knew; but then again, he didn't. Kribs sat unsmiling, fidgeting, sitting forward and leaning back—having an adrenaline attack. He didn't look Ross in the eye.

"As the board authorized," Neville began, "Mr. Squire has completed a thorough audit of the Foundation books and all related financial accounts." Neville looked at Raymond Squire, and the two men exchanged impotent smiles. "Normally," he went on, "we would receive a complete written report in due course. However, in this case Mr. Squire has discovered a matter of some severity. The fact of the matter is that somewhat over ten thousand dollars is missing…or rather, is unaccounted for."

Ross felt the air grow thin in the stunned silence.

John Knox was the first to speak. "Mr. Squire, you mean the Foundation balance sheet is short by ten thousand dollars and you cannot find a trail?"

"Well that's close," said Squire calmly. "Not short in one sense because there are records that indicate such an amount was dispersed. Let's put it this way: I can't find where it went, but I know where it was. You see, there are two separate bank accounts, both of which can be drawn upon using Foundation checks. Both accounts receive infusions of cash as a result of activity stemming from drawdowns of the Foundation's port-folio earnings and other liquid holdings. I understand this was done on an as-needed basis. My analysis indicates that, as you know, one account is used primarily for Foundation overhead expenses: rent, salaries, utilities, and so forth. The other account is used exclusively to pay grants awarded by the Foundation."

"Is the shortage from one or both accounts?" asked Miss Emeline.

Squire referred to his notes and ran a forefinger down the page. "Just checking my conclusions, Miss Armbruster. I'm quite certain that all of the discrepancy is in only the one ac-count, the one that pays out grants. And it shows up through duplicate checks."

"What's that mean?" asked Kribs.

"Simple enough," Squire said. "Let me give you an actual ex-ample. I brought a couple of cancelled checks along. Here's one made out for fifteen hundred dollars to the Salvation Army and on the memo line it says Christmas Fund. Now here's another check made out to *cash* in the same amount, and this time the memo notation says Salvation Army Christmas Fund."

Ross felt a cold ice pick drive into his innards. "What was the date of those checks, Mr. Squire?" he asked.

Squire held the checks up, one in each hand. "Both are dat-ed November 15 of 1958. I checked with the Salvation Army people, and according to their records they received one check for fifteen hundred dollars but no cash gift in the same amount from the Foundation here." Squire looked in Neville's direc-tion. "That was the method used to divert all of the amount in question. Some amounts were less, five hundred dollars or so, but most were a thousand to fifteen hundred."

"Over what period of time?" John asked.

"A couple of years," Squire said. "From early '57 to spring of this year. Little more than two years."

"Odd," said Miss Emeline. "How would someone continue to cash these large checks without being noticed? How could that be?"

Squire was warming to his task. "Well, I looked into that." He sat forward and became a bit more animated. "The Foundation checking accounts are with the Douglas County State Bank. I talked with John Carlisle, the manager, and interviewed his tellers and discovered how it happened."

"I know how it happened," Ross said.

The silence around the mahogany table was a form of suspended animation. Every face pivoted toward Ross. Raymond Squire's expression was one of disappointment at being cut off, as he was about to make his revelation—an accountant's euphoric moment.

"I'm sure Mr. Squire knows that I'm the person who cashed the checks," Ross said. His chest had tightened as he realized that he was being maneuvered into a ridiculous position. The expressions on their faces would have been humorous on any other occasion, but the only one smiling was Kribs.

"Yes," said Squire, "you did."

"*You* did?" said Neville. "What on earth…"

"Wait, Neville," said John. "What's the story, Ross?"

The scene blurred for Ross because his eyes were watering under the rubber band tension in his body. He was grateful for his father-in-law's even hand.

"Yeah, I got to hear this," said Kribs. Neville shot him a cutting look, but it did not diminish his smugness.

Ross wiped his hands on his pants legs and brought them up and laid them on the table, one on top of the other. He had been thinking about how to explain this absurdity for many hours. The only thing he had come up with was calmness. Maybe if a fool appeared calm and rational he would seem less of one. Oddly, what entered his head right then was the squeal of tractor treads coming in through the open window. While he was in the dock facing an inquisition, someone was playing with a bulldozer, something Ross had always wanted to do. Why couldn't he be doing that instead? Neville cleared his throat.

"Yes," Ross said and looked around at the huddle of faces. "Well. Neville called me yesterday about the shortage."

Kribs snorted. "Shortage. Shortage is a leak. This s a gusher."

Ross paused and breathed in slowly. "May I?"

Kribs shrugged and tilted his head, still smiling.

"Let me piece this together as best I can," Ross began. "One of the reasons I came to work here was to bring most of the bookkeeping and the disbursement of grants in-house. I understand that was what the Colonel wanted." He looked toward Neville and got the nod he was looking for. "That left Dick Arthur to do a quarterly balance sheet. So, like I say, except for that we did everything right here. I wrote checks for our expenses and for grants and kept two sets of books."

"Who signed the checks?" asked Miss Emeline.

"The Colonel. He was authorized to sign all of our checks. Day-to-day bills and grants approved by the board. Gordon would sign the checks for rent, telephone and such, and I mailed them out. Except for our salary checks, that's the way funds in that account were handled." Ross paused and drank a swallow of cold coffee and fought back a gag reflex. He had to cough hard twice.

"Excuse me," he said and drew a palm across his mouth. "So uh…but the grants account, that was handled differently."

"Seems like," said Kribs.

Ross ignored him and went on. "I cut each check as directed by the Colonel. After every board meeting, he'd give me a handwritten list of grantees and the amounts they were to receive. Thing was…and I know this is going to sound odd—it did to me. The thing was, pretty often he would ask me to write two checks that would total the amount going to a grantee."

"I don't understand, Ross," said John. "Why two checks for the same grantee?"

"I know, unorthodox," Ross said. "Well, here's the way it would go. Say the Buckhorn Boys' Ranch was to receive three thousand. Gordon might ask me to make out two checks, say one for two thousand made out to the school and one for a thousand made out to cash."

John's eyes narrowed. "What for?"

"Well," Ross laughed; it wasn't a real laugh, more like a release valve. "That's the thing. Asked him that myself. At first." Another squeal of grinding tractor treads rose up, but all eyes and ears were on Ross. "He said... he thought it would be special to present part of the grant in person in actual cash." Ross squeezed his hands together, saw his knuckles go white, quickly let go, and flattened his palms on the table.

"Surely you both knew that was a questionable practice," John said. "I mean, handing out large sums of cash with no fiscal trail."

"I was concerned," Ross said. "First couple of times I said that to the Colonel, said we probably shouldn't be handing out cash like that. Wouldn't look right, I said."

"His response?" John had taken on the role of questioner. Neville and Kribs were sitting back watching, listening, and Miss Emeline was nodding and letting John ask the questions.

"Gordon, the Colonel, he has this way of setting the boundaries," Ross said. "Who's in charge, who's responsible for what. Didn't actually tell me to tend to my own business. Instead he'd say, *Not to worry, Ross, it will be fine.* That was the first time. Next time it happened, and I pressed him, he was standing right over there by that window, and I remember he had this little pocket knife and was cleaning his nails. Calm as could be about it. That time he said one word: *trademark.* Told me every man had to have his trademark, a characteristic that set him apart. He wanted his to be the act of putting substantial amounts of cash in people's hands in the name of the Emeline and Jonah K. Armbruster Foundation.

"Then he put his knife back in his pocket and looked over at me and said clear as could be: *Last time we discuss this. Just do it.* And that's how it went. I'd go over to the bank, cash the check—there was only one each time—and bring the money back. I would write the name of the grantee on an envelope, seal the cash inside, and put it on his desk. That's it. Until Neville called yesterday, never thought about it. Just the way he wanted it."

No one spoke for a protracted moment. Raymond Squire was seated next to Ross; he shuffled his papers and squared them up nicely and acted as if he were studying a row of figures. Kribs, heavy-lidded and calm, slouched in his chair and stared at Ross, who found that vexing. Someone slammed a car door down in the alley; that broke the trance.

"My, my," said Miss Emeline. "So simple back when it was just Jonah and me doing this. Never seen it fail—start adding more folks, and you get complications."

"So Raymond," said Neville, "what's your recommendation at this point? What do we do next?"

Squire smiled a *You're asking me?* smile. "Up to you people," he said. "Far as dealing with what has already happened, that's your decision. I can recommend some operational procedures you can adopt." He looked around at the still-stunned faces. "So for now, why don't I leave you all to sort things out? Then, Neville, if you want our firm to help you further you can contact me. How's that?"

Neville nodded, and everyone watched in silence as Raymond Squire collected his papers and inserted them into his black leather briefcase. He rose, thanked Miss Emeline, nodded to the men in turn, and excused himself. The moment the door latch clicked, it seemed everyone took in a breath as if the hall monitor had gone out of sight.

A moment later Kribs blundered ahead. "You ask me," he said, though no one had, "this is crazy. This story…this fairy tale we been told. You say the Colonel did this, stole money from under our noses. And him in a coma, unable to call you a damn liar."

"Hold up, Wendell." Neville raised a hand and waved Kribs off. His face was scrunched into a frown. "What I don't get," he said as he lifted his glasses up and rubbed his eyes, "is why the discrepancy never showed up. We award money to Buckhorn for example, why didn't the difference show up somewhere? I mean the grant's for a couple of thousand, say, but they only get a check for fifteen hundred. Got to come out in the wash sooner or later."

"I know why," said Ross.

Kribs snorted. "Neville we aren't going to let…"

"Kribs, you're not helping things here," said John. "Go on, Ross."

Ross looked around the table ending on a silent exchange with Kribs. "Started with whatever amounts the board decided to award. Gordon recorded the approved grants and later entered them in the minutes. Then, like I said, he gave me a handwritten list of grantees and the amounts they were to receive. Say you granted two thousand to the school. On the list he gave me, the amount for Buckhorn might be listed as three thousand."

"Says you." Kribs was surly.

"Surely you must have noticed this pattern," said John. "What about the letters that went out with the checks to the organizations? The actual amount would have been cited, would it not?"

"Colonel did all that," Ross said. "Handwritten notes with each check, I never saw them."

"Still," said Neville, "you're the one who cashed the checks."

"Yes, but they were signed by Gordon McKenzie."

"Didn't you prepare all checks for his signature?"

"Sure, Neville, but…"

"So you'd put a stack of checks on his desk to be signed, get them back to be mailed and so forth," Neville said.

"Yes," Ross answered.

Neville looked around at the others. "Do that all the time myself. The controller prepares checks, I get a pile of them every day and scan them as I sign. I'm primarily counting on my guy to have verified every check I sign—wouldn't get squat done if I personally scrutinized every one of them."

John chuckled. "But you're comparing a complex company to a two-man shop. The Colonel could easily have studied each check. I mean, we're only talking of a few grant checks every other month or so. Maybe not that often."

"Well sure," said Neville. "But it's still a routine. Not excusing it, but you put ten or twelve checks in front of a person, same payments you see every month, mix in a few grant checks, hell, you just sign them. Your mind is somewhere else. Probably the way it happened."

"If you believe that," said Ross, "then you're saying I'm a crook."

"Didn't say that," Neville said. "Just saying, well, saying we don't know, can't assume the worst about the Colonel."

"Or me," Ross said.

"And that too." Neville struggled to get the words out.

"Ross," said John, "did you keep those handwritten lists Gordon gave you?"

"No." His voice was small. "I looked again this morning. See, I'd write the checks, post them, and toss the note. Never occurred to me to keep them."

"There you go," said Kribs. "You got nothing, mister. Not a thing to prove you aren't a thief."

Ross leaned forward and looked hard into Kribs's red face. "You're getting the truth, the cold hard truth, like it or not. Don't think so, then I demand that each and every grantee be interviewed and their records checked for the past two years. Then we'll see who's honest and who's a scoundrel. I've never," he paused and looked down the table, "Miss Emeline, I have never taken a nickel from the Foundation."

Miss Emeline's face was blank, and her only response to Ross was to blink. He swallowed and ended by saying, "And I thought I was working with a man of honor."

"Don't you dare smear the Colonel's good name," said Kribs. "Man has more honor in his little pinky than a hundred Nebraska Cornhuskers."

"That's enough," said Neville "I think Ross's suggestion is a good one. We'll table this matter for now and continue to look into all the angles. I'll have Ray Squire do some more work, and we will speak with each grantee that received funds over the past two years and compare records and such. In the meantime, unless there's an objection, Ross continues his duties as usual. I'll call us all back together as soon as we have some answers to this mess."

Ross sat still as chairs scraped back and everyone in turn rose and quietly shuffled into the outer office. John came to Ross, shook his hand, and patted him on the back. His words of assurance did not penetrate the dread Ross felt.

After they had all gone, he stood in the emptiness and remembered that he had never wanted the damn job in the first place. He swore at his nemesis, a man unconscious, a man unable to confess, a man unable to defend himself, and a man revered for his thin shell of unconfirmed valor. Ross stood at the back window, looked out at the brownness on the hillside, and leaned on the sill, head down. Tears formed, and he laughed bitterly at the absurdity of it. There was a moment when he thought of calling Maybelle but abandoned that idea. Instead he spun around, determined to go over every record and reconstruct what had happened, then remembered that Raymond Squire had all of the records.

For a while he sat at the desk, body slack, mind leaping and shrinking, looked at a blank yellow pad and tried to recall details. There was nothing. He wiped away tears and paced the office and went down the hall to pee. Came back and sat with his arms folded and was an empty vessel. Ross, in a dream state, seemed to see Gordon McKenzie appear by the same window once again cleaning his nails with that little knife: the same smile, the same assured arrogance; then he said the names. Ross wiped at the moisture on his brow and began to write, as it came to him, of the times he had cashed checks and for which grantees. He wrote rapidly, the pen digging into the paper, and reconstruction emerged; first he reclaimed three grant recipients, and after those he tweaked his recollection for another.

After two hours he sat depleted. He had detailed five grants dead-on accurate and a couple that were fuzzy but valid. He was certain that the financial records of those organizations would prove they never received cash from the Colonel. Fine, but where the hell did the money end up? What did he do with it? Until that was known, Ross wouldn't be clear of suspicion. Couldn't prove he didn't steal. Damn, he thought, *they'll want to go through my bank records—and May's, for god's sake.*

About one fifteen the phone rang. It was a counselor from Roseburg High School saying she had lost her scholarship guidelines for the Foundation. Ross promised to mail her a new copy. He hung up and said to himself, *If I'm not indicted for embezzlement first.*

12

At ten minutes until two, the Snappy Service Café had three customers, now four as Ross took the booth closest to the front door. He plucked the menu out from behind the sugar dispenser and looked up at the chalkboard with the daily specials neatly printed on it: chili, corned beef sandwich, or chicken fried steak with mashed potatoes and green beans. He decided on chili.

"Coffee, mister?" Jill smiled down at him, the ever-present Silex pot in one hand, the other hidden in her uniform's patch pocket.

He didn't speak at first, only locked onto her blue eyes; they held that connection for a moment. "Okay," he said.

She set a cup down, tipped her wrist over, and poured with precision from a good foot above the cup. She looked around when two men said her name as they were leaving; she waved and called out their names. "Say," she said to Ross, "going to take my lunch break right now. Okay if I join you?"

Ross thought about that. "Sam doesn't mind you fraternizing?"

"That's a yes then," she said. "So what you having?"

"I thought chili," he said.

"We're out. Corned beef sandwich's good," she countered.

Ross agreed and smiled as she hustled off. So far, he thought, being invited to have lunch with a blue-eyed waitress was his highlight of the day. When she breezed up balancing their food on two forearms, he couldn't help but grin. Her eyes were bright, and she was breathing fast.

"What's that?" Ross asked, looking at her food.

"Chili," she said.

"Thought you were out."

"We are," she said. "I put dibs on the last bowl before you came in. Honest. You want it, though, that's okay with me. I'll take your corned beef instead."

He smiled, said no. She smiled back and dipped a big spoon into the simmering chili with a glob of cheddar cheese and fistful of diced onion on top. Ross bit into the sandwich, enjoyed the mellow tang of the corned beef, and there they sat, eating and sharing gentle smiles. Blanche came by and poured warm-ups, smiled at Jill and winked at Ross.

"What's that for?" he asked Jill. "Blanche. The wink and all."

"Nothing. Just foolishness. We tease one another whenever we're sitting with a customer. We only bother the solos. You lonely guys," she said.

"So you think guys alone are always lonely, then?"

She crumbled a soda cracker into the chili. "You should see some of them. Pathetic hangdog faces. Drumming their fingers on the table and looking around, reading the menu two, three times. Oh yeah. Jump at the chance for some company. Then," she patted the air, "and then they tell you their life story or their problems. It's like being a bartender, I swear."

"So you ready to hear mine?" he said.

She looked up and licked some chili from her lips. "Life story or problems?"

"What do you have time for?" he kidded.

She looked up at the wall clock. "Depends. You're quick, maybe both."

He laughed and forgot the partly eaten sandwich on his plate. "I wouldn't bore you with my tale of woe. And certainly not my life story."

"That's okay," Jill said. "No, really, I 'd like to hear about you…." Her voice trailed off.

"Okay then," he said, "how about problems? I'll go first, then it'll be your turn. Game?"

Jill lowered her spoon back into the chili and looked over at him, smile turned off. "Doesn't work that way," she said. "Customers only. Tell you what, let's talk about something that's not personal, like the blast."

"Tired of talking about that." He looked into her eyes until she looked down.

"How's your sandwich," she said, nodding at the remnants.

"Okay. Really wanted chili," he said.

She laughed and shoved the bowl at him. "Here, finish it off."

"Nah. Think we're done eating," he said. "Don't you?"

She shrugged. "Okay, I'll clear this away, then."

"But I still have time on the clock, don't I?"

"Guess so, if you want." She settled against the booth's cushioned back.

He inhaled and for a long moment thought about laughing it off. Then he told her—about the trouble he was in. She listened like he was the most interesting person she had ever heard. Her eyes stayed on his the entire time it took him to tell his side of things. Neither of them took note of the three times Blanche came by to warm up their coffee or refill their water glasses. When he was done, he sat back, put his palms down on the table, and instantly felt the flush of regret run up his neck and color his face. How reckless, sharing the most threatening episode in his life with a waitress with blue eyes.

Jill sat very still in her pink and white waitress uniform, a thin gold-link necklace twinkling at her throat. Finally, she reached out and drank deeply from her water glass. "My gosh," she said. Her voice was a whisper. "What can you do?"

He shrugged and blundered on. "They can't prove I took the money—because I didn't. Then again, I can't prove I didn't because I don't know what he did with it and he can't say, now can he? Real mess, huh? Any of your customers' problems match that?"

Her smile was sad. "No, mostly they gripe about their jobs or their wives—hear a lot about wives."

Ross laughed. "I haven't told you the wife part yet. But now it's your turn."

She looked up at the wall clock. "I should be getting back to work. About coffee break time. We'll be busy."

"Still have fourteen more minutes. I kept track," he said.

"Really, I don't have anything to say, I…"

"What about Gordon?" he asked.

"You mean the Colonel?" Her voice dropped.

"But you called him Gordon," Ross said. "Why?"

She looked up as a customer walked by. "No reason," she said. "His name was in the paper is all."

"Who's your friend, the one who knows the Colonel real well?"

Jill twisted a paper napkin, looked down as she did, and sighed. "Well," she began and spoke slowly, "I know that he wasn't hurt in a car wreck. Know that for sure. So do you, isn't that so?"

Ross felt the feather in his stomach again but said nothing in response.

"Doesn't matter if you say so or not. I know where he was when that truck exploded," she said, "and it wasn't in a car out to the country club. Wasn't."

Ross hesitated, swallowed, then asked, "Okay, where, then?"

"But you already know where he was," she said.

Ross moved his coffee cup around in a circle. "Tell me anyway," he said.

She blinked, and her eyes moistened. "No."

"Because of your friend?"

She bobbed her head and wiped a finger beneath one eye when a tear broke loose.

"I know who she is," he said.

She looked up, eyes wide.

"Mona, right?" Ross said. "Mona Johnson."

"Oh," she said and wrapped her arms around her torso. Then she slid out of the booth, collected their dishes, and left Ross juggling truths and lies and contradictions. He left the café without looking again for Jill and returned to the office, taking the elevator and listening patiently as Charlie Beamus pressed the latest gossip on him. Beamus was ebullient with a tale that one of the Roseburg Merchant Police was certain that the Gerretsen fire was one of a number of arson fires that occurred in the days before the blast.

"This here guy, the merchant cop, Lloyd's his name, he even knows who done it," said Beamus, jiggling one leg on the rung of his stool. "Says so, anyhow. Thinks was some little gal lived close by near the tracks. Remember the Flegal Building fire? And the sewage plant? They was set fires. Arson. Merchant cop, he swears this girl was at the scene of both them fires. Saw her running the night of the blast, too. But hell, everybody was so busy then that no one followed up on her maybe setting the Gerretsen fire. Funny thing though, Mr. Bagby?"

"What's that?" Ross asked as he stood at the elevator's open gateway.

"The girl's family? They's gone. Cleared out not more than a week after the blowup. Funny, huh?"

No not funny, thought Ross, *tragic is more like it*. He was getting used to tragic. As he was picking up three envelopes and the latest *American Legion* magazine that had been shoved through the mail slot, the phone rang. It was Emeline Armbruster. She wanted to see him that afternoon, if he could find the time. It was already three thirty, so he told her he would come right away.

Miss Emeline lived in a historic farmhouse out old Melrose Road. The house sat on a plot that used to be part of the old Stryckland farmstead, just large enough for her roses and vegetable garden; she had sold the rest of the acreage years ago. And there she had lived all by herself for nearly six decades; never married or had a beau as far as anyone knew. Worked by Jonah's side at the corporate office until he retired—they both quit on the same day and, except for the Foundation, never participated in the Armbruster Lumber business again.

Ross met Miss Emeline coming out of her flower garden holding a fistful of spectacular deep pink roses. Ross stepped through the gate of a low white picket fence and waved. She was wearing a pair of man's dungarees and a white linen blouse with the sleeves rolled up on her sinewy arms. She held the flowers aloft and smiled.

"I thought Maybelle might enjoy a bouquet from my garden," she said.

"Amazing color," Ross said. "May will love them. Here, let me smell. Wonderful."

"Let's go in," she said, "and I'll put them in water until you leave."

She strode past him straight as a hoe handle. He followed her up the walk into the coolness of the house. The aroma of the place was oddly pleasing, part settled-in older person and part energy of someone who was still living life. The hardwood floors were alive with richly colored scatter rugs, offset by the more reserved tones of the upholstered furniture. In one corner sat an old pump organ; the rear wall of the living room was floor-to-ceiling shelves, every inch filled with books.

Soon she was back from the kitchen with a large vase containing the roses. She set them on a side table, fussed with the blooms for a moment before turning her attention to Ross, who was standing with his hands in his pockets watching her with interest and curiosity; she was so vigorous. She gestured for him to be seated across from her on the sofa.

"Can't recall, Ross," she said, "you been here before?"

"I have," he said. "Just thinking about that. It was on your eighty-fifth birthday. Whole Armbruster clan was here, must have been what, two years ago?"

"So much fuss over getting old—older." She laughed and pushed at her hair with one hand. "Didn't really feel it in my bones until then. Must have started with that party, my arthritis I'm speaking of here." She flexed a hand studded with enlarged knuckles. "If that's the case, I don't need more birthday parties."

"I'll spread the word."

"Would you, please?" She studied him. "Thank you for coming out. Probably know why."

"Not hard to figure," he said.

"Uh-huh. So, how are you doing? Darn tough morning you had," she said.

"Not so good," he said. "Can't believe it, really."

"I'm sure." She studied him. "Say, would you like something cool to drink? I'm a bit dry. Ice water in the fridge, or I can make lemonade."

"Water's fine," he said.

She was back in minutes with two tall cobalt blue glasses tinkling with ice cubes. She saluted, and they each took a long drink.

She swirled the glass in her hand as she spoke, veins nurtured through years of work in her gardens stood out on the back of her hands and up her thin, wiry forearms. "Talked with Maybelle yet? About all this?"

"Haven't been home," Ross answered. "Didn't call her, either. Rather tell her in person."

Miss Emeline studied him for a moment and took another drink of ice water. "Life here in the county, it been good to you? You're from Kansas?"

"Nebraska," he said. "How do you mean, good to me?"

Miss Emeline bobbed her head. "Nebraska, I knew that. I mean, are you content? Feel like this is home? Have friends? Doing things that speak to your innards and so on?"

Ross tipped his glass so the ice cubes moved around in a circle. He looked up at her and smiled but didn't know what to say.

"As I figure it, you and Maybelle have been married eleven years," she said.

"Twelve," Ross responded. "Married in forty-seven. You were there."

"Deary, I been to more weddings than I've taken baths. Couldn't pick one from the other if the fate of the world counted on it." She studied him some more. "Twelve years, plenty of time to decide if a person's where he wants to be. Frankly, you've been a shadow to me. There when Maybelle's around, not when she's not. Just who are you anyway, Ross Bagby? The man with the last name his own wife doesn't use."

"She isn't even a Knox," Ross said. "Least I have company."

Miss Emeline laughed and crossed a lanky leg. "Child puts too much stock in the Armbruster name."

"Hey," Ross said, "it counts big around here, Miss Emeline. You know that."

"I didn't get you out here to talk about Armbrusters," she said. "Need to know how you are. You contented?" she asked again.

"Contented?" Ross drained his glass and set it down. "I don't know, guess I never think of life that way. Hardly think of life much at all. Not l-i-f-e." He spelled it out. "I just get up every day and go do something then come home say hello to the woman I married, if she's around. May's quite involved. Then we eat, read or watch a little TV, go to bed. Next morning, guess what? Do it again."

"My, my," Miss Emeline said, a cheerless smile on her mouth. "Living can get in the way of a life, can't it? Whatever happened to your grand plan?"

Ross cocked his head. "Grand plan?"

"Everyone has big ideas when they're young," she said. "Some are small, some are enormous, but they're all grand in the mind. Trick is not letting the juice run out of them. So tell me, Ross Bagby from Nebraska, did you have some big plans?"

He picked up the glass again, rolled it between his palms and chuckled. "When I was a kid, all I wanted was the paper route Harvey Nettles had. Guess that was my first *grand plan*. Harvey was four years older than me, and I wanted to be him. He delivered the *North Platte-Herald*, rode a gleaming Shelby-Eagle bike, and collected money every month from my dad. Harvey impressed my dad. He said over and over, *That Nettles kid is a sharp cookie.*

"When Harvey finally gave up his route, I applied and got it. Well, Harvey Nettles was a sharp cookie, but my dad said I was in over my head. Turned out I was damn good at it. Mr. Richards, the route manager, told my father I was the best carrier he ever had. All my father said was *Hope he don't mess up.*"

"So," Miss Emeline said, "all of the juice ran out of your plan right then because your daddy knew you were going to go a long ways farther than he did."

Ross hesitated. "He hated his job, know that much. Grocery warehouseman for thirty years. Union man, angry. Biggest thing in his life was being promoted to forklift driver. I hated him sometimes, but he worked like a mule for us, my mom and me. What was his grand plan? Doubt he had one. If he did I'll never know, had a heart attack when I was a teenager. Drove his forklift right into a stack of pallets and died with Gold Medal unbleached flour up to his waist."

"I had a grand plan," Miss Emeline interrupted. "Very long time ago." She smiled like a little girl. "Wanted to teach. Went to teachers' college and taught school in northern California. Little school, tiny. That was 1895. I was twenty-three. Wait."

She raised a forefinger, pushed herself up out of the chair, danced over to the pump organ, and picked up a framed photograph, took a blue and white handkerchief from her back pocket and wiped the picture glass. When she held the photo out for Ross, her expression was one of delight and anticipation. He held the small wooden frame in both hands. It was a picture of several children and a young woman standing on the steps of a tiny frame building.

"Schoolhouse," he said. "That you?"

"That's me." Her eyes were bright. "Me and my five pupils on the steps of the Little Sequoia schoolhouse. That was 1897, the last year I ever taught."

"Why?"

"Jonah. He called me to come help him fulfill his grand plan," she answered. "I did, and his plan became mine." When she saw him studying her, a small frown on his face, she said, "That's what happens sometimes. Grand plans are a photograph on the shelf, and real life takes over."

He looked at the picture again. "Too bad for you."

"Oh no," she said. "You see, I'll always have them. Always have Sarah, Hope, Ephraim, little Nellie, and Charles." She pointed to each face as she named them. "And the frame, it's made of redwood, made for me by Hope's father. They gave me this before I came north."

"But you'd only begun," Ross said. "Playing out your grand plan, I mean."

"I had a piece of it though, didn't I? What about you?" She put the picture back on the organ and sat again in the armchair and smiled at him. "You had a piece of dream yet?"

"You're getting after me, aren't you?" he said. "Why?"

"Since you're watching over the Foundation, figured I'd better find out more than I know about the real Ross Bagby, not the one who shows up at Armbruster turnouts."

Ross crossed a leg and gripped his ankle with both hands. "I thought you asked me out here to grill me about the money."

She waved a hand at him. "The money? I know you didn't do that. Not about that. Also, I know you were shanghaied like I was. Brought here because…well what else could you do? Jonah says come, what could I do?"

"May and I chose to come here. We did," Ross said. "We talked about it, discussed the options, where we wanted to settle, where I could work, if she wanted to pursue employment. Came down to going back home for both of us, Roseburg or North Platte."

Miss Emeline's eyes softened. "You really think Maybelle would have settled in Nebraska with you, Ross? Not on the hair of your chiny-chin-chin. She's an Armbruster. You imagine an Armbruster playing second fiddle to an accountant in North Platte? You were set up, Ross, like I was before you. And what could we do? We love them. You came west for love, not a career. I came north for my big brother, whom I love dearly. Thing was, we had a world to conquer and I had equal say, equal power and equal respect. I was needed, Ross." Miss Emeline gently shook a finger at him. "Nobody needs you, do they? By marriage you're part of the Armbruster clan. You're in the holding pen, shall we say. Beyond that—what?"

Ross felt the redness of humiliation course up his neck. He clenched his jaw several times but didn't know how to respond. But there she sat, waiting him out.

"Tell me," she said when he didn't reply, "what do you get out of bed for? You said *go do something*. What's that mean?"

"I don't know what you're after here, but I'm finding this slightly insulting," he said, an edge to his voice.

A chirp jumped out of her throat. "Slightly insulting, you say. I would think so. I've been running you down, and you're only slightly insulted? Goodness man, you haven't misplaced it, you've dug a hole and buried it deep."

"What?"

"And don't even recognize it," Miss Emeline blurted. "Your pride! Your ego! Your balls, man!"

Ross dampened a flash of anger and gripped his hands together. "Where are we going with this?"

"Ross Bagby, I'm probing your innards. Want to know what's in there. And I have a good reason. Heard you talked with Jonah. How's he seem to you?"

"I don't know," Ross said. "Okay, I guess. Frail."

"Not strong as a bull then?" she asked.

"Course not, but he's ninety years old."

"And I'm eighty-seven," Miss Emeline said. "In better condition than Jonah but still older than everybody I meet come the other way down the street, let me tell you. Time is not on my side or Jonah's. But we still have plans. Plans we'd better tie down pretty darn quick. That's the way it is when every sunup is a surprise. And *you* figure in our plans."

"Me?" Ross was totally confused.

"Colonel's not coming back," she said.

"You think he's going to pass on?"

"Doesn't matter," she said. "He's not going to run the Foundation. Jonah and I have talked and made up our minds. Like I said, we don't have a lot of time left between us, and the Foundation is our one remaining grand plan, Ross."

"Doesn't Neville pretty much control the Foundation?" Ross asked.

Miss Emeline sniffed. "Thinks he does. Foundation isn't part of Armbruster Lumber. It's a separate charity. Original funds came from Jonah and me. When we retired, we spent our time on the Foundation, had a wonderful time until Jonah's health caved in. That's when Neville offered to put a board together and hire someone to run things. At the time, that was a relief. But never liked that man, the Colonel. And Jonah and I, we know Neville doesn't respect the Foundation, not like he should."

"So what are you suggesting?" Ross asked.

"Become permanent director." She smiled. "Make the Foundation your grand plan. The time you spent with Jonah the other day made him feel good about you, Ross. Told me, *He's a good man, Emeline, a good one.* I agree. All I need to know is if you're willing to take the job and if need be to fight for it. Neville is going take some convincing."

Ross felt something roll over in his stomach just before he said yes.

13

Ross drove home with Miss Emeline's roses on the seat beside him and wondered how best to tell Maybelle that the earth had tilted since breakfast. But she wasn't there, just a note on the kitchen table: *Golf tournament meeting at country club. TV dinners are in the freezer. See you around nine.* He found a vase in the cupboard above the sink, plunked the roses down in the middle of the dining room table, preheated the oven to 350, then let a sliced ham Swanson frozen dinner incinerate while he watched the local news on television. With the manager of the Chamber of Commerce declaring that the blast might prove to be a blessing for Roseburg, Ross threw the burnt mess and warped aluminum tray in the garbage. He snapped the television off, mixed a bourbon and seven, and went out on the patio; he was still there when Maybelle came home. He heard her car door slam and felt his body tense. She called his name a couple of times before finding him, sitting calmly, looking down into the lights of the town.

She plopped onto the lounge next to him. "I'm exhausted. What you drinking? Ugh, not that. Would you be a dear and fix me a gin and tonic? Thank you." She kicked off her heels as he walked off, rubbed each foot, and sighed.

He returned with her drink and sat down again. A late summer dusk settled in, and the warm day began to cool; it was quite pleasant. They sat together, sipped their drinks and seemed to be living the good life; at least the neighbors would say they were. After all, they were Armbrusters.

"I never asked you," he said, breaking the silence, "why Carleton. Of all the colleges you could've attended, why there?"

She laughed. "Where'd that come from?"

"I don't know," he said, "just popped into my head. Why did you?"

She swallowed some more gin and leaned her head back on a plastic pillow. She laughed again. "You want to know the truth? It was simply so I wouldn't end up at Oregon State where all the local boys went. And to find you, dear."

"That might have been true—once," he said.

"Now, now, don't pout," she teased, "doesn't become you. Life moves, on and we grow up. You didn't expect to live the college life forever, did you? That was a playpen. Where we were in our prime, when we were absolutely the best physical animals we would ever be. God, we had fun. Even learned something. Carleton was small, far away, and Sally Nichols, a girl I knew from Eugene, went there. So I did. Simple, really. Had to go to college, couldn't be who we are in this town and not go to college. So all that and to be able to outtalk the boys at the dinner table." She swirled the ice cubes in her glass. "And I have ever since. Now why'd that pop into your head?"

"Oh, Miss Emeline asked me to come out to her place this afternoon to talk about the Foundation," he said.

"That's where the roses came from, then," she said. "Thought you were being romantic. Fat chance, huh?" She chuckled. "So, what about Aunt Emy?"

"We got into this discussion about life's grand plans," he said. "She wanted to know what mine was."

"I can tell her," Maybelle said.

"Oh, and what is, or was, my grand plan?" he asked.

"Go to Carleton, marry a rich girl, and take life easy," she replied.

Ross turned his head to look at her. "You really think that?"

"Sure," she said. "Same reason everybody was there. Get that degree, marry up, and enjoy security and position."

"You really thought that of me, May?" he asked again.

"Don't be hurt," she laughed. "No, not in so many words at the time, but when it all began to come together—us, marriage, where we'd live—then, yeah. Why not? Life is ninety-percent strategy, ten percent passion I say. And Ross, honey, we used up our whole ten percent at Carleton."

"That's cynical," he said. "So what we're doing now, this is the strategy part?"

"Now you're being petty," she said. "I'm going in, take a bath and go to bed. Coming?" She swung her legs around and stood holding her glass and her shoes.

When she started for the door, Ross said, "A lot of money is missing from the Foundation." He felt her pause in the shadows. "They think I took it."

She turned at the patio door and stared back at him in the dimming light. After a moment, she tiptoed in her shoeless nylons back to the lounge and dropped down on it like a sack of meal.

"You didn't know?" he said. "Was sure your father would call to fill you in."

"He didn't," she said in a quiet voice. "I mean, no I didn't know...Ross, how much?"

"Ten thousand."

She dropped her shoes. "Ten thousand! How? I mean, where'd it go?"

"Colonel," Ross said. "Proving it will be something else."

"The Colonel took it? Then why do they think you did it?"

"I was his dupe," he said. "Had me write the checks, cash them, and give him the money."

The shock on her face was the first honest reaction he had seen from her in a very long time. It made him smile.

"Why are you smiling?" she said.

"Such a fucked-up mess, that's why," he answered. "I handled the money, and the one person who knows I didn't steal it is in a coma and may be a vegetable for the rest of his days."

"So what will happen?" Maybelle asked and massaged one foot again.

"Everybody is running their own little investigations," he said. "Neville. The accountant. Probably Kribs. And I'll sure have to dig into it myself to protect my backside. When there's been enough backtracking, Neville will convene the board, and they'll hash out what to do about it."

"So tell me," she said and leaned toward him. He was still stretched out on the other lounge chair. "Truth, Ross. Did you take it? Now wait, before you get riled, I need this one time to clear the air between us, just us now." She paused to study his face. "Did you do it?"

"If I tell you yes, what then?" He smiled at the long pause before she spoke.

She sat still, not even swatting at the black fly that landed on her bare arm. "Yes?" she said. "You're saying you did it? Why? We have money."

Ross rose up and set his feet down. "You aren't even sure if I would do something like that."

"I didn't say that. But you said..."

"Miss Emeline knows I didn't do it," he interrupted. "She was at the meeting this morning and heard all of the damning evidence from the CPA, and it sounds bad. She knew instinctively that I am innocent of this thing. She knows it and told me so."

"Ross, I'm not accusing you."

"Do you know my character, May?"

"Character? You mean, are you honest and such?"

"And such," he parroted. "Yes, do you live with an honorable, ethical man?"

"Yes, I think you are an honest person."

He laughed. "I am in deep shit. My wife *thinks* I am an honest man. Not that she *knows* I'm an honest man."

"Damn it, Ross," she said. "We have to get clear here, between us, you and me. We have to agree on the story we will stand by when the accusations start flying. This is Armbruster business, for god's sake."

"Yes, Armbruster business," he said.

"Ross. Did you steal the money?" she demanded.

"Of course not." He said the three words calmly.

She stood and inhaled and let it out all at once. "All right, then. I know where I stand."

"And where's that?" he asked.

"We'll deny all charges," she said.

Ross watched her limp off on sore feet. When he heard the tub filling, he went down to the basement and lifted weights for a few minutes; it always helped him sleep. Maybelle was reading by the time he came up to the bedroom. She lowered her book and watched him hang up his clothes.

"My father called while you were downstairs," she said.

"Oh? What did he want?"

"Asked if we'd talked about the Foundation. Actually he said the *mess* at the Foundation. I told him we had, and he said he was behind you, didn't for a moment think you'd do such a thing. Said he just wanted you to know."

"Your dad is a good man," Ross said. "Not only because of that. He just is."

Maybelle blinked before saying, "I know."

"Do you?" He slid into bed, rolled over, and shoved his fist into the pillow. Sleep came grudgingly.

14

Mid-morning of the following Wednesday, Neville called Ross and told him that the board would be meeting at nine the next morning; Neville had already notified everyone by phone. In a voice devoid of energy, he let Ross know that nothing was required of him: no agenda, no financial statement, no minutes. "Just be there," he said. The tone of Neville's voice sent a chill across Ross's shoulders and inspired him to go back over his own reclamation of the money trail. A couple more bits of data came to mind; he added them. He was certain that what he had reconstructed would jibe with the actual financial records held by Raymond Squire. But he also knew that that wasn't the issue. The damning point wasn't an accurate record of cashing checks; it was *did he pocket the money*?

With the office empty and nothing particular to do, Ross was dead cold alone. As he sat in the Colonel's chair, he felt a disconnection, a powerlessness, the isolation of floating without oars. He picked up the phone. When Monte Coe answered, Ross said, "I need a friend, and you're it. Meet me for lunch in fifteen minutes at Snappy's."

He had just shoved back from the desk when the phone rang. It was Kribs.

"What'd you do with the money, Bagby?" he said.

"What do you want, Kribs?"

Kribs laughed. "You're sweating, aren't you?"

"You want something in particular," said Ross, "or are you just killing time on the Armbruster clock?"

"I know you done it," Kribs said.

"You mean you know I *did* it. Thought you went to college," Ross said.

"Listen mister, just wait until tomorrow. Won't be a grammar lesson then."

"Bring your own maple bars," Ross said and slammed the receiver down.

He sat with his hand on the receiver for a moment, swore, and then walked up the street to the café. Monte was already there, sitting in the rear booth in soiled coveralls, drinking ice water.

He grunted when Ross dropped onto the seat across from him, glowering. "Thought you meant today," he said and cracked an ice cube with his teeth. "Why the ugly face?"

"Got a call from my favorite son-of-a-bitch before I could get out the door," Ross said. "Why? Take you away from anything important?"

"Livelihood. Stuff like that. But damn, when a man calls says I'm his friend, I'll kiss off most anything."

"Did I just say friend? I should've said *only* friend."

"Hey," Monte said, "guess that means you're buying, then."

Ross laughed. "Okay. Anything on the menu."

They ordered burger baskets and vanilla milkshakes from Blanche; Ross didn't see Jill and didn't look for her. The two men sat quietly, Monte cracking ice and Ross worrying the salt and pepper shakers with his left hand.

"You know," Monte said at last, "I divine water, not minds. Guess you'll get round to spilling what's on yours 'fore I lose the rest of my hair."

Right then, Ross told him about the missing ten grand. Burgers came. They wolfed them down with the vanilla shakes and squeezed in a word here and there. Ross fleshed out the Foundation crisis between bites. Afterward, they sat wiping burger grease off their fingers and finished the milkshakes.

"Okay, for starters, know you didn't do it," Monte said, dipping a fry in catsup. "Take the money. Not in your blood. Trick's going to be finding out where all that cash went to. Ideas?"

"No," Ross confessed.

"Come on now," Monte said. "You got to have a suspicion or two. Think."

"Monte, I've been doing nothing but think about this for a solid week. Day and night I've been thinking. Can't sleep. Gives me plenty of time to consider the possibilities."

"Okay," Monte said. "Eliminate stuff. New car?"

"Nothing out of the ordinary." Ross shook his head. "These people get new cars as often as I get a new bottle of bourbon."

"But stuff like that," Monte pressed, "boat, bunch a new furniture, you know, expensive stuff."

"I wouldn't know," Ross said. "I mean, nothing you wouldn't expect from a man with his ego and connections. The Colonel, he kept up. Ten thousand's a hell of a lot of dough in one lump, but you spend it over time probably doesn't stand out with the likes of the McKenzies."

"That's it," Monte said. "His wife. She been spending like crazy?"

"Again, I wouldn't know," Ross said.

"Big house remodel? New house?" Monte kept on.

Ross shook his head.

"Hmm." Monte chewed on more ice. "Got to be something we're not thinking of. Hey, gambling. He go to Vegas or Reno much? No? Thought I had something. Guy likes to run with the money crowd. Can't you picture him in the casinos, playing twenty-one, poker, with a dame on his arm?"

Ross sat up, his eyes widening. "Jesus," he said. "Maybe that's it." He slapped a palm against his forehead. "How dense can I be?"

"Knew it." Monte rapped a knuckle on the table, rattling the glasses.

"He was seeing this beautician," Ross said. "That's where he was the night he got zapped in the head. Mona's her name. Mona Johnson. Staring right at me. Monte, you're worth your weight in mill ends."

"Thanks," Monte grinned, "I feel warm all over."

"Now if you'd just take a bath, I'd give you a big hug," Ross laughed.

"That'll keep me away from water for a spell," Monte said.

"Coffee for either of you fellas?" It was Jill.

Ross looked up and felt his chest go tight. She was looking right into him, smiling; one of those low-wattage smiles that crawls inside a man. She held a coffee pot that was three-quarters full in one hand and dangled two cups from the fingers of the other. He nodded, and she poured; Monte kept his mouth shut and chewed on a toothpick. She turned her eyes on Ross again before moving on to the next table.

Monte dumped a squirt of cream into his cup. "There's a cutie pie," he said. "Course, it's obvious that you already know that."

"What?" Ross had been watching her back. "Don't be an ass. She's just a kid."

"Kid my butt," Monte said. "Growed woman with life behind her. And you're taking notice, I can tell."

"Damn it, Monte."

Monte stirred his coffee and smirked. "Mighty pretty thing. Dead duck blue eyes."

Ross looked down the aisle and followed her movement. "Tell you something that has me wondering about her, though."

"I'd be careful, I was you," Monte cut in. "That kind of woman can be dangerous. Cute as hell and all, but she can get in a man's head, and he becomes a dang fool. I speak from experience."

"Get off it, Monte. That's not what I'm talking about," Ross said.

"Man thinking from his crotch up not rational," Monte went on. "Wake up on the scrap heap if you ain't careful."

"Don't even know why I called you," Ross said. "Come on, I have to get back to the office to prepare for my execution tomorrow. Plan the menu for my last meal."

"Shit." Monte made the word three syllables. "They ain't going to do nothing to you. Wife's got Armbruster blood. Not gonna humiliate one of their own."

Ross looked up as a man he knew came out of the men's room in the corner. They nodded at one another when he passed, but neither spoke. "There's a lot of ways to be punished. Could kick myself for being the Colonel's pigeon. Being pitiable is worse than being horsewhipped."

Monte sucked on his front teeth. "So they probably not going to turn the law onto you, but let the shunning and funning begin. That it?"

"Monte Coe, the water-witching philosopher," Ross said. "Let's get out of here." He slid out of the booth and strode up to the counter. Jill came over and tapped out his bill on the cash register. They traded money and eye contact.

After exchanging a couple more insults, Ross and Monte parted ways out on the sidewalk. Ross walked to the Foundation office mulling over his guesswork on the connection between the Colonel and Mona Johnson and what Jill knew about it. That all went out of his head when he found the office door unlocked and Germaine McKenzie sitting at his desk. They regarded each other quietly for several moments before Germaine pushed the leather chair back on its rubber rollers and stood.

"Not very comfortable," she said. "Thought it would be more comfortable than that. Used to see Gordon sitting in it and wondered why a man needs a big chair. Make him feel bigger? That it?"

Ross looked at the chair. "Could be. Don't know. It was just there when I sat down. Wouldn't have been my choice."

"Really?" She turned and examined the chair. "Thought every man coveted that kind of chair."

"Too pretentious, all that tufted leather, brass tacks, and then the high back. Like being on display," Ross said.

She laughed. "Thought that was the idea."

"For some, I guess," Ross said.

"Hmm. Well, I guess you're wondering what I'm doing here—in your office," she said. "Least your office for now."

"How is Gordon? Better?"

"No. There's no change," she said. "Not yet."

"Sorry."

"Yeah, well." She sighed. "I apologize for just barging in. Fact is, I thought you'd be here. When you weren't, I used Gordon's key."

"Entirely all right. As you say, I'm only using that chair for the time being. Something you wanted?" he asked.

She glided over to the conference table and sat down. Ross watched. When she walked, it was nearly impossible to ignore Germaine McKenzie. She had perfected a slow rolling gait that accentuated her hips and her very narrow waist, a waist she kept cinched up with a collection of wide belts. Wide belts made her waist seem even tinier. She wasn't a beauty, but she had a sensuality that caused most men to look. When she was seated and had wiggled herself comfortable, Ross sat across from her.

She fingered her wedding ring. "Heard about the problem here."

"Oh?"

"Oh?" She chuckled. "Ross, I know everything that goes on here."

"Not surprised," he said. "Expect you would."

"So about this missing money, was told you're trying to pin it on Gordon. Wait a minute—before you say anything, let me say this." The smiled faded from her face and her eyes. "If you do anything to taint the Colonel's name, I will make sure *your* name is trashed in this town. Don't care if you're getting transfusions of Armbruster blood. I'll put you in a boxcar back to Nebraska."

Ross didn't speak right away. He inhaled her tart perfume and chose his words.

"Kribs is your tattletale, isn't he?" he said as calmly as he could.

Her eyes flickered. "What if he is? I have a right to know about this outrageous allegation of yours."

"I've made no allegation, Germaine. All I've done is explain my part in all of this. And I know one thing for certain—I did not take the money. I wrote the checks, cashed them, and gave the money to the Colonel. The way he wanted. After that, I don't know where it went."

"Listen here, Ross," she said, leaning over the table, "I know you can't prove any of that. Can you? And if you can't then, by god, you'd better not be insinuating the Colonel even held a dollar of it in his hand."

"But it's true, Germaine," Ross said. "And I think you know it's true."

"I don't give a damn if it is true." She sat straight up. "I have to live in this town after the bastard's gone and I will not do it as the poor widow McKenzie who suffered humiliation because of her husband's indiscretions. I won't. I won't." She paused and added, "I just won't."

"What happened to the money, Germaine?" Ross asked.

She sat back and pulled a handkerchief from the purse she had laid on the table and dabbed her eyes. Her color had risen. A frail smile edged onto her face. "Look, Ross." She altered her voice, and Ross knew a chameleon of personalities was working on him. "I don't know about any money. Really I don't. Besides, it doesn't matter now does it?"

"What do you mean?" he asked. "Of course it does."

She lowered her eyelids and smiled. "No, it doesn't. They'll fuss around a bit, but if they can't figure it out, Neville will just make a donation from ALC to cover the loss."

"You don't know that," Ross said.

"Oh yes, I know that." She pushed the hankie back into her purse.

Ross studied her. "Wait. This has happened before, hasn't it?"

"Ross." She reached across the table, put a hand on his and squeezed. "Ross, life's a game. Don't you know? And a game is all about moves. We're playing chess, only it's with folks. Need pawns for it to work, but the trick is to use them, not to be one." She patted the back of his hand then began to lift each of his fingers slowly, let one drop, lift the next, and let it drop. When Ross pulled his hand away, she smiled at him through mascara-laden lashes.

"Understand now?" she said. "Don't want you messing with my reputation. Colonel's all I got no, matter what an SOB he's been."

Ross ran damp palms over his thighs. "Can't be a pawn now can I, Germaine?"

"Ross honey, hate to tell you this, but you already are. Have been all along."

15

Ross listened to Germaine's high heels tap out her departure on the tile floor of the hallway and, with her aroma still hovering like insecticide, decided on a course of action. Something he should have done a week ago.

He made a call, said he was coming, and drove northeast out of town to Buckhorn Road and the Boys' Home. He idled along up a long gravel entry road until he came up on an assemblage of rambling buildings: old farm house, barn, sheds, cabins, corral, and a fenced pasture where several horses and perhaps fifty head of Hereford cattle grazed. Richard "Red" Pritchard, the founder and headmaster of the school, greeted Ross as he got out of the car. He did a quick finger-pointing description of the grounds before leading Ross into the former farmhouse that served as an office and dormitory. A bedroom served as Pritchard's office.

"So," Pritchard said, "what's the story on the Colonel? Making a recovery, is he?" The man was leaning back in a wooden office chair with one leg propped up on the corner of a battered desk.

"No," Ross offered, "sorry to say. He's in a coma, you know, has been from the time of the accident. Still no change. Cause for concern, really."

"That so?" Pritchard held a hand up to a boy who started to enter the office. "See you later, Billy. Okay? Busy right now. After chow, how's that?" He looked back at Ross. "So that doesn't sound promising then for Colonel McKenzie. Well, we'll hope for the best. Sure it'll work out like it was meant to. So what brings you out our way, Mr. Bagby? Think I know."

Ross wiggled his butt around on the hard wooden chair and crossed a leg. "Who contacted you?"

Pritchard studied Ross for a moment before he spoke. "Got a phone call a few days ago from Neville Armbruster, the big gun at Armbruster Lumber. Guess you know that, though."

Ross nodded. "What did he want?"

"Look, I sure as hell don't want to mess up our thing with the Foundation," Pritchard said. "Before I say anything else, would you kindly tell me just what's going on?"

"My name come up when Neville spoke with you?" Ross asked.

Pritchard waited a moment before answering. "Fact it did."

"In what way?"

Pritchard chuckled. "Nah, I don't want to get between you fellas now. Something doesn't smell right here and...well, I just don't know which way the wind's blowing."

"Let me ask you this, then," Ross said. "When was the last time you saw Colonel McKenzie in person?"

Pritchard drew a hand across his mouth and looked off. "Geez, let me see now, last time I saw the Colonel in person. You mean face to face? Okay. Face to face. That would have been at the Rotary Club last fall. Club gave us a nice check and a certificate for community service. Saw the Colonel then, and we spoke afterward for a few minutes. That's it."

"Okay," Ross said. "Did Neville ask you that same question?"

"Nope, asked me when's the last time I saw *you*," Pritchard said. "Told him I'd never met you before at all. Wouldn't know you if I saw you on the street. Until now, of course."

"He didn't ask you about seeing the Colonel?" Ross pressed.

"How about receiving cash gifts from the Foundation?"

"What you mean?" Pritchard's eyebrows shot up.

"Did you ever receive any gift or grant from the Armbruster Foundation in the form of cash? Ever?" Ross said, tapping the edge of the desk.

Pritchard's face puckered up, and he looked at Ross as if he had asked him if he was selling boys into slavery. "Cash. Actual folding green? That your question?"

"That's it," Ross said. "Have you ever been handed cash by anyone from the Foundation? Anyone. Me, the Colonel, Neville Armbruster, Wendell Kribs, or Jonah Armbruster? Anyone?"

"Holy cow." Pritchard sat up straight. "This doesn't sound good. Answer's no, not one red cent. Money always comes to us by check. There some money missing?"

"There's been some bookkeeping errors," Ross said, carefully, "and we're backtracking every money trail we have, to find out what happened. With the Colonel out of the picture, we don't have his knowledge of things to help clear up the discrepancy. Didn't Neville ask you about receiving cash gifts?"

"Did not," Pritchard answered. "Can I ask you something, Mr. Bagby?"

"Sure. Call me Ross."

"Okay, Ross. This problem, it going to have any effect on our recent application?"

"You can relax on that. Board approved your last grant request a short while back. You'll be getting a check soon." Ross smiled when the man's face softened and his smile re-emerged. He left Pritchard standing in the yard with his arm resting across the back of a skinny little guy who wanted to wrestle.

Back at the office Ross made two phone calls, jotted some notes, and went home around six thirty. He was in the middle of a workout that evening when Maybelle yelled down that he had a phone call. He lumbered up the stairs, a towel around his neck, and used the extension in the living room. It was Miss Emeline; she wanted to know about the meeting the next morning. Did he have his head on? Could he do a better job of staking out his version of things? How were his innards? Before hanging up she said, "You're ready now, aren't you? To be the one?" He swabbed the tacky sweat from his face and neck and thought about being a pawn. "Yes," he said.

Maybelle was standing in the doorway watching him when he hung up. She started to say something, but he held up a hand and shook his head. He had had enough talk from enough people about what he ought to do. He showered, went to bed, and dreamed he was in high school in North Platte trying to get up his courage to ask Felicia Stone out on a date.

At six o'clock he got up groggy, puzzled over the weird dream and the fact that he could remember every detail. He shaved, dressed, left Maybelle sleeping, and drove to breakfast.

Snappy's was busy. The breakfast crowd was beginning to resemble the usual downtown customers as the town slowly returned to normal, although what *normal* meant for Roseburg had been changed—maybe for a very long time. Ross sat at the counter. Jill took his order and poured him a cup of coffee; they didn't talk.

When she stopped to refill his coffee cup for the third time, he whispered, "I know where your friend is." Her body froze for an instant before she took a step back. "If you don't already know," he added. She moved her head side to side once. "Do you want to know?" he asked.

She looked away, toward the front window for a long moment, then set the coffee pot on the counter. "Yes," she said.

Ross leaned forward a bit. "Far as I know, Mona is in Redding."

"Redding?" When he nodded, she whispered, "That's where her mama lives. I wondered where she got to. Beatrice, the apartment manager, you know where Mona lived? She wouldn't tell me. Just said Mona was on a trip. Didn't make any sense."

"She's on a trip all right," Ross said, "one way."

Jill tipped her head down as tears came into her eyes. At the call of *Order up!* she snatched a napkin from the holder, dabbed at her eyes, and walked away. Ross waited until she had delivered the order and was coming back. He motioned for her to stop.

"What time you get off?" he asked.

"Four," she murmured.

"I'll meet you at the Timber Room," he said, referring to the cocktail lounge a block away.

"No, I can't," she said.

"Think about it," Ross said. "I'll be there if you change your mind. We can talk."

She walked away, and he left the café. He had a dragon to slay—or at least wound. He tidied up the office one more time, pulled a file folder and legal pad from the top drawer of his desk, and waited. The arriving faces were unsmiling; even Kribs was sober.

Neville wasted no time with pleasantries.

"Meeting's called to order," he said, thumping a loose fist on the tabletop. He looked at Ross who was already dating a yellow page to record the proceedings. "Ross, no minutes. Now, as we left things last week," Neville said, folding his hands on the table, "we'd make another run at sorting this mess out. Have Ray Squire go over the books again with a magnifying glass. Then Wendell and I, we would contact most of the organizations that received funds over the last two years. All that was done. Results? Well," he sighed, "they're a big fat nothing. Ray didn't find anything new except an itsy bitsy posting error here or there. Wendell and I didn't learn a thing that would shed any light."

"So, where does that leave us?" asked John.

"Nowhere," said Neville. "Inconclusive is the only professional verdict I could get out of Ray Squire. We know the money's missing, we know how it was done, and we know the parties involved: Ross and the Colonel."

"What now?" asked Miss Emeline. "You accusing one or both of these men, Neville?"

"Not but one person to accuse," said Kribs, "the way I see it." He stared at Ross and then at the others. "Don't look at me like that, John. No, wait just wait a minute, will you? Ross wrote all the checks, including those sneaky ones made out to cash. Colonel signed them. Ross went to the bank and pocketed the money. Then Dick Arthur sees a check made out to cash, but referred to the Salvation Army by the memo, posts it, and it's gospel." Kribs pointed a finger at Ross. "And we'd have you dead to rights if the Colonel was able to talk."

Ross's heart was beating noticeably by this time, and he could feel nervous sweat building beneath his shirt. He did his best to appear calm by keeping a benign expression on his face and seeming to make important notations on his pad.

When Kribs ceased his tirade and the room was calm, Ross raised a hand and looked to Neville. "May I?"

Neville assented with a dip of his head. "I did a little investigating on my own," Ross said. "First, I made a visit to Buckhorn Boys' Ranch. Talked with Red Pritchard. Now Neville, you talked to Red, too, didn't you?"

"I did," Neville responded. "He was among several I spoke with. Why?"

"Funny thing. I figured that you would," Ross said, "you know, ask the same questions I would ask. But you only asked Red one question. Why was that?"

Neville inhaled sharply through his nose. "Just had the one question. I was looking for a pattern of information so I...I asked each grantee the same question. You see, if—"

"What was the question?" asked John.

Ross had never seen Neville with a red face. He sat back and waited for John to press the point. Neville looked down at his hands, interlaced his fingers, and tapped his thumbs together before answering.

"I asked Red Pritchard when was the last time he'd seen Ross Bagby."

"Why just that question?" John asked.

Neville played more thumb gymnastics. "Trying to see if there was any kind of pattern to this thing. Who saw whom when, how often, and...and like that. Process of elimination, John. Process of elimination."

"Well, I did ask Red Pritchard other questions," Ross said. "I asked him about the last time he saw the Colonel in person. Turns out it was last year at a Rotary function. Oh, I forgot. Neville, when was the last time Red had seen me in person? He say?"

Neville stalled, rotated his neck. "Guess he's never met you before. Said he wouldn't know you if he saw you."

"Until yesterday," Ross said. "Just to keep things straight, I also asked Red if he had ever received cold cash from anyone connected with the Armbruster Foundation: me, Gordon, Neville, Kribs, Jonah—any one of us."

"You got no right throwing our names out like that," said Kribs.

Ross laughed. "Really? Relax, Buckhorn folks have never ever been given actual cash. Not by any of us—or by the Colonel. Oh, and I made two other calls. Salvation Army and the Red Cross. Guess what? The directors there told me the same story. Except this time it was Kribs who called each of them and asked the very same question about me. One had seen me at a recent motion picture. The other vaguely remembers us crossing paths at a fund-raising dinner they had a while back. Both had seen the Colonel many times at meetings and functions."

"So?" Kribs challenged.

"So nothing," Ross responded. "And neither of them recalled ever being given a cash donation of the size in question. Said they would have remembered that for sure."

"Neville, I don't like the smell of this," said John. "What's going on?"

"Yes, Neville," Miss Emeline spoke sharply, "I'm with John. You aren't trying to pull something, are you? Be mighty disappointed if you were."

Neville sat quiet for a moment. "Thought I had this nailed," he said finally.

"Hell, still—" Kribs raised his voice.

"Shut up, Wendell. For once will you keep that yap of yours clamped?" Neville glared at his sycophant. "Thing is, even if it seems I wasn't being square, I still think the trail leads back to Ross. Can't imagine the Colonel doing this."

"Well that's a hell of a note," John said. "I happen to think it's the other way around, Neville, and for the same reason. Can't imagine Ross stealing money, either. You saying he has to sit idly by under your cloud of accusation, no way to clear himself with the Colonel out of commission? Just be a stout fellow? I say that's unacceptable. So now what?"

"Simply don't know. Damnable situation." Neville swabbed his forehead with an open hand. "Tell you all one thing, got me a lumber company to run. Can't be spending all my time fussing with a hand in the cookie jar here. Now don't get riled, Emeline, but I've got bigger fish to fry. A corporation worth millions, you may recall."

Miss Emeline raised her chin and gave Neville a cool stare. When she didn't respond, he shrugged.

"Regardless of our disagreement, we have to get a handle on this mess," Neville said. "I've been thinking this over." John grunted and leaned back, his smile cynical.

"Damn it, John, let me lay this out now. Okay, here's my thinking. Ross takes a leave of absence and—now doggone it, at least hear me out. So Ross, he takes some time off, and Wendell steps in as director just for a while. Figure Maybelle and Ross are due for a long vacation, Europe maybe, and I'll pay for it. How's that?"

"Ridiculous," said Miss Emeline. "You haven't got the answer, but you're expecting Ross to politely step aside like he's guilty. Neville, I never heard of a more dishonest approach to a thing."

"Can I ask one more question?" said Ross, trying to ignore the turmoil in his gut.

"Okay, sure." Neville raised an arm. "Shoot."

"Has money come up missing before? Here? At the Foundation?" He jabbed a forefinger into the tabletop.

Neville took off his glasses, held them out, flicked something off one of the lenses, and hung them back on his ears. His sigh was chest deep. "Where'd you hear that?"

"It's true isn't it? How much, and when?" No one spoke. Ross looked at each person, one at a time. "You all know about it, don't you? You do. I can see it. I'll be damned."

"Not the same thing at all," Neville said. "Someone's talking out of school. We had an agreement that wasn't to be broken."

"So I'm left hanging while you protect your backside?" Ross pushed his chair back and stood up. "That's it. You want me out of here, fine. You can have Kribs as your director."

John was laughing. "Wait, Ross." He grinned at Kribs's red face. "Sit down. Come on now, sit down. You're not resigning. No, Neville, fair's fair. He has a right to know. Hey, scowl all you want. I'm telling him. Okay, Ross, here's the story. Happened before you came on board. Dick Arthur was doing the books, and we came up a thousand dollars light. Short version, neither Dick nor the Colonel could vouch for what happened to it. Each blamed the other for messing up. It was a standoff. In the end, ALC made up the difference, and all concerned agreed to put a lid on it and chalk it up to a lesson learned."

"Small change compared to this," Neville said.

"Like hell, just more zeroes," said Ross.

Neville growled and pushed his chair back. "I've got a mill to run. Meeting's over. We'll work on this later."

"Need you to sign some checks," said Ross. "Grantee checks."

John laughed. "Look out for those made out to cash, Neville."

By the time Neville had signed the checks the others were gone. He thumbed through the pale green rectangles one more time before holding them out to Ross. "We need this to go away, Ross. No blame, just restore things."

"You mean replace the money," Ross said. "ALC like before?"

Neville stood and shook his head. "Can't—not this time. Before? That was pocket change, trivial mix-up, close to the vest. This, it's too much, gone too far. Lots of people know, too many. Got to clean it up, make it go away." He stared hard at Ross. "Fact is, want you to think about accepting responsibility and moving on to something else."

Ross blinked at the heat behind his eyes; he stood for a moment with his mouth hanging open. "What? You can't be serious. Damn it, Neville! Make me the scapegoat? Gordon did it. Don't look at me like that. You know he did."

"Whatever, doesn't matter," Neville sighed. "Can't be Gordon. Can't. It's about corrosion. Seen it before in companies. Lose trust, or there's animosity between certain people, you can't ever get back to level ground—gears won't mesh like before. Besides, Ross, you can do better. Remember Randy Smythe? Introduced you to him out at the country club. He owns Smythe Logging Supply. He's looking for a chief accountant. His guy is retiring. If I put in the word for you, the job's probably yours. Think about it. Be a good move for you."

"I'll bet," Ross said. "Saying Smythe would be willing to hire an accountant who's admitted to stealing from his employer? A thief? Guess you promised to make good on anything I steal, that it?

"Don't be a ass" Neville frowned.

"You know," Ross said, "there wouldn't be any corrosion if you pulled it together like last time. Clean up the Colonel's misappropriation. Then make things all shiny again by booting Kribs off the board. He's the weak link."

Neville sniffed and hitched up his pants. "Don't get it, do you?" He held up four fingers and began ticking them off. "First, Wendell and I go back to the Stone Age, not going to dump on him. Second, the Colonel's reputation is tied to Armbruster, Inc. Blacken his name it blackens ours. That isn't going to happen. Third, I control everything Armbruster. Everything. Emeline can make my life difficult if she chooses. I know she's taken a liking to you, so it's best you aren't involved in the Foundation from now on. Fact, Ross, you won't be. So fourth, I'll be in touch about the Smythe job. Grasp my meaning here?"

Ross fanned the checks in his hand and tried to appear unperturbed. "I understand what you're saying."

"Let's hope so,' Neville said. "Hate to have this thing get public attention, have the court get involved, charges filed and the like. None of us want that—do we? By the way, like I said, no minutes of this meeting. It was off the record, no action taken. Destroy anything you may have written down in there. Let's keep it in the family. Now I have to get out to Tenmile."

On an impulse, Ross grasped Neville's arm as he walked past. "Neville," he said, "you ever read the Foundation's mission?"

"You mean that human potential business? What about it?"

"Extraordinary, wouldn't you say?"

Neville pulled his arm free. "You getting religion, Ross? A puddle of goodwill, that's what the Foundation is, nothing more." He held up his four fingers again. "Don't forget."

"Oh, I won't forget anything," Ross said.

Neville studied Ross for a moment and left the office. Ross stood in the emptiness and mulled over the ultimatums he had been given; then he sat down and wrote everything he could remember of the ludicrous meeting. He trembled with rage when he re-read what he had written and considered what lay ahead—if he chose to contest his accusers.

He went looking for the brown leather briefcase he had brought with him the first day on the job. The briefcase had gone unused because there had been no reason to. It was wedged between a file cabinet and a bookcase in the outer office. He wiped it off and shoved in the papers on which he had recorded the events and data in question. That leather case, he determined, would not be out of his sight from then on.

16

Ross left the office, carrying his briefcase, and walked up Jackson Street to the U.S. Bank building and presented himself at the Smith and Squire office. A curious Raymond Squire came out to meet him and was visibly nonplussed when Ross asked for all of the files Squire had taken from the Foundation office. Squire stared at Ross as if a fuse had blown. After an odd interim, the man's mouth opened, closed, and opened again before actual words came out.

"You've caught me by surprise, Mr. Bagby," Squire said, his face reddening. "Frankly it would take some time to gather it all together."

"I can wait, Mr. Squire," Ross said. "Took you less than an hour to gather up our various files. Can't imagine it taking more than say, what? Fifteen or twenty minutes now that you have them all lumped together? Is that about right? I can sit right here in your waiting room and read a magazine." He picked up a copy of *Argosy.* "How about this one?"

Squire turned to see his receptionist in an open-mouthed stare and quickly ushered Ross into his office and gestured him into a chair. He nestled himself safely behind his desk.

"You know," said Squire, almost giggling, "this is a bit awkward, but does Mr. Armbruster know about this? I mean you getting the files?"

Ross leaned forward in his chair and propped his elbows on

the arms. He waited until he was certain that the accountant was truly uncomfortable before he spoke. "We had a meeting of the board this morning," he said, speaking slowly. "Neville reported your findings, or should I say your negligible findings?"

Squire rearranged three Eversharp pencils on his desk, lining them up in a row, each one a different color. "I completed my further analysis exactly as requested," he said.

"I'm sure you did. Thing is, you didn't uncover a smoking gun relative to the missing funds, am I right?"

"That's true, but…" Squire hedged.

"But what?"

"Look," Squire said, "I can't just release these documents to you, Mr. Bagby. Not without authorization from Mr. Armbruster."

"Is that right? Neville gave you specific instructions to hold on to the Foundation financial records? Now is that just to hold them from anyone, or me in particular?" Ross pressed.

Squire ran his fingers along the edges of his desk pad. "Well… he used your name specifically." His face had grown pink.

"So he told you, *Don't let Ross Bagby have these files?*"

"Something like that."

"When did he do that?" Ross kept his voice even.

"After my meeting with the board," Squire said. "Last week."

"But before you turned up nothing, zilch, zero," Ross said. "Zero that is, if you were intent on implicating me, Mr. Squire. Is that not right?"

"Mr. Armbruster gave me specific instructions, and unless…"

"May I use your phone?" Ross asked.

Squire sat up straight and looked at the phone on his desk.

Ross pushed himself up out of the chair. "Which line may I use?"

"Uh, well any not lit up," Squire said. "But really, can't we just wait?"

Ross was already twisting the dial with enough force that the phone hopped around on the desk. Raymond Squire settled back in his chair and appeared to be in pain.

"Neville Armbruster's office, please," Ross spoke into the mouthpiece; it had the faint aroma of Listerine on it. "Yes, Ross Bagby." Ross looked at Squire, smiled, and toyed with the phone cord while he waited. He stood straighter when Neville came on the line.

"Neville, I'm in Raymond Squire's office. I came over to retrieve our records, but he says I can't have them."

"I told him to hang on to those files for a while," Neville said. "What are you doing there anyway?"

"Since the audit is done," Ross said, "I thought we ought to have our financial records back where they belong."

"You're testing me," Neville said. "This isn't over, and you know it."

"I'm not testing you," Ross said and winked at Squire to cover his nervousness.

"Well then, those papers stay right there in Squire's office," Neville said. "You got that?"

"Look, Neville," Ross ventured, "regardless of how this turns out, the Foundation has to conduct business. And the man found nothing, am I right?" Ross waited for a response and looked at a U.S. Bank calendar on the opposite wall; the picture for August was of Crater Lake.

"Doesn't matter, Ross. Those files stay right there."

Ross looked down at the floor, toed a leg of the desk, and thought, *what the hell?* "Okay, but I used the last of the checks I had today, those you signed. Bills are coming due."

There was a pause. "Does Squire have the Foundation checkbook?" Neville asked.

"Yes," Ross said. "I have an idea. Why don't I send all of the bills to Mr. Squire here, get him a signature card with the bank, and we can…"

"Damn you, Ross."

"I mean, since you don't trust me, wouldn't that…"

Ross smiled and handed the phone to Squire. "Wants to talk to you."

Squire took the phone as if it would give him an infection and sat at attention. "Ray Squire," he said. "Yes, Mr. Armbruster. Well, I know, but he…Mr. Bagby just arrived…well, I wasn't expecting him." He raised his eyes to meet Ross's. "Of course. I'm only too happy to accommodate. You know that. Everything then. Certainly. And thank you as well…" He held the receiver out then set it back in the cradle. "He hung up."

"He does that," said Ross.

Squire adjusted his gold-rimmed glasses. "All right then, if you'll just wait right there." He held out both hands, palms opposing, and pointed exactly where Ross was to wait then moved off in brisk strides.

In less than five minutes Squire was back carrying a distended accordion file held closed by an elastic band. After Ross signed a receipt, Squire ushered him to the outer office. The clack of the door latch echoed in the hallway, and Ross stood alone, an ejected undesirable. He laughed, walked down the hall and, with the folder under one arm, pushed his way into the waiting room of Chapman, Hughes, and Knox, Attorneys at Law. He asked to see his father-in-law. A prim receptionist advised Ross that Mr. Knox was with a client; Ross waited.

Fifteen minutes later, John emerged accompanying a well-weathered man wearing bib overalls. They conspired in whispered words for a few moments before John patted the man on the back, eased him out the door and turned to greet his son-in-law. As usual, John Knox was impeccable, starched white shirt, nary a wrinkle, matching white teeth, striped tie perfectly knotted and cinched. Ross ran a hand through his thin, uncooperative hair and thought, *That's the best I can do on short notice.*

John saw the file at Ross's feet. "What's that, the missing cash?"

"Not funny," Ross said.

"Everything is funny as long as it is happening to somebody else," John said. "A Will Rogers quote, I believe. What do you have there?"

Ross pushed the accordion file with a toe. "Foundation financial records. Had to arm-wrestle Ray Squire for them and call Neville's bluff."

"Sounds curious. Come on in." They entered John's spacious corner office and sat in matching leather chairs in front a hockey-rink-sized desk. "So you arm-wrestled Ray Squire. What for?" John asked.

"Evidence," Ross extracted a ledger book, check register and a bundle of cancelled checks. "You have one of those thingamajigs that'll copy stuff?"

"Our Thermo-Fax? Sure. Here, give me what you want copied. I'll have the receptionist take care of it while we talk." He stepped out. "Now, what's this about bluffing Neville?" John asked on his return.

"Decided to drop by Squire's office, you know, down the hall?"

John nodded, and his face turned lawyerly.

"Thought I'd better get the records Squire absconded with," Ross said. "But Neville had given him strict orders not to let me have them."

"That so? Just you?" John asked.

"Just me," Ross reiterated. "After that lynch party this morning...hey, you know that's what it was. Anyway, figured I'd better get my hands on those records as soon as possible. Decided to just go get them, but Squire seized up. So I got Neville on the phone. He balked at my taking the records until I called his bluff. Said, okay, Squire can do the books." Ross leaned toward John. "Got the records."

"Don't get too cute with Neville," John said. "Man's not used to being outflanked. Has no sense of humor when it comes to his ego and his authority. By the way, what went on after I left this morning? You and Neville had a huddle?"

"That's why I'm here. Neville has a game plan. Want to run it by you."

John shifted in his chair. "What is it?"

"Flat out, I'm to be the villain. Wants me to accept the blame for the missing money and move on to bigger things. I'm guessing ALC will make up the shortage. Oh, and there just may be a job available for me with Smythe Logging Supply. All kept in the family, of course, but I'll still be the culprit. On the record. The threat is that if this thing doesn't go away, charges could be filed against someone. Can't imagine who that'd be."

John had his elbows on the chair arms. He made a tent of his fingers and sat quietly.

"Ridiculous," he said after a moment. "The intention of serving you up as the fall guy is intolerable. I don't like threats, even hollow ones. Neville's probably just rattling his saber about legal action. Still he's a skunk for doing it."

"There's something else." Ross cranked his mouth into a self-conscious smile. "Miss Emeline, she and Jonah have been plotting, and they want me to become the permanent director of the Foundation. No matter if Gordon recovers or not." He hesitated. "I…said I would do it."

John folded his arms and looked hard at Ross. "Is that what you want?"

"Yes, I do. I like the work. It's growing on me."

"Tweaking Neville's nose is not good," John said. "He's possessive of anything with Armbruster attached to it. Tell me, do you think she's got it all together?" He tapped the side of his head. "Miss Emeline, still sharp?"

"Oh yeah," Ross said. "I'd say anyone underestimating Emeline Armbruster is looking to walk away carrying his head at waist level breathing out through his neck."

"That's vivid enough," John laughed. "Hope she's up to it—taking on Neville, I mean. Her prerogative, of course, if she wants a good fight."

"Think we'll all be in for a fight," Ross said. "You know, I may have just been the Colonel's water boy—drifting along. Then the town blows up, shit hits the fan, and I'm covered in it. On top of that, I've been letting Kribs dictate to me like he is something more than a brownnosing buffoon. Well, that's over." Ross paused. "And another thing, I think I know where the money went."

John's body stiffened. "What? You kidding me? After all this falderal? Where?"

"Pretty sure it went to the woman," Ross said. "Spent on her I'm almost certain. The one the Colonel was with at the time of the blast? Mona Johnson? Beautician. You knew about that?"

"Well, he has a history of that sort of thing, but I hadn't heard of this. I'll be damned."

"Thought Maybelle may have told you. She knows a little."

"No, not a word," John said.

"Neville's really kept a lid on it, then," Ross said. "Told me to keep what he calls the *sleaze* between us. That's amazing. Neville and me sharing a secret—keeping mum about Mona Johnson. The hell with that, if the man wants to take me down, all bets are off. That's where the Colonel was the night of the blast, in an apartment down on Mosher with this young beautician."

"I'll be," John said. "So you think Gordon spent the money on this beautician? But how can you prove that?"

"That's what I intend to find out." Ross said. "On top of that, she was pregnant."

"Really? How you know that?"

"This Mona, she sent a letter to the Colonel," Ross said. "It was in the mail delivered to the Foundation after the explosion. She wrote that she was pregnant and wanted to know what to do." He laughed. "Really screwed up Neville's original scheme. Planned on getting the woman out of town quick, easy, and cheap. Should have heard him sputter and curse over that letter and lament his role of cleaning up the sleaze."

"So what did he do?" John asked. "You know?"

"Yes," Ross said. "Told me what he ended up doing and for me to keep my yap shut about it. Done deal, he said, no more woman, no kid, end of story."

"What?" John's voice went up. "Does that mean what I think it means?"

Ross took a couple of breaths. "What do you think? One of Neville's boys drove her to San Francisco. Took care of things. Guess it wasn't pretty."

"Meaning?" John asked. "You're not talking about an abortion?"

"Oh, but I am," Ross said. "Neville told me it was a botched job, complications. The woman nearly died. Had her in some out-of-the way clinic for nearly a week, then the guy they sent down drove her back to Redding. Neville said they paid out a bundle to keep her shut up tight about it."

"So that's where she is, Redding?"

"That's right," Ross said. "Got her a job there, paid her off."

"God almighty. And Neville told you this?" John was incredulous.

"I was on the inside. Had to tell me when I pressed him. That's the trouble when you widen the inner circle—more people to keep quiet. And who knows, might run deeper than that."

John was gripping the arms of his chair. "You think there've been others?"

"Who knows? But like you said, that's a lot of money. Just my gut theory."

"Damn." John got up and walked to the window, looked into the street then came back and stared down at Ross. "Can't figure why in hell Neville told you all the gory details. Took the risk. You'd think he would have kept his mouth shut."

"Because," Ross said, "I told him I wanted to know the whole thing, insisted, actually. In case anything backfired, I thought I needed to know the complete story. That seemed to fit Neville's brand of survival tactics. He didn't fight me on it. Just kept pointing his finger, reminding me to keep my mouth shut. Guess he figures I'd want to avoid ugly complications like he does. Except for one thing."

"What?"

"Neville has a lot more to lose than I do."

"Can you prove any of this, about the woman and the money?" John asked again.

"No, not yet, still a theory," Ross said. "That's it, though, has to be. Thinking on taking a trip to Redding to visit Miss Mona Johnson. Want to come?" Ross smiled at his father-in-law's look of uneasiness.

"No, and I strongly advise against your going down there, either," John said. "I wouldn't do it, Ross."

"Yeah, well, I'm just considering that for now."

John looked up and smiled over Ross's shoulder. The receptionist had come into the room with copies of the financial records.

Ross put the documents back into the file. "Thanks for the copies. Thought I'd better have my own set of records."

"Probably a good idea," John said.

"And thanks for listening."

"Sure. But, Ross, a word of advice," John said. "You have your adrenaline roaring. I might feel the same if I was in your position, but don't be reckless. I'll try to back you up but you need to play this smart and be judicious."

"Lawyer's talk for *watch your butt*." Ross stretched the elastic band over the file.

"Don't worry, John. I know I'm on my own with this. But it

is my neck. I'll do what I have to do. Besides, if I need a good lawyer, I know where to go." Ross hefted the folder up under one arm and grabbed his briefcase.

John's smile was weak. "Don't even joke about that possibility."

"Isn't a joke, John. A knot formed in my stomach the minute I opened that letter from Mona Johnson. It hasn't gone away."

John ran a hand down over his tie and turned on his lawyer face again. "Like I said, be careful. And I'd forget about going to Redding, not a good idea."

Ross grinned, said, "*Judicious,*" and left Chapman, Hughes, and Knox, Attorneys at Law. On his way back to the office, he stopped by Doctor Jackson's for a moment.

17

The office was warm and stuffy when Ross returned with the financial records. He raised a window, its glass brightly new, and looked out toward the sights and sounds of Roseburg taking out its revenge on the ravages of the blast. He remembered the head of the Chamber of Commerce declaring that he felt an air of sober optimism and that there would be a master plan for reconstruction—for a new Roseburg. Ross wondered about that and breathed in the now familiar odors then began separating the copies of the records he wanted from the originals and put the copies in his briefcase along with his unauthorized notes from the board meeting. Later he left the building and wandered down a couple of blocks to see *sober optimism* at work. He watched a dozer push around chunks of concrete that had once been the walls of the Coca-Cola bottling plant. A job foreman came up and told him he was in a hardhat area. Ross waved and walked away.

He carried the briefcase up the street and entered the Timber Room a bit before four o'clock. It had just reopened for business, and sheets of plywood still covered the windows. He slid into a booth, looked around to see who else was there, no one he knew for sure, ordered a beer, and waited. He had dawdled over two beers and consumed a dish of peanuts by the time Jill showed up. It was nearly five o'clock. She sat opposite him, smiled, and wrapped her arms about herself; she was still in uniform.

"Hi," Ross said. He found himself looking around again, but no one was paying them any attention.

"Sam had me stay late to clean up," she said in a quiet voice.

"Uh-huh," Ross responded.

"No, that's not true," she confessed. "I wasn't going to come. Almost to my apartment when I came back."

Ross picked up his glass and drained the last drops from it, studying her face. "What's wrong?"

"I don't know," she said, her face unsmiling. "Guess it's thinking about Mona."

When the cocktail waitress came up, Ross ordered two more beers then sat quietly and waited for Jill to open up. The waitress reappeared, put down two coasters, and set the beer glasses on them. Jill picked up her glass and drank from it; she didn't seem ready to talk.

"Tell me about Mona," Ross said, not willing to sit in silence. "How do you know her?"

"I met her a couple of years ago," Jill began, "at a party. She was dating this guy, a real creep, I thought, but she was goofy over him. Anyway, we liked each other right away and Mona, sweet Mona, said I should come by the beauty shop she worked at, and she'd give me a free permanent." Jill laughed. "Thought my hair needed work. But geez, after she worked on it, my head felt like it was in a vice. No more permanents, that's for sure."

"I like your hair," Ross said.

"Yeah well, I let her cut my hair. She's good at that."

Ross drank deeply from his glass. "So you've known her a while, then."

She nodded and grew quiet again. The waitress brought by another dish of salted peanuts.

They each took some and nibbled. Someone suddenly laughed loudly across the room, causing Jill and Ross to smile at each other, relieved by the distraction.

"She a good friend?" Ross asked. "Mona?"

"I guess. I mean, yeah. It's not like I have a ton of friends. There's a couple of other gals I do stuff with. But I guess Mona's maybe my best friend."

"What about fellas?" he asked.

Jill fixed her eyes on his. "Mona or me?"

Ross felt his face warming. "I was thinking of you. Figure we already know about Mona."

"Uh-huh." She raised her glass again, took a sip then set it down carefully, right in the center of the coaster. "There's a guy…or was. Tony. He's in Alaska making more money. Look, Mr. Bagby, what about Mona? You said she's in Redding. In California, right?"

"Thought I asked you to call me Ross," he said.

"Ross, then," she said. "But what about Mona?"

"You tell me."

"What…what do you mean?"

"You know why Mona is in Redding, don't you?"

She sat up straight. "I have to go to the ladies' room," she said and scooted out of the booth. She looked down at Ross for a moment before walking away.

When she came back she found that Ross had ordered two more beers.

"I don't want any more beer," she said.

"Okay."

"Look I should be going, I—"

"You knew…know Mona's pregnant, don't you?" Ross interrupted.

She looked away and watched a man shoving coins into the big jukebox. "Yeah," she said, "I know. She told me."

"How long ago?"

"I don't know, three or four weeks." She reached for the fresh beer after all. "She was a mess. Just cried and cried. That bastard!"

"Who?" Ross asked innocently.

"What do you mean, who? The Colonel, of course," she said.

"So Mona told you the Colonel was responsible?"

"It was him, all right."

Bobby Darin's voice, singing "Mack The Knife", suddenly blanketed the room. Jill took another drink from her beer while the music gave them a moment of deferment from Mona Johnson. Another selection boomed from the jukebox before it was quiet again. By then the glass of beer Jill didn't want was empty and the peanuts were gone.

"I'm going to Redding," Ross said out of the silence between them. "Find Mona."

Jill nodded through her tears.

By the time Ross was facing Maybelle in the doorway of the kitchen, she had been waiting dinner for an hour. She pointed to the oven to where a casserole dish resided on low heat. An aluminum foil tent covered a congealed mass of hamburger, cheese, and egg noodles.

When he asked what the dish was, she said, "Call it experimental."

He laughed. "I'm sure I'll like it."

"What courage," she said. "Where've you been, anyway?"

He was lifting the Pyrex dish out of the oven with a potholder in each hand. "Uh…quite a day, let me tell you."

"Do then," she said.

She sat at the kitchen table and listened to Ross describe his day while he ate a repentant serving of stiff noodles, gummy cheese, and gray hamburger as if it were prime rib. Her eyes were locked on to his as he told the tale of defending himself against charges of thievery. He left out the part about a woman who was getting into his head.

"So do you think you can get clear of this thing?" Maybelle asked.

He shrugged, set down his fork, and gratefully took another swallow of red wine. "We'll see, won't we? By the way, Doc Jackson gave me this." He pulled a vial from his pocket and set it on the table between them.

Maybelle reached for it, turned it in her hand, and unscrewed the cap. She saw his goofy grin. "This what I think it is?" she asked. "Are you really going to do it?"

"Up to you."

They looked across the table at each other, grinning. Maybelle twisted the cap back on and slid the bottle back to him. She watched Ross toss the bottle in one hand.

"So," he said, "what'll it be? Time's a wasting for a woman of thirty-five who wants babies." He laughed. "I don't want to do this just to humiliate myself."

"Women in their mid-to-late thirties are having babies—it's not that rare anymore," she said.

"That right?" he asked. "Where did you read that?"

"*Scientific American*," she said.

"*Scientific American*? When have you ever read *Scientific American* in your life?"

"Mercy, she gave me a copy," she said. "Don't look at me like that. She did."

"And it just happened to have an article on fertility in older women. Okay, not older—on the outer edge of the fertility curve—that better? So Mercy's eager for more grandchildren. Does that mean we have to submit our bodies to strange medical practices?"

Maybelle sat back. "Do I have to hear this again? You going to do it or not?"

"Are you serious about getting pregnant?" he asked.

"I have to take a pledge just so you'll donate a sample?"

"You really want to carry something around for nine months, scream it out of your body, let it suck your gorgeous tits, change shitty diapers, all so it can say it hates you when its hormones kick in?"

Her grin flashed white teeth. "You bastard, all that ranting just to get me mad so you don't have to deliver a couple of squirts of your manhood? Tell me, where are you going to do it? In the basement looking at a *Playboy* centerfold? Don't look so shocked. I know where you keep them. No woman on earth looks that good."

"You do, Mazie." He leaned toward her and wiggled his eyebrows.

"Oh sure, in your dreams and for thirty seconds about the time we met."

"You're still something," he said and growled.

She laughed and reached for the bottle again. "Want some help?"

"Might work," he said.

They sat looking at one another, smiling like they used to, until Maybelle stood up and walked away; a moment later he followed.

18

Friday morning the air was still and dry. The temperature had dropped overnight, but the sun was pressing down early; it would be yet another hot day. Ross barely noticed and couldn't have cared less. He and Maybelle had eaten a hasty breakfast before he left carrying the vial, keeping it warm and cozy in his pants pocket, and drove to Doctor Jackson's office. They had snickered about their collaboration, teased one another, and laughed to the point of breathlessness. Ross was moved by the loving moment, reminiscent of other days and times gone by. Still, it pained him that such times were uncommon. Before he'd left, carrying their precious sample, they lingered at the front door, hugged and kissed and laughed some more.

The doctor's office wasn't officially open, but Doctor Jackson had told Ross that he was always in by eight. By knocking firmly several times Ross roused the office nurse. "He'll want to see me," he assured her. The woman looked him up and down and strode off, leaving Ross standing out in the hall. One look at the vial brought a smile to Henry Jackson's lined face. He patted Ross on the arm and said, "I'm just heading over to Mercy for my rounds. I'll get this to the lab pronto. Call you when I know something," he said and winked.

Ross drove to the Foundation office thinking about how many million sperm he needed to be a normal guy. Doc Jackson had said anything over forty million was good as long as sperm motility was high. Forty million? Damn! He sat at the desk thumbing through the day's mail and laughed, thinking that he'd probably be coming in at thirty-eight million.

There were five proposals for funding in the mail, along with an invitation for the Colonel to attend the next board meeting of the Humane Society for special recognition. Everything else went in the wastebasket.

Ross decided to go home for lunch and ease into telling Maybelle about going to Redding the next day. He stuffed all of his notes for the day into his briefcase, along with every other document he safeguarded, and drove home around twelve thirty. Maybelle wasn't home, so he changed into a tee shirt and shorts and went to the basement for a workout.

When Maybelle came in, she shouted, "You down there?" He grunted a response and did a quick mental rehearsal of his reasoning for the trip. She was in the kitchen looking in the refrigerator when he climbed the stairs swabbing the sweat from his face.

"Ugh, you're soggy," she said.

"You didn't say that last night," he replied.

She lifted a package of sliced ham out of the meat drawer. "That was different. You deliver it?"

"I did. Doc says we'll know something in a day or two. How many million I'm ahead or behind."

She turned to him, held her body away from his sweat, and kissed him lightly on the cheek. "You're a good sport. I was thinking," she said, "maybe we ought to get a case of those little bottles just for our own amusement."

"You are awful," he said. "Target practice, you mean?"

She punched him on the shoulder.

"By the way," he said, "I'm driving down to Redding tomorrow. Welcome to ride along if you want."

"Redding," she said, "whatever for?"

He was spreading mayonnaise on a slice of wheat bread. He

clamped it down over slices of ham and cheese and said, "The woman the Colonel was sleeping with lives there now. Going down there to see her. Part of clearing my name."

"Ross, you can't do that," she protested, standing over him as he ate. "Embarrassing us by traipsing after that woman. There are other ways to handle this mess."

He set his sandwich down, reached up, held her by the arm, and patted her. "I'm up to my nose in *this mess*. And I'm not going to just roll over for Neville and Kribs so they can protect the Colonel—should I say the Colonel's memory? Because he's not coming out of that coma and won't be able to stand up like a man and admit he stole the money. So I'm going to Redding to look up that beautician and prove where the ten grand went and get it off my side of the ledger."

"Won't make any difference, will it? Even if she tells you he gave her money, how can you prove it was the missing money and not his own money? Running down to Redding will be just a waste of time."

"If I don't figure this mess out somehow, I could end up on the hook for the Colonel's embezzlement. I'm serious. And you're not being any help."

"What am I supposed to do?" She raised her arms.

"Ever call your uncle and decry my guilt?" he asked.

"What good would that do? I don't know a thing. I don't know if you have some secret bank account somewhere."

He grunted. "You're my wife, damn it. Wives stand up for their husbands no matter what. Or is it because you wonder if I am guilty of this…this pilfering? I'm going to ask you again: do you think I'm a thief?"

She looked into his eyes for an instant before answering. "No, of course not, I told you that before. Come on, Ross, what's the big deal? Neville can cover a puny amount like that. This is just a family squabble. You're making too much of it. And you don't need to drive all the way to Redding to prove nothing."

"That may be," he said, "but so far I'm the only one looking out for my hide. What if it comes to charges being filed?"

She patted him on the shoulder. "Comes to that, I'll pull the right strings."

"Why wait, for god's sake?"

Before she could answer, the phone rang. She turned her head. "Why don't you get that, probably the boogey man for you."

It was Kribs. Ross laughed out loud and looked at Maybelle.

"Something funny?" Kribs asked.

"Private joke," Ross said. "What's up Boogey Man?"

"What the hell does that mean?" Kribs grunted.

"Never mind. Something on your mind, or are you just hassling me?"

"Just wondering why the Foundation dye-wreck-tore isn't on the job," Kribs said. "What are you doing at home in the middle of the day?"

"Been taking lessons from you, Kribs," Ross said. "You know, how to put in a full day without really working. You're my idol. No one works less than you."

"Listen," Kribs breathed into the receiver, "listen real close. I were you, I'd be watching my behind. And don't spend all that money you stole—you might need it for a lawyer. I sure hope so. The thought of you being indicted makes me smile."

Ross looked around to see if Maybelle was still in the room; she wasn't. "The Colonel raided the Foundation," he said. "I know it, and you know it. In fact, Kribs, I'm pretty sure you've known that all along. And if you think I'm just going to hang around waiting for Neville and you to decide my fate, think again. This is my life you're screwing with, and I'm taking that very seriously. So whenever you can't see me, I'm working very hard to nail the Colonel—and if you had any piece of this—I'm going to scrape your hide as well. Think on that and sleep well tonight."

Just before he hung up, he heard Kribs sputter something, but he didn't catch any of it.

<hr/>

Ross rolled out of bed Saturday morning at five, tiptoed to the bathroom to pee and run the Remington razor over his face. When he came back out, Maybelle was awake; she rose up on one elbow and watched him. A deep sleep line ran across her right cheek.

"You're still going?" she asked.

He nodded. She watched him dress. When he buckled his belt and turned her way, she rolled over and closed her eyes. For a long moment, he looked at the prone hump of her body beneath the light blanket. He thought of saying something, but he didn't.

At five forty-eight, he backed the Chrysler out of the driveway, his briefcase beside him on the seat. He drove south, and as the miles ticked by scenes from his suddenly complicated life played in his head—over and over.

He drove slowly into the Redding city center in near one-hundred-degree heat and gassed up at a Flying A station, where he managed to get directions to Rhonda's House of Beauty—the name he had pried out of Neville. He drove out South Market Street until he found the tiny beauty shop. He parked across the street, pulled his damp shirt loose from the vinyl seat back, stepped out of the car, and stood blinking in the intense sunlight. There was one car parked in front of the salon. The shop had three chairs, a couple of those hair dryers that women sit under, and at least three years of *Photoplay* magazines. Rhonda was a woman in her fifties, dyed blonde hair piled high, white plastic-rimmed glasses with rhinestones embedded in them, and red lipstick so thick Ross wondered if she put it on with a putty knife. She was sitting in one of the beauty chairs thumbing through a magazine, smoking a filtered Kent cigarette. The place had the rotten egg smell of permanent solution and the volatile tang of hairspray only partially diminished by the cigarette smoke.

Ross smiled at her and stepped over to an oscillating fan sitting on a counter and plucked at his damp shirtfront. It was cooler inside but not cool. The woman licked her thumb, flicked the pages of the magazine, and looked at him over the top of her glasses.

"Something I can do for you?" Her voice rasped out over vocal cords that had endured a thousand times ten thousand inhalations of smoke.

"Hot," Ross said. "Thought everyone had air conditioning down here."

"And you came all the way from where to tell me that?" she asked.

Ross smiled. "Roseburg. Oregon. Hot there too, but not like this."

She stopped thumbing the magazine. "Air conditioner went kablooey last week. You say Roseburg?"

"Yeah," he said. "You been there?"

"Haven't had the pleasure," Rhonda said. "On my list, though, right after Paris."

"Yeah," he said, "I was in Paris last year. This is Redding's year."

"Touché," she said. "So you here for a perm? Getting a little thin there."

"Be kind, now." Ross turned around and let the fan dry his back some. "I understand Mona Johnson works for you. That right?"

Rhonda reached over and stabbed her cigarette out. "Did."

"She doesn't work here now?"

"Nope. Not anywhere, honey. She's dead."

Ross faced the woman, and they stared at one another for a long moment. "Dead?" Rhonda nodded. "When?"

She examined her very red fingernails. "Just who are you? Coming all the way from Roseburg? On a Saturday? Asking about Mona?"

"Sorry, I'm Ross Bagby."

"Any more clues?"

He hesitated. "The Armbruster Foundation."

"Uh-huh." She tapped another Kent out of a pack and thumbed a lighter. "Someone up that way made Mona's life miserable. That you?"

"No. I only met her once. How'd she die?"

Rhonda tipped her head back and blew smoke at the ceiling. "Suicide."

"Suicide?" Prickles danced across Ross's shoulders. "When?"

"Little over a week ago."

Ross took two steps back and lowered himself into a chrome-legged chair and immediately stuck to its plastic upholstery. His mind began chugging through everything he knew about Mona; he locked on to a poster across the room with umpteen photo squares of beautiful hairstyles and tried to swallow back the sourness that rose in his throat.

"Went to the funeral," the woman said, like it was worth a merit badge. "Pitiful."

"Her family, they're from here, isn't that right?" Ross asked.

"Yep, right here, Redding. She was living with her mom and a sister."

He looked into the sequined glasses. "Mona, did she work here long?"

"Not long." Rhonda sucked on the cigarette, her upper lip wrinkling like crepe paper, and studied Ross.

Ross plucked at his shirt again.

"Odd little gal," she said. "Seemed sad most of the time. Tried, but I never could cheer her up."

Ross got up and went to stand in front of the fan again. "You have the mother's address?" When the woman just looked at him, he said, "Want to pay my respects."

"Suppose it'll be all right." She rummaged around and wrote the address down on a Rhonda's House of Beauty memo pad, drew him a map, and printed the mother's name: Myrtle Johnson.

Ross thanked Rhonda and stepped back out into the white light.

19

Myrtle Johnson lived in a poor neighborhood in a dingy, white stucco, flat-roofed bungalow trying to look Spanish. The yard was two dried scraps of dirt with brown tufts of grass separated by a narrow strip of warped seesaw concrete. Ross stepped from one tilted wedge to the next and knocked on the screen door. The front door was open and the radio was on loud. Connie Francis was singing "Who's Sorry Now?" He knocked again harder; the unhooked screen door bounced in the frame. After a third knock, a woman Ross thought to be in her early twenties strolled up and peered at him through the mesh. She was chewing gum with her mouth open.

"We ain't buying nothing," she said in a flat nasal voice.

"I'm not selling anything," Ross said. "I wonder, is Mrs. Johnson in?"

She stood looking at him and chewing. "You sure you ain't selling nothing?"

Ross held up his hand. "Scout's honor."

She stood in a slouch and looked at him for a drawn-out moment then walked off like it was hard work. A couple of minutes later a short woman, stout, with wiry gray hair, came to the door. She looked up at Ross through thick glasses.

"Mrs. Johnson?" Ross asked.

"That's me."

"My name's Ross Bagby. I came down from Roseburg today and wondered if I might have a moment of your time?"

"Bagby, don't know no Bagby," she said. "What you want?"

"Well, you see, I'm with the Armbruster Foundation and…"

"Armbruster!" She stepped back, gripped the edge of the door, and slammed it so hard dust flew.

Ross stood at the door for a minute thinking she might open it again, if only to give him a piece of her mind. She didn't, so he knocked once more and waited. After several minutes of knocking and waiting, the door opened; it was the younger woman. She pushed the screen door open and stepped out part way.

"Mama says she's going to call the cops if you don't leave." She chawed on her gum some more. "What you want, anyway? You really from that Armbruster Company?"

Ross decided to go with what worked. "You folks getting money from Armbruster Lumber Company?"

She blinked at him and stopped chewing for the first time. "Come on in," she said. "I'll tell Mom you're here about the money. Are you?"

"Yes, I'm here about money," he said carefully.

He followed her and sat where she pointed, on an old brown couch with prickly upholstery. It was hot in the house. There were no fans, and the odor of previously consumed food hung in the air, something fried and greasy. He sat quietly, his hands resting on his knees, sweat beading on his forehead, and listened to the sound of the two women arguing in another room. When they finally came into the living room, Ross stood and smiled. Myrtle Johnson strode past him, plunked down in a platform rocker, and glowered.

"Rachel says you're here about the money," she said. "You better not be thinking of cutting us off, mister. Better not be. 'Cause you do, and we'll make a real stink for you."

Keeping his composure, Ross sat back down slowly. "First let me say how sorry I was to hear about Mona's death. You have my sympathy."

Myrtle Johnson looked away then back and reached up to wipe at the moisture in her eyes. She sniffed and laid her hands in the lap fold of her housedress. "Your sympathy ain't worth spit you thinking of going back on our agreement." The woman talked tough, but Ross could see she was nervous and assuming the worst.

"Ma'am," he raised his hands, "I'm not here to cancel any agreement."

"Better not be, that was for ten years no matter what. No matter what," she repeated. "Didn't say nothing about stopping them payments if Mona died. Man said we'd be getting that money—family now, not just Mona—get that money to help us 'cause she had to come back home. Ten years, and we ain't even into this first year but a little bit."

"What man?" Ross asked. "Who was this? The one who told you about the agreement?"

Myrtle Johnson squinted and rocked. "Thought you said you was with them Armbruster people."

Ross smiled. "Well, I'm with the Armbruster Foundation. We're a charitable organization, support charitable work in the community."

"This ain't no charity thing." The old woman snorted and looked at her daughter. "Let me tell you. No, this ain't about charity. This about a snake in the grass, that's what. That sumbitch. Right, Rachel?"

The young woman bobbed her head and snapped her gum. "That's right, Mama."

"Got my little girl pregnant then run her out of town and made her go to San Francisco to get fixed. And...and she got so sick down there. Hardly recognized her when they dumped her off." Myrtle Johnson swallowed and looked away from Ross. "And that's just what they did. Hardly stopped the car.

Big black car stopped out front, some man set Mona's suitcase on the curb, and he drove off leaving her standing there. She could hardly stand up, and that bastard didn't even see her into the house."

"Sorry," Ross said.

"Bet you are, sorry as all get-out," Myrtle Johnson said. "Well, this here money we been getting, it's blood money now. My sweet girl, she started dying from the inside soon as she come home with an empty womb. She dried up from grieving about the child and…and that man. Couldn't get her to stop moaning about him even though he messed up her life."

"You speaking of Mr. McKenzie?" Ross asked.

Myrtle Johnson laughed and rocked harder. "Mister McKenzie, he says. You mean the Colonel, now don't you?"

"That's right, the Colonel."

"Bastard," she said. "Get my hands on him, I'd kill him. I would, and take my time doing it."

"Mama," Rachel admonished.

"Don't you *Mama* me. I mean it. Since we got one of them Armbrusters right here in our house, I'm going to tell him what I think of all their sorry asses." Myrtle Johnson rocked hard some more. "Mona, she come home like I said and started shriveling up like a prune in the sun. Had her to the doctor, and he knew right off what'd happened with her, knew she'd had that abortion. But said she would be okay, just take time for everything to heal up. But that wasn't what was dragging her down. It was how she felt in here." She poked herself between sagging breasts.

"She took her own life, then," Ross said. "That right?"

Mona's mother drew her mouth in and blinked the tears out of her eyes. "Cut herself. Right back there, in the tub. Rachel and me, we was to the grocery store when my little girl used the boning knife on herself. Time we got home she was too gone, so weak. Got her to the hospital but she was already cold, knew she was gone." She raised a hand to her mouth and sobbed without making any sound, sobbed and squeezed her eyes shut, sobbed until she stopped like she'd thrown a switch on her grief.

Ross looked down at the sorry gray carpet. It was quiet in the house except for the sound of Rachel chewing on her wad of gum. Myrtle Johnson blew her nose and stuck the hankie back in the pocket of her cotton housedress.

"So, mister—what'd you say your name was?" she asked.

"I'm Ross Bagby."

"Okay, Mr. Bagby, if you aren't here about that money we're getting—and will keep getting, by-god—what are you here for? Long drive from up there. So get on with it," Myrtle Johnson said. "Why you here? You didn't come all this way just to watch Rachel chew on that wad of gum. Honestly, Rachel, drive a person to distraction. Get rid of it."

Rachel ducked her head and rolled the clump of gray gum out into her palm and, seeing her mother's glare, got up and went into the kitchen. Her mother waited until she came back and sat in the same chair as before, red-faced.

"That's better," said Myrtle Johnson. "Now then, Mr. Bagby, you want something. What is it?"

"I'm here to ask you about the Colonel." He ignored her squint and told her about how the Colonel was hurt—the real story, not the car accident—and that he was still in a coma and not likely to come out of it alive or with his senses straight. The woman listened stony-faced and didn't say a word until he was finished.

"Knew most of that," she said. "Mona told me and Rachel about what went on up there. The big explosion and all. And I know she was messing with a married man. Just grief when you do that, nothing but grief comes out of them kind of shenanigans. She wasn't proud of what she done, but danged if she wasn't plain goofy over that Colonel fella. Couldn't get her to let go of him. Lordy, I tried. Was like she was possessed, voodooed."

"You know how long Mona and the Colonel had been seeing one another?" Ross asked.

"Ha!" Myrtle Johnson chirped. "Seeing one another, he says. They wasn't seeing one another, son. The way I sized it up, my daughter was on standby, you know what I mean? She was standing by until he needed something to poke his business into."

"Mama!" Rachel pleaded.

"Oh shush," Myrtle Johnson said and waved a meaty hand at her daughter. "Man didn't come down here for fairy tales. Now Mona, she was silly enough to think that a man like that was going to one day leave his society wife and take up with her. She was my little girl, but when it came to men she didn't have a lick of sense. Damn the misery of it, the pain you men can heap on a woman."

Ross leaned forward, elbows on his knees. "Mrs. Johnson, I drove all this way to ask you one question."

"Let's have it." She gripped the arms of the chair and rocked and worked her mouth.

"Okay." He inhaled. "Did Mona ever tell you that she received money from the Colonel while she lived in Roseburg? Not talking about the money you're receiving now or that Mona got after she moved back. This would be a significant amount of money over a couple of years."

Myrtle Johnson swiveled her head at Rachel, who suddenly needed something to chomp on, but her mouth was empty. Ross waited while the old woman thought something over. He could see her eyes wandering; her mouth was working some more and her dentures clicking.

"Like I said," Myrtle Johnson began, "Mona had big ideas about her and that man. Had these dreams, she did, about him and her living in a nice house. She came to visit me and Rachel, you know, regular like." She sighed. "And when she was here it was always, *Me and the Colonel, we're gonna do this or that.* Never talked a lot about him climbing all over her body. Rachel, stop that look now. That's what he was doing. That's all he wanted, damn it. But Mona, she loved the skunk. Thought he really loved her.

"Anyhow, part of her storytelling was convincing us that her Cinderella story was real, so she bragged about every little crumb he gave her. And like you said, yessir, some of that was money. She'd tell us about the money, and the amounts was always more'n seemed reasonable."

"Like how much?" Ross asked. "What kind of numbers did she use?"

"What's this all about, anyway?" Myrtle Johnson's eyes narrowed. "You ain't angling to get some of that back, are you, or using that to cut us out of our deal?"

"Absolutely not," Ross said. "This is about an unrelated matter."

"Unrelated," she repeated. "How can I trust you? I'll make life miserable for you people, splash stuff all over the papers up there if you trying to cheat us."

Ross studied her face for a moment, not seeing anything likeness of her dead daughter in the woman or the younger daughter. "Okay, here's what's behind my questions," he said. "I'm filling in as director of the Armbruster Foundation while the Colonel is out of commission. You know he is director of the Foundation. Anyway, with all the change and turmoil it was decided that there should be an audit." When she frowned, he said, "A check of the finances, Foundation books. But when an accountant went over the books, he discovered that a large sum of money is missing."

Myrtle Johnson moved her mouth around again. "How large?" she asked.

"Ten thousand dollars," he said.

"Lordy," Rachel said.

"Mona never had no ten thousand dollars," Myrtle Johnson said. "Lemme tell you that. Never."

"Now, wait a minute." Ross patted the air with his palms. "Let's look at this in pieces. You say Mona would talk about large amounts of money the Colonel gave her. Give me examples of those figures."

Myrtle Johnson rubbed her forehead. "I don't know. Been a while, can't really recall."

"Just think of any numbers you can recall," Ross said. "This is important."

She stared back at him. "Maybe important to you—not us. I ain't gonna tell you stuff that could hurt our arrangement."

"Sad to tell you, but Armbruster's a huge company," Ross said. "They have resources that can turn your arrangement inside out. And your threat to expose them depends on people willing to print what you say. Who do you think the newspapers are going to believe?"

"You can't talk to my mama like that." Rachel stood up.

"Rachel, sit down," her mother said. "Sit down, I say, and be quiet. You wanting to bargain with me, Mr. Bagby, that it?"

Ross sat back and wiped at the moisture on his forehead. "Could be like that, yes. You a haggler, Myrtle?"

She grinned. "Known to be. What's the deal?"

"I wrote the checks, cashed them, and gave the money to the Colonel. Money that was supposed to go to local charities—it didn't. Thing is, we don't know where the money went for sure. I think he spent most or a lot of it on Mona, but I don't have any proof. Others are saying I stole the money. I didn't. With the Colonel in a coma I can't force him to fess up." He wiped at the moisture on his forehead again. "That's why I drove two hundred and fifty miles on a Saturday morning."

Myrtle Johnson studied Ross through her thick lenses. "If I can give you what you want—can't say I can, now—but if I can, what do we get?"

"If, and this is a big if, Myrtle," Ross said. "If I get information from you that will help clear up this mess, I will do everything I can to assure that your deal is honored."

"Hell, that ain't nothing, *do all you can*." Myrtle Johnson squirmed. "I want a guarantee."

"Can't give you one," Ross said. "And you can't give me one, either. All you and I can do is give each other what we have and hope it works. What do you say, Myrtle?" He heard her dentures click again.

"You pretty good haggler yourself. All right, then, what do you want to know?"

Ross drove north out of Redding at five fifteen with his briefcase a little fatter. Myrtle Johnson's memory was a sponge of details, significant and insignificant. She and Ross had sat at her kitchen table, and he wrote while she recalled each of Mona's trips home and cited her brags of money she had been given by the Colonel, a car, trips, clothes, and furniture. Quick addition brought up a total of over six thousand dollars. More importantly, Myrtle Johnson brought out a shoebox containing letters Mona had written to her. Among them were many that told of wonderful gifts she'd received from the Colonel or of trips they'd taken. There were twelve such letters.

A few minutes shy of ten thirty that night, he pulled into his driveway and killed the engine. He scoured the house before finding Maybelle out on the patio fast asleep in a chaise lounge with a book spread open across her stomach and a flurry of moths agitating the patio light. He left her sleeping, poured a tumbler of bourbon on ice, then turned off the light and settled into the chair next to her. When the bourbon was gone, and he had reconsidered his day several times over, he shook Maybelle gently until she woke, startled and disoriented in the near dark. Her book spilled off onto the patio. She looked up at him, blinking, licked dry lips, and smiled before evidently remembering she was mad at him and stumbling off to bed.

20

For Ross, Sunday morning always began with him rising first, putting the coffee on, retrieving the Sunday morning *News-Review* from the front stoop, scanning the front page, and then cooking breakfast while enjoying his first cup of coffee. Breakfast was usually his time-tested specialty: buttermilk pancakes, scrambled eggs with chopped green onions turned in, and link sausages. As he chopped onions and blended pancake batter, the bizarre turns, the sudden wrenching events that had changed everything, played in his head again: the explosion, the Colonel in a coma, him accused of thievery, and Mona Johnson dead by her own hand. It took him a moment to realize that he had nicked his finger. He scrutinized the small drop of blood then put the finger in his mouth and fumbled for the box of Band-Aids they kept in a kitchen drawer. He was wrapping the wounded finger when Maybelle came down in her bathrobe. She looked at his bandage, yawned, poured herself a cup of coffee, and started reading the Sunday paper at the table. Ross finished scrambling the eggs and filled their plates. They ate in silence. There had been no mention of going to church; they weren't in a spiritual mood.

After ignoring one another, passing sections of the newspaper back and forth across the table without comment, Ross finally asked Maybelle if she wanted to see what he had brought back with him from Redding. She told him she didn't care, but after a vacant few moments she relented with a shrug. He retrieved his briefcase from the dining room and laid it on the kitchen table, but before he showed her any of it, he said her name and waited until she looked at him.

"Mona Johnson is dead," he said. "Suicide. She cut her wrists." He felt Maybelle shudder, waited a bit, then he told her all of it and let her read Mona Johnson's letters and Myrtle Johnson's recollections written in his hand and signed by Myrtle. When she listened, Maybelle's eyes danced, dismay written in them, and she read everything crouched over like she was taking an exam.

"So now what?" she said afterward. One of Mona Johnson's letters lay open in front of her, the loopy childish handwriting running uphill.

"Guess we'll find out, won't we?" Ross answered. She folded the letter and put it back in the envelope.

"Damn his hide, coma or not," she said. "Are you going to show this to Germaine? God no, you can't do that. Can you?"

"No," he said, "I can't do that, even though she threatened to bury me if I sully the Colonel's reputation."

"She's probably scared as hell," Maybelle said. "Can't blame her, I guess."

"Don't know if Germaine's ever afraid of anything," he said and put the papers back into his briefcase. "She's a survivor, tough as they come. When she finds out about this, and she will, I wouldn't expect to escape her wrath no matter the truth of it. Not something I'm looking forward to. Before that happens I'm going to ask Neville to get the board together so I can clear up this mess. Defend myself. I have the goods now."

Maybelle started to say something but fell quiet; she reached out and centered the vase of daisies she'd cut from their flower bed behind the house to replace Emeline's roses that had dropped their petals.

"So," he spoke when she didn't say anything, "what's up for the day?"

She inhaled at the change in topics. "Oh, I have a golf date with the girls." She looked up at the kitchen clock. "Oops, better get going."

He followed her up to the bedroom; they took turns in the bathroom. She went first and was already putting on makeup by the time he emerged, toweling off. He always found it fascinating to watch her pencil her eyebrows, thicken her eyelashes with petite upward strokes of the mascara brush, and spread redness onto her upper lip and transfer that onto the lower lip by rolling them together. *Much more interesting than the dullness of shaving, sensual even*, he thought.

"What about you? What you up to?" she asked as an afterthought, realizing that she had left him out again.

"I don't know. Wash the car, mow the lawn, maybe watch a ball game." He paused in the seesaw motion of drying his back. He knew what else he would do. He took a breath before saying, "Then there's a waitress at the Snappy Service Café. Mona Johnson was her best friend. She doesn't know that Mona is dead. Thought I should tell her."

Maybelle stopped brushing her hair and looked at him in the mirror, skeptical. "Why you?" she asked.

He stepped into his boxer shorts and fumbled for an answer. "Don't think there's anyone else to tell her. Besides, she told me some things…about the Colonel and Mona Johnson. I owe her."

"You owe her?" Maybelle continued to look at him in the mirror. "Who is this person?"

"Name's Jill. Like I said, she's a waitress. See her most every day." He could see Maybelle waiting for more. "At the café, I see her at the cafe. Jill, last name's Luckett, Lockhart, something like that. A while back, she and I were talking about the explosion and I mentioned the Colonel's accident."

"You mentioned the accident?" Maybelle said. "Just out of the blue? To a waitress."

"No," he said. "It wasn't like that, May, for crying out loud. I was chewing the fat with her...about the explosion. Like everyone's been doing. And she asked if I knew anybody who'd been hurt or killed. And I...well, I said no but mentioned the Colonel's automobile accident in passing."

"Ross," she said, "I can't believe you."

"She'd already read about it in the paper," he said. "And believe me, she didn't buy the car accident story. Not even a little."

"Why not?" Maybelle asked.

He sighed. "Because. She knew different. From Mona, her friend. She knew where the Colonel actually was when things went blooey."

Maybelle finished brushing her hair, went to the closet and took out the capri pants and sleeveless blouse she would wear. "The café is closed on Sundays, isn't it?" she said.

"That's right." He ran a belt through the loops on his pants. "Hadn't thought about that. I'll have to call her, then."

"You do that, dear," she said.

Turned out Jill's last name was Lockner. She was surprised by Ross's call. Sensing her skepticism, he told her that he had been to Redding and had news of her friend Mona. When she pressed him about what he knew, he hesitated and said that it might be better to talk in person. She took in a breath. "It's bad isn't it? I know it's bad." Ross calmed her and asked where they might meet. She told him she was just about to go out to the duck pond, and if he wanted they could meet out there. He didn't know where that was, so she gave him directions out Garden Valley Boulevard to the Adventist Church. She would meet him in the parking lot.

Jill was sitting in her Chevrolet waiting when Ross parked alongside her. She stepped out of the car holding a brown paper bag. Her expression was questioning, and it did not change just because Ross smiled. She turned away quickly and took an obscure path at the back of the lot, through the scrub and trees until they came into the clear and saw the pond. A cluster of ducks was paddling about; their contented quacking rose to an alarmed cackling as soon as the two humans were noted. Jill looked back at Ross and opened her mouth to speak, but instead she walked to the water's edge and began tossing breadcrumbs into the pond. Ross stood back, watching her for a bit, and noted how different it was to see her out of uniform. It was like seeing a different person. She was wearing blue cotton denim pants, a white blouse, and open-toed sandals; she stared unsmiling as the ducks fluttered about snapping the bread from the surface of the pond. When Ross came up beside her, she tossed more crumbs into the pond and watched the birds feeding.

"Jill, about your friend," Ross said, "I'm sorry, but—"

"My most favorite place," she said, cutting him off. "Especially now with the stink in town and the mess. So peaceful and natural here. There's talk of filling it in, the pond, and putting a motel here. Makes me want to cry just thinking that they might do that. It should stay like it is. Where would the birds go? They should make it a park or something."

"Nice spot," Ross said. "Never been here before."

He stood quietly observing the ducks and waited her out.

She threw more crumbs. There was a flurry of feathers before she spoke. "I'm scared to ask, but tell me about Mona."

"That little patch of tall grass looks like a place we could sit," he said, gesturing. They flattened the grass with their feet and sat and were quiet.

"Mona is dead," Ross said finally. "I'm sorry."

She raised a hand to cover her mouth and moaned. "Oh no." Tears came quickly. "Mona, no." She tipped forward, almost leaning on her knees, and sobbed and said Mona's name again.

Ross sat and didn't say more. After a time, Jill got up and walked off. He let her go and didn't look to see where she went or how far. The ducks eventually swam away after cleaning up all of the crumbs; he watched them paddle aimlessly out and about and back again. Some minutes passed before Jill returned and sat back down in the grass. Ross glanced at her and waited.

"So you really went to Redding?" she asked.

"Yes."

"So tell me," she sniffed, "what happened...How did she die?"

"She took her own life," he said.

"What?" Her eyes widened. "No...not Mona. She wouldn't have done that. No. She wouldn't have, no."

"Well," Ross said softly, "she did. I'm sorry."

"How?" she asked, brittleness in her voice.

"Jill, you don't want to know," he said. "It's not nice, it's ugly."

"Ugly?" she blurted. "It's already been ugly. I want to know... all of it. Please."

He told her—all of it. She listened, stared straight ahead, not seeing the ducks, not seeing anything. She just listened, her face frozen and resolute. When he had finished telling her what he knew, they both fell silent. Jill wiped her eyes. Sadness hummed in her chest, and she cried silently one more time.

"Those bastards," she spit out finally.

"Who?"

"What?"

"What do you mean, *those* bastards?" he asked. "Who are you talking about?"

"Never mind."

"No," he said. "What do you mean? The Colonel?"

"No," she said. "Not him. Well, him but..."

"Who then?" he pressed. "What are you talking about?"

She crossed a leg, removed a sandal, and shook out a crumb of dirt.

"What can I tell you? That's what I'm talking about," she said. Gone was the sweet, bouncy waitress. Her voice had turned cold; the tone came from some other part of her, deep and unfriendly. "This about Mona...what you found out...it's not, well, there's more to it."

"Okay," he said. "Tell me."

"No." She shook her head. "I shouldn't have said anything."

Ross stood and walked the few steps to the edge of the pond. He reached down and picked up a pebble and threw it. A duck paddled madly away when the stone plunked into the water near it. When he turned back, Jill was standing, holding her paper sack.

"So?" he said.

"I'm leaving," she said. "Thanks for telling me about Mona."

He took three quick steps and stood in front of her. "Tell me," he said. "You must."

Her eyes didn't have the sparkle Ross was used to. He looked into them, searching for some reflection of the woman who had played games in his head. She wasn't there, not right then.

"I...maybe later," she said. "I have to think."

"You can tell me, Jill."

"Please, Ross," she said. "Let me pass."

He stepped back and she moved by and kept walking. He was still watching her when she paused and turned. She didn't return his wave, just walked back up the trail to the parking lot. Ross followed and heard the starter grind; the engine came alive, and she drove away, a thin stream of blue smoke following along behind the car.

Ross drove home, trying to judge Jill's intimation that there was something more to know about Mona Johnson and the Colonel—and who else? Later, washing the car, Jill's, *What can I tell you?* continued to replay itself.

A slight reprieve came when the snarl of the rotary lawn mower dulled the conversation in his head. Afterward he hosed the green mush buildup from under the mower shroud, put everything away, and went to the basement to clean up. With the warm water fanning out over him, he went right back to the scene with Jill at the pond. Whatever she'd withheld from him was something he ought to know, but maybe didn't want to know.

Standing in the quiet of the basement, looking in the mirror above the wash tub, wet hair, sad eyes, a towel wrapped around his midsection, his feet planted on the wet coolness of the concrete floor, he felt an aloneness, like being in total darkness. He was caught between two truths: the truth of his own innocence and the more obscure truth that something else, something ominous was still out there. Who were the bastards Jill had referred to? In his stomach, he knew that whatever it was, it would likely further complicate his life.

He combed the front strands of thin moist hair, lowered the comb, looked into his reflected eyes, and considered the word *dread*. That's what he felt.

21

Ross's day was made complete when Neville Armbruster came knocking. He didn't use the doorbell; he pounded with the heel of his fist—that was the sound, the thudding Ross heard from the living room where he was watching the tail end of a baseball game between the LA Dodgers and the St. Louis Cardinals. Neville's eyes were glassy marbles when Ross opened the door. They stabbed at Ross for a moment, before Neville shoved past into the foyer and walked to the living room, where he stood looking at the television screen until a Gillette razor commercial came on. He turned on Ross.

"I want to see what you brought back from Redding," he said.

Ross walked deliberately to the television and turned it off. "How do you know about that? Me going to Redding?"

"Maybelle, saw her at the golf club."

"She told you about that?" Ross bent his head forward in time with the question. "May told you?"

Neville had his hands on his hips; he nodded and turned toward the television again, saw the gray screen, and turned back. "Yeah, she did."

"I can't believe...how did it even come up? She really told you?" Ross asked again.

"Ran into her in the pro shop," Neville said.

"And she just came up and said, *Hey, Uncle Neville, guess what?*"

Neville stared at him and fidgeted, shuffling around in a half circle and back. "I want to see what you have, Ross." He paused. "Let me have it."

"May just up and volunteered it?" Ross held his arms out. "How'd she do that?"

"This is getting us nowhere," Neville said. "Look, Mazie pulled me off to the side and told me you'd gotten evidence on the Colonel. I want to see it. What you have." When Ross didn't move Neville said, "I insist."

"My dick's in a wringer, and you're the one holding the crank," Ross said. "You think I'm going to give you evidence that will exonerate me?"

"Not going to argue with you." Neville raised a forefinger "Besides, it's not just about you. Maybe what you have will clear up the whole mess. I want what you have, or..."

"Or what?" Ross said.

"Look, I'm your employer," Neville threatened. "I have a legal right to see anything related to your employment and the Foundation. Not going to argue with you. Give me what you brought back."

"And what do I have?"

Neville swung his head back and forth and pulled his lips back in anger. "The letters, damn it, and what you wrote down... what the girl's mother told you."

"She did tell you," Ross said. "Jesus, betrayed by my own wife."

"That's for you to handle. Now come on, Ross." Neville was tempering his tone. He conjured up a smile. "It'll be okay. I just need to see it so I know...so I can protect all of our interests." He widened his smile. "By the way, you given any more thought to the Smythe job? Should. That's the way out of this whole fuss."

"Sorry, Neville," Ross said, shaking his head. "I'm the one on the outside looking in, but not for long. I know what happened, and I can prove that I'm not the thief around here. And forget the pissant job deal."

"You're going to regret this," Neville said. "Remember…"

"Regret what?" It was Maybelle. She was standing in the doorway to the living room. "Neville, what are you doing here? Ross?"

The two men looked at her but didn't answer. Neville grunted, cast a withering look at Ross, and brushed past Maybelle, slamming the door on the way out. Ross stepped over to the side bar and poured himself a drink.

"You want something?" he said to Maybelle.

She shook her head. "What was that all about?"

"What do you think?" he said.

For a long moment they stared at one another. Ross sipped from his drink and saw the window shade roll up on Maybelle's face. She slumped into the closest chair.

"It was me, wasn't it?" she said. "At the club."

"Uh-huh."

She stared dumbly at nothing.

"And I thought I was naïve," he said. "Don't you know, May?"

She squinted. "Know what?"

"They've known about this all along," he said. "Neville and Kribs. Went along with it. Screwing me was a way to keep their skirts clean."

"The money…"

"Not about money," he said. "About the game they were playing and the stink of it and about power. They need to clean things up because the Colonel is not coming back, doubt he makes it, period. They knew that eventually the money shortage would show up and they had to create an answer. Hanging it on me was probably Kribs's idea. I'd bet on it. Get me out of the way, and he could become the titular head of the Foundation, clean up everything, and leave me spread-eagle. I'd have to go along with being the guilty one or face legal consequences. That'd save the Armbruster face—blaming it on that outsider Maybelle brought home."

"This is crazy," she said. "You can't believe all of that. It's nonsense."

"Why do you think Neville charged over here immediately after you spilled the beans to him? He wanted everything I'd brought back from Redding or, else."

"But, Ross, all I told him was—"

"May, why did you tell him anything? You betrayed me."

The expression on her face, mouth hanging open, eyes like headlights on full beam, almost made him laugh, except there was no humor in it.

"You showed my trump card," he said, "to the man who wants to tag me with embezzlement."

Her mouth snapped shut on a spring. "I did not betray you, Ross. I...well I thought Neville should know, that you would want him to know that you aren't a thief."

"Not what he wanted to hear," Ross said. "That the whole thing could now be explained. Neville wanted the confusion, needed it so he had leverage on me."

"This is ludicrous," Maybelle said, "all this scheming and treachery over this...this itty-bitty anthill. It's a joke, Ross. You guys," she laughed, "I...well, I can't believe the misery being trumped up."

Ross inhaled and swirled the liquor in his glass. "Not how big a thing is," he said. "It's all relative to the size of your world and to the intensity played out inside its fence line. To Neville and Kribs, and even me, our anthill is the world—one of our worlds, anyway. People will go to extreme lengths to protect their patch of dirt, and they'll strut even if elected president of the West Side Manure Spreaders. It's all about the things you invest your soul in and what you'll do to have power in that sphere."

"Still, it's just ludicrous," she said.

"May, tell me," he said, his smile patronizing, "does it make any difference to you who's in charge of your golf tournament committee? Talking about anthills. You care if you're not the one calling the shots? Ah, I see by the look on your face that it does matter. But to me *that's* ludicrous, I mean all that fuss and months of planning over how far a bunch of people hit a little white ball. And the pecking order, that's what really matters on any anthill. It's never really about the issue in contention. It's about who's in power. And if it takes a sneak attack to stay in power, that is what people will do, whether it's the Chamber of Commerce or daily vacation Bible school."

"My husband the cynic," Maybelle said.

"My wife the cloistered child of wealth and power," he responded.

"You really think that?"

"You bet," he said. "I'm not blaming you, but, May, you've never had to worry about anything other than what to wear."

"That's just not true."

"Don't make me tick down the list," he said. "You don't want to hear it."

"No, go ahead," she said, leaning back in the chair. "Enlighten me. I want to hear this, Ross. Tell me. No, I mean it. I want you to."

He swallowed the last of his drink and held the glass in his hand. "Okay. Let me put it this way: wealth and power are the great insulators, to such an extent that you don't even know that you're insulated, not really. For instance, you've never been hungry—I mean without food in the house and not knowing where the next meal is coming from."

"That's not a good one," she said. "Neither have you."

He smiled. "Oh, but I have. My father's union went on strike when I was still in grade school. It lasted for a very long time. No way could we live on the strike stipend. For a time I went to bed with an empty belly, had one meal a day. I was scared we might starve to death. Of course, we wouldn't have, but as a kid I didn't know that. You want me to go on?"

She blinked and said yes.

"All right," he inhaled. "You've never had to worry about a roof over your head, clothes that fit you when you grew, not even new clothes, just some that fit. You didn't know what it was like to not have access to the country club, a place to play tennis, or to travel outside of your own town let alone to Europe. But mostly you've never had to work for a living or be the dutiful spouse who hopes her man can work hard, succeed and better the life of the family. And you have always known privilege in a town where your family is important and in control of a lot of people's lives and futures and the food on their tables. Where your name has always opened the way and made your daily life seamless. You didn't have to scrimp or work your way through college.

"I fell in love with a bright, beautiful young woman," he went on. "Back then, we were on an even playing field. Only later, back here in Armbruster country, did I find that I was only a lower-middle-class kid who had married a woman who didn't understand where I came from. No, not North Platte, but where I lived, on what strata. There were no parallels for us after college."

"Oh come on, Ross," she said, "you're being melodramatic. So you missed a few meals as a kid. Hey, I cut my finger and needed stitches once and broke an arm when I fell off my horse. Did I have to be poor to be worthy of marrying you? I thought falling in love with you and you being smitten with me was all it took."

"Smitten," he said. "Now there's a frivolous word."

"Frivolous? It's a truly enchanting word," she said.

"Enchanting? Fits right in there with perky and cute and charming," he responded. "Thought what we had ran deeper than that."

"Meaning that I am a shallow child of privilege?" she said.

He stepped to the sideboard and considered pouring another drink but didn't, put the glass down, and turned back. "Do you know how much I want to love you—no, I do love you—but how much I want to be passionate about you?"

Maybelle looked up at him. For a long moment they stared at each other; then she grinned. "Ain't life a bitch?" she said. "My white knight never came in, either."

Ross winced and shook his head.

"Come on now," she said, "I'm joking. You've had a rotten day. Let's give it a rest, okay?" When he didn't answer, she said, "All right, how about a time-out then? I'm pooped. If you want to keep going on with this, I'll give you the first swing in the morning. How's that?"

"Look," Ross began, "this isn't a boxing match, I..."

Maybelle got up, came over to him, and gently put a forefinger over his lips. "Tomorrow, bright and early if you want," she said and gave him a kiss on the cheek.

22

But the next morning Ross didn't even get the first word. When the phone awoke them, he stumbled out of bed to answer it. It was Neville. The Colonel was dead; there would be a reception for Germaine that evening. Be there. Ross and Maybelle sat beside each other on the bed and stared in silence at nothing.

"Well," Maybelle broke the quiet, "that's it, then. He's gone."

"The Colonel is dead," Ross declared. He stood, pulled up on his shorts, and said, "Long live the Colonel."

Maybelle sighed, and they took turns in the bathroom. Breakfast wasn't appealing, so they sat in the kitchen over coffee; Maybelle reached across the table and touched Ross's hand. He looked up in surprise then squeezed back and held on.

"People are dying," he said and spoke of those who had perished in the blast, and Mona Johnson, and now the Colonel.

Maybelle pulled her hand back and picked up her coffee. "Well, maybe with the Colonel gone it's over with, all the ruckus at the Foundation."

"You kidding?" he said. "Now I'll be going up against a *dead* war hero."

Her chest dropped with a heavy sigh. "Ross, the man's dead. Let it go, no one's going to care anymore."

He drained his cup and got up from the table. "Want a refill?" he asked.

She held her cup out.

"You don't get it, do you, May," he said, handing the filled cup back to her. "Someone still has to walk the plank for this. Someone has to lose. You want me to be the loser?"

"Ross, let things run on out. After the Colonel's in the ground, if you still want a go at those guys—do it," she said. "Put on the gloves."

"Might be nasty," he said. "Could mean airing some Armbruster laundry."

Maybelle studied his face. "Bagby's a good last name," she said. "Do what you have to do. I'll be with you."

"I'll be damned," he said.

"Might be exciting," she said.

"No, May, it won't be that." He told her about his meeting with Jill and his certainty that there was something beyond Mona Johnson and the Colonel.

"What do you think she meant, there's more to it?" Maybelle asked.

"I don't know, but I fear we'll find out soon and that whatever it is, it will be bad." He leaned over and kissed her on the forehead. "Thank you, May."

The reception for Germaine McKenzie was held at Jonah and Mercy's house, just another *show-up gang*, as Jonah called such events. Neville organized the formal party so that Germaine would have friends around her while she was grieving.

"Grieving? Germaine will be grinning—least on the inside," Ross said that evening as they dressed for the event. "Having the end come while people still know who the old Colonel was gives her a passel more hero worship to bank on. And believe me, she'll be milking the Widow Colonel McKenzie role until the day she dies."

"You're awful, just awful." Maybelle laughed.

"So," he said, "it's command performance time."

"No, in spite of your cynicism, it *is* to support Germaine. Hurry up now. We need to leave by six. By the way, while you were in the shower, you had a phone call."

"From whom?" He felt an electric flash across his shoulders. Who now?

She smirked. "Doctor Jackson. Bet it's about your test results. Think he'll need another sample some time soon? Glad to help. He's still at his office, said you could call."

Ross grunted and went downstairs to call Doctor Jackson's office. Sure enough, the tests were in. Henry Jackson came on the line laughing and told Ross he could hire out for stud. His sperm count would make a jackrabbit weep. "Suppose you'll be celebrating this news some way," the doctor chuckled before hanging up. Ross stood with his hand on the receiver, smiling, and decided he would keep the news to himself until later. He wondered how Maybelle would take the news that the question of fertility was now on her biological tree.

The Colonel's vigil that evening was a subdued affair. Germaine McKenzie held court with each person as they arrived; she was seated in a big wingback chair with a picture of the Colonel in full dress uniform on a table beside her. While her parents and the Colonel's relation's shook their heads and clucked remorse in the background, Germaine surprised people by being upbeat; in several cases she was the one who had to console someone and assure them that the Colonel's passing was for the best. When she and Ross caught sight of one another, their eyes lingered for a long moment; there was a knowing between them that required no words. Ross stood off where he could watch the widow and knew that she was relieved that her husband had not lived and, he imagined, even glad that he died as vengeance for his philandering. In fact, she was already basking in the light of being the widow of a man of high esteem—deserved or not—and the celebration of his life was only the beginning. It was great theater.

While Ross was taking in the spectacle, Neville walked past with Kribs right behind. Ross and Neville locked eyes, the umbrage simmering between them as if they were a couple of schoolyard combatants. Neville went on by, but Kribs stayed holding a plate heaped with food.

He looked around and leaned close to Ross. "Colonel's gone, and we got you in the crosshairs. Count your days," he said.

"But you're not keeping up," Ross smiled. "Guess you didn't hear about my trip down south? To Redding? Figured Neville would've told you. No? Guess you're not in on everything after all." Kribs blinked his ignorance. "Yeah," Ross went on, "I drove down there last Saturday, saw Mona Johnson's mother and sister. Mona's dead—suicide. You didn't know? Yeah, about a week ago. Tragic. Gruesome. Anyway, came back with the whole story. About the money, I mean. Was the Colonel, all right. Sure was. So Neville didn't tell you?" Ross said again. "Guess with the Colonel passing on and all he hasn't had the time. Anyway..." Kribs turned and walked off.

Ross was lowering a medium rare cut of prime rib onto his plate when Germaine came up. Actually, her perfume arrived first, so he wasn't totally surprised. He kept putting food on his plate.

"Touching, isn't it, Ross?" she said.

He turned to her, holding a fork above his plate.

"The outpouring of sympathy for Gordon. You know," she said, plucking a carrot stick off a vegetable platter. She bit down and snapped it in two. "I think some of these folks are actually grieving for my fallen warrior. But then, it's all really play-acting, isn't it? Like right now, you and me, we're acting things out, aren't we?"

"Could be," Ross said. "Guess we're all acting part of the time, some of us all of the time. Isn't that so, Germaine?"

She leaned close and breathed into his ear. "You know, they all think we're sharing a moment of grief. Watch this." She raised the hankie in her hand and dabbed at the corner of one eye, then sniffed and swiped daintily at her nose. Ross peeked past her shoulder; she was right. Several chronic mourners were indeed watching her every move, and when Germaine did the dab, sniff, and wipe routine they looked at one another and turned even more sorrowful. When she leaned her head on his shoulder for a moment, a couple of women almost burst into tears.

"Damn it, Germaine," Ross muttered, stepping back, juggling his plate.

Kribs suddenly appeared behind them. "Now, isn't this touching," he said, moving his tongue around in his mouth to dislodge a leftover.

Germaine turned to Kribs, a fraudulent smile gracing her mouth. "I'm so glad you'll be one of the pallbearers. Gordon would be pleased."

Kribs's smirk faded. "Be my honor," he said. "I loved the man."

"I know." She patted him on the arm. "We all did. It's so special to have everyone here, means a lot to me."

Kribs swung his cow head around and took in the room. "Uh, yeah." He nodded grimly before turning his eyes on Ross. "Course Bagby here, he's not so respectful of the deceased. Now, are you?"

Germaine twisted her neck, her too-showy earrings swinging, and looked at Ross. "Whatever could you mean? Ross is heartbroken."

Kribs missed the sarcasm. "Yeah, I'll bet. Snake in the grass. Germaine," he kept staring into Ross's eyes, "this here heartbroken fellow has been sneaking 'round on the Colonel, setting him up."

"What *are* you talking about?" she said.

"About..." Kribs lowered his voice, "about the money, you know, Germaine. You know." He tipped his head toward Ross conspiratorially.

"For crying out loud, we all know about the money," she said. "What about it, anyway? Gordon's sure not worried about it."

"Yeah, but," Kribs blinked at her, "but this son of a buck's been sneaking around setting the Colonel up to be blamed for it. Don't get any lower than that, bismerking the name of a dead man."

"Word's *besmirch*," Ross said.

"Damn you," Kribs said to Ross, "you and me are gonna—"

Germaine had stiffened. "Shut up, Kribs," she hissed and squared up in front of Ross.

"The hell is he talking about? Better not be what I'm thinking. You do remember our little talk, don't you?"

"I do, especially the part about putting me in a boxcar back to Nebraska," Ross said. "Very vivid. I was claustrophobic for days. I know, not funny. Thing is, Germaine, it's come down to me or the Colonel—one of us is going to take the rap for the missing ten thousand."

Ross could see the stiffness of Germaine's posture, but he was not expecting her to turn on him and drive two of her pointed nails into his chest. But she did, and with eyes of wrath that bulged in their sockets. She opened her mouth to speak but stopped and looked at Kribs who was hunkered over to eavesdrop.

"I want to talk privately to Ross."

"But I…"

She inhaled. "Leave us."

Kribs's face reddened even further, and he stumbled away only to pause in the arched doorway to the living room and look back. Germaine flicked the back of a hand at him, and he obeyed. Ross wanted to reach up and rub the tender spot on his chest, but he didn't. She threw her shoulders back and raised her chin. The effect made Ross feel smaller than she was, and when he looked into her eyes, he swore the color had changed from hazel to green. Her face seemed longer than it was due to her high forehead and the exposed length of her neck. They stood like that, toe to toe.

"You do this," she said, flat and in control, "and I'll cut your liver out and have it with onions. Told you not to mess with me on this."

Ross fought not to blink. "No, you won't do that."

"Like hell I won't," she hissed.

"No." He raised a forefinger. "You won't."

A flicker of doubt skipped across her face. "And why not?"

"Because I have the truth, Germaine," he said. "Documented."

23

Coverage of Colonel Gordon Butler McKenzie's death filled the front page of the *News-Review* on Tuesday, driving ongoing stories of the blast recovery to page two. There was a military-issue head-and-shoulder photograph of him in dress army uniform and an old army photo where he was leaning over a map on the hood of a Jeep in Korea as if he were planning a military offensive. (The real story behind that photo was that he was getting directions to a restaurant in Seoul.) The paper embellished his army career and his service to the community after his retirement, and documented his pseudo tragic death. Among those quoted were Neville Armbruster and the Colonel's brave widow. The funeral was held at the Armory to a packed audience followed by full military honors at the Memorial Gardens Cemetery where he was interred. Germaine had declined having the Colonel buried at Willamette National Cemetery in Portland; the paper said that she wanted him nearby where she could visit him regularly. Ross marveled at Germaine's tactical maneuver of having the Colonel's remains close at hand where his memory would continue to give credence to her position as the inheritor of all rights and privileges commensurate with her icon hero's rank.

There was an abnormal calm within the clan between the consoling dinner at Jonah and Mercy's and the funeral. The only respite from the ritual was the evening Maybelle suddenly remembered the call from Doctor Jackson. Ross was watching

James Garner and Jack Kelly connive another scam on *Maverick* when Maybelle brought him a cup of coffee and sat next to him on the couch. She sipped from her own cup for a minute then asked him if he really wanted to watch television. He looked at her, quizzical, and asked why.

She smiled. "Just remembered Doctor Jackson's call. About the lab test, wasn't it?"

He nodded, turned his eyes back to the television screen, and evasively slurped more coffee from the heavy brown mug.

"Well?" she asked. "Results?"

He shrugged.

"So why haven't you told me?"

An ad came on for Carnation evaporated milk. Ross got up and turned the set off and stood looking down at Maybelle, hands in his pockets. "Slipped my mind, Gordon dying and all that."

Maybelle's smile was teasing. "Going to get around to sharing the news with me sometime, were you? Or maybe you'd rather not?"

Ross puckered his mouth. "It's just that I haven't quite figured how to word the ad yet."

"Ad? What ad?"

"That I'm hiring out for stud," Ross said. "Got any ideas how I can put that in a civilized way? Like: *Bagby Breeding Services, Sir Sire,* or maybe *Procreation, Incorporated.*"

"Ross Bagby!" Maybelle cried out, laughing. She threw a couch pillow at him. "Sir Sire," she laughed some more. "So I guess that means you're fertile."

He grinned and tossed the pillow back. "Yep, Doc says my count's in the kajillions."

"Really. Kajillions." The glee gradually faded from her face, and she slumped back on the couch. "Well that's a bunch now, isn't it?"

"Sorry," he said.

"For what? Oh, you mean it has to be me then," she said.

A rueful smile played over his mouth.

"Stop that," she said. "I hate it when you do that—what you're doing now. Like you're pitying me."

He sat down beside her and propped the pillow behind his head. "I'm not pitying you," he said. "It's just that you were so insistent on this."

She laughed, but not like before. "A game. That's all it was. Wasn't serious you know."

"Maybelle!" he said. "What about telling me every time Mercy asked about grandkids? Or those articles on fertility she gave you?"

She pulled her feet up on the couch cushions and hugged her knees. "Want to know the truth? Always thought it was you, not enough little swimmers. Of course, I never wanted to get pregnant anyway. Not really."

"Like hell." He raised his head up off the pillow and looked at her. "We've talked about having kids since before we were married."

She turned her head toward him, still holding onto her knees. "The truth. Can't imagine waddling around for nine months like that. Ugh. Then the diapers, snotty noses, and then it goes on for years. My friend Nancy, her oldest is thirteen. God, the stories, the anxiety—not for me, thank you." She saw his stunned expression and laughed deep in her throat. "Should see your face. Hey, no big surprise, is it? I'm one selfish bitch. I like my life, my freedom."

"Yeah? Well, looks like that's guaranteed." Ross got up and turned the television back on; James Garner was doing something tricky with a hand of playing cards.

Maybelle quietly collected their coffee cups and took them to the kitchen. Ross found her standing at the sink, crying quietly. He put his arms around her; she leaned back into him, and it was as if he could feel something within her fading away.

They stood that way for a while, the television performing impotently in the background, until she patted him on his hands as they held her and turned to face him. Her cheeks had dried streaks of tears on them. She clung to him for a bit then pulled away, kissed him lightly on the mouth, and went upstairs. Later, when Ross came up, she was lying on her side facing away from him. He looked at her and considered one irrefutable fact—the two of them was all there would ever be between them.

He undressed slowly and looked over his shoulder as he sat on the edge of the bed; the light blanket rose and fell with her shallow breathing. He saw her hair spread out on the pillow and was surprised when tears filled his eyes. When did they stop loving each other, he wondered? Last year? The year before that, or was it even longer ago? Maybe it was when they sensed there would be no children. He pulled his socks off and rubbed his feet and couldn't pin it down. She was the strong one, always had been. After all she had the power—at least, that had been his rationale. So he had never before felt any guilt over the deadening between them; tonight he did. He even thought of making love to her right then, as something affirming to do, as something to grasp on to and not let Maybelle's promise to stand with him slip away. And something to show that whatever they had wasn't gone because they would be childless.

He lifted his legs and slid them between the sheets. For a time he lay quietly before turning off the lamp on the nightstand. When he turned on his side facing her back and tried to draw her close, she tensed.

"Don't," she said.

24

The Colonel's funeral had been a test of endurance for Ross. His deliberate shunning by the widow and the head of the Armbruster clan and his chief minion was laughable in its exaggeration. Ross was amused by the averted eyes and turned backs. Maybelle saw the spurning too, and would give her husband a sympathetic smile and an occasional squeeze of the hand.

By that next Monday morning he was eager to get out of the house and begin reclaiming his honor. He turned down Maybelle's offer to fix him breakfast, but he hugged her before he left and reveled in a return to affection long missing between them. Still, he was out the door by six and sitting at Snappy's counter by six fifteen. Jill was serving a couple of construction workers down the counter, laughing at something one of the men said. She skittered by Ross, scribbling on her order pad, and they shared only weak, obligatory smiles; it had been like that ever since the day at the duck pond. He ordered a cup of coffee to go, decided to call it breakfast, and left the café without looking at Jill.

A potted azalea plant was waiting bravely by the door to the office with a card stuck among the pink blossoms. Ross squatted down and plucked the envelope out. It was from the Buckhorn Boys' Ranch. Red Pritchard had written one word, *Con-*

dolences, and signed his name. Ross took down the notice he had taped on the office door window about the Colonel's death, shoved a mound of mail aside with the door, and carried the plant inside. The mail made quite a pile on the conference table. There were cards of sympathy from other organizations that had been funded over the years, the Chamber, the banks, and other businesses. Ross set the sympathy cards aside, tossed advertisements, sorted out bills and new funding requests—some now requesting blast-related assistance.

There were two envelopes addressed specifically to him. One was from Myrtle Johnson. Her unschooled hand had printed his name in block letters. Why was Mona's mother writing to him? He slit open the envelope with the Colonel's silver-bladed letter opener. The missive on an awkwardly folded piece of lined school paper was short, written in pencil with several smudges and erasures. The letter had to be read slowly, both to decipher misspelled words and to interpret Myrtle Johnson's vehement accusation of *You Armbruster people weezling out on your word.* He refolded the letter and slid it back into the envelope, chagrined that due to factors out of his control she was madder than hell and threatening to see *All of you shown up for the scoundrels you is.*

The other envelope was also hand-addressed to *Ross Bagby, Director, Armbruster Foundation, City.* To the left of his name the word *Personal* was underlined. The writing was in a neat cursive hand; there was no return address. Ross opened the envelope expecting an appeal for funding of some sort. There was one sheet of paper; the writing used less than half of the page. It read: *Dear Mr. Bagby, Something shameful is going on. Mona Johnson is not the only woman who's been mistreated. Things are in a bad way. We're in a desperate situation and want to get out of it. Will you help us? You know who to talk to.* There was no signature. Ross read the six short sentences twice and felt a chill each time before putting that letter, along with Myrtle Johnson's, into his briefcase along with the documents that never left his side.

Neville took Ross's call immediately and grunted his agreement that the Foundation board be convened right away. Ross convinced him to hold a meeting the next morning at nine o'clock. They spoke in clipped sentences and hung up abruptly as soon as there was nothing more to say. Ross made the calls. Every board member could attend. No one complained; the promised drama was too great to miss. Afterward he wrote down some additional notes to himself, put the yellow tablet into the briefcase, and wondered if he would still be standing when it was all over.

And now there was the gravity of the anonymous letter asking him to help unknown women out of an unknown desperation. He didn't know what the letter was referring to, but a fuzzy premonition clawed at his stomach, warning of something odious.

That evening Ross drove out Del Rio Road to attend a board meeting of the Humane Society, where he had been invited to accept a certificate of appreciation for the Foundation's support. He thanked the board members, who smiled too much, encouraged them in their work, and praised them too much. By eight thirty seven he was turning onto Brockway Avenue. He slowed the Chrysler when he drew opposite the apartment building where he knew Jill lived and parked the car across the street. He kept the engine running and wrestled with his apprehension and his temptation. He had been determined to avoid what he was drawn to, but now he had no choice, or so he thought. The dusk had lowered a salmon pink veil over the town; there were lights on in the apartment building, and the neighborhood was quiet. He suddenly wanted a cigarette. He'd given up the addiction long ago, but there were times when he craved just one freshly lit Lucky Strike. This was one of those times. *After a couple of puffs, maybe four,* he reasoned, *I could stub out the glowing butt, snuff this hankering from my veins, and drive away.* Simple as that. Instead, he turned off Frankie Avalon and the ignition, put the envelope containing the anonymous letter in his shirt pocket, and walked across the street.

The apartment foyer was a tiny enclosure with a rubber floor mat and eight mailboxes embedded in one wall. Jill was in apartment six. He pushed through the second door into the hallway and stood listening; it was quiet, and there was the stale smell of linoleum and dust and old paint. He ran a comb through his hair, checked his shirttail, and started up the stairs on his toes. When he reached the landing, one of the four doors popped open and a short older man with steel wool gray hair came out and looked at Ross with baggy eyes. A woman's voice yelled out, "Don't forget my cigarettes, ya hear! Cecil!" The man turned and called back, "Yeah, yeah!" and yanked the door closed. He shook his head as he passed and eased himself gingerly down each step.

Ross watched until he had exited the building before rapping lightly on the door to Jill's apartment. He heard movement, the door opened a crack, and her blue eyes peered out at him. He smiled, and she opened the door wider.

"Mr. Bagby…Ross. What are you doing here?"

He dropped the smile. "We have to talk."

"What about?" she asked.

He looked down the hall then back. "I got a letter today," he said. "An anonymous letter."

She studied his face then turned, left the door ajar, and walked away. He wandered in and looked around the small, tidy apartment. She had gone to sit in a saggy overstuffed chair and was watching him warily. He tried smiling again; she didn't smile back.

"Nice apartment," he said.

"So you got a letter," she said.

"Yeah." He reached in his shirt pocket and pulled out the envelope. "This one."

Jill bit on a fingernail. "What's it got to do with me?"

"Okay if I sit down?" She nodded, and he walked over to a rose-colored couch. An errant spring pushed up against his bottom when he sat down. He rearranged his rump and held the envelope in both hands.

"The person who wrote this letter said I'd know who to talk to," he said.

She hesitated before saying, "And you think it's me?"

"Yes, I think it's you."

She reached out. "Can I see it?"

He stood, handed her the envelope, and watched as she opened the flap and pulled out the sheet of paper. She looked over at him once before beginning to read. He leaned back against the couch cushion and watched her. Her expression didn't change. She lowered the letter after reading it.

"You know who wrote that?" Ross asked.

"No," she said too emphatically.

"I think you do."

She pushed herself up out of the chair and padded past him on bare feet and went into the kitchen. He waited until he heard running water and followed. She was filling the percolator.

"Coffee?" she asked.

"Yeah, coffee would be good." He leaned a hip against the counter and watched her scoop coffee from a red Folgers can into the percolator basket, set the thing on the stove, and turn up the dial under the burner. He watched each motion she made and chided himself for his pathetic fascination. It had been easy to excuse his self-deception when it seemed that he and Maybelle no longer mattered to each other. Because he had convinced himself of that perceived reality, he freely indulged in his delusions about a young woman. But with one clear act, what had been missing returned. When Maybelle said, *I'll be with you*, Ross had been shaken by her simple expression of belief. *It may be the beginning*, he thought, *of finding our way back*. But he wasn't sure.

Still he watched Jill fuss about. He followed her with his eyes, getting cups and spoons and the sugar bowl. He partook of those moments of distraction, bits and pieces that softly delayed the real words that would have to come. They sat over a tablecloth with red and white squares and doctored their coffee and sipped.

"Your wife was in the café today," Jill said. "Mabel, that her name?"

"May-belle." He looked away as if it didn't matter. "She was?"

"Yeah, Maybelle. She's a pretty lady."

He moved his head affirmatively. "I agree."

"She came to see me, I think," Jill said.

"That so?"

"You should see your face," Jill laughed. "Yeah, she sat in a booth, ordered coffee and a piece of lemon pie. Invited me to sit down for a minute."

"What for?"

"Boy, the guilt on your face," she said. "Should see it. Now it's red, too."

He drank more coffee and waited.

"Anyway, your wife was sorry that Mona had died. Said she was glad that you were the one who told me what really happened. You being gentle-like and all." Jill paused. "Odd her doing that, though."

Ross toyed with his coffee cup. "She's just curious, that's all."

"You love her?"

"Of course," he answered too quickly.

"She love you?"

"Jill," he stopped her. "Who wrote the letter, and what's it mean?"

She stood up suddenly from the table and went to the kitchen window above the sink and looked out.

"You told me there's more to it," Ross said. "Out at the pond, you said that. Now this letter comes and says something is shameful and that things are desperate. Jill, whoever it is wants help. Damn it, you've got to tell me now."

She spun around and leaned over the table, hands planted, and put her face close to his. "All right," she said, snapping out the words. "All right." She sat down and inhaled deeply. "Give me a minute, collect my thoughts."

Ross sat upright and waited.

"It started out for fun," she said a moment later. "That's all, just fun, crazy, risky fun."

"Risky?"

"Yeah," she said. "You know, like when you do something a little improper and you feel all shivery because it's fun but a little bit naughty, too. It was going to be that way, just spicy fun."

"Just what the hell are we talking about here?" Ross asked.

Jill became still. She traced the checkered squares on the tablecloth with a finger. Then she began to rock in her chair and bob her head and finally to hum. Ross watched her for a time and then abruptly spoke her name.

"Jill!"

Her head snapped up, and her eyes looked into his.

"The *spicy fun* part," he said. "Tell me about that."

"*How'd you like to go to Reno, honey, and have a fun time?*" she said in a soft voice. "*See some shows*, they said, and *gamble with our money*, they said. *We'll drive you down*, they said, *a long weekend of exciting fun*, they said. They said all that."

"Who are they?" Ross asked. "Who are you talking about?"

"Nope, just listen," she said. "The first time it *was* fun...kind of exciting. We got out of town on a Friday afternoon, drove right on through crowded into this big old car, had drinks in the car, ate on the road. We stayed at the Mapes Hotel in Reno—every time that's where we stayed, at the Mapes. Had our own rooms. We went to shows and saw Frank Sinatra and Sammy Davis Junior, even Milton Berle. They gave us money so we could gamble in the casinos, slots mostly. We ate and drank and it was…a party." She paused and breathed in. "Sunday, we drove back and got in at one or two in the morning. Exhausted and dopey, but we'd had fun, really lived it up."

"Then it wasn't fun," Ross said.

"No." She paused. "Things changed after that."

"How'd they change?"

Her eyes met his. "I don't know about telling you this."

"Sure you do," he said. "Someone you know wants help. They're desperate. Who wrote that letter? Who told them to write me? You did, didn't you?"

"No names," Jill said. "That's the rule."

"Whose rule?"

"Their rule, of course," she said.

Ross sighed. "So what happened? What made it not fun anymore?"

"The next time we went to Reno," she said, "maybe a month later, it was different."

Ross started to ask her what she meant but stopped and just waited her out. Let her breathe and calm herself.

"We saw a show," she began, "like before. We had dinner, we gambled—it was fun, like the first time. One of them won over five hundred dollars, and he divvied it up with us gals. That was something. But then…then we were paired off with them. Not like before when we girls shared our own rooms. They had each of us stay with one of them. They sweet-talked and arm-twisted until we all went along with it."

"They forced you to sleep with them, didn't they?"

"Wait, just let me tell this," she said. "I…I remember that the next morning," she went on, "Caro…the youngest one was in a daze. Her eyes were red, she barely touched her breakfast, and she would often cry to herself on the long drive home...that long, gloomy ride back. That was the first time."

"What about you?" Ross asked. "Were you...paired off?"

"Yes," she said. "No, don't ask me who with. Don't. Or what it was like."

"Were you mistreated?"

"Don't do that, I said," she answered.

Ross got up and took the percolator off the stove and poured fresh cups for each of them. He straddled his chair, sat down, doctored his coffee then leaned over and stared into the cup. The sound of a car accelerating outside filled the silence for a moment.

"I never went again," she said. "Just told them no."

"They pressure you any?"

She nodded. "I more or less threatened them, though. *Leave me alone or else*, I told them."

"Or else what?"

She smiled. "I don't know. I was bluffing. They left me alone, though. But Mona and the others, they kept doing it. And it got worse..." She raised a hand to her mouth and closed her eyes; tears seeped out, and she wiped at them.

"Why didn't the others just quit?" he asked softly. "Like you."

She sniffed and wiped at her eyes again. "I asked Mona that same question, told her to stop—couple a times I told her that. Wouldn't do it. Just wouldn't."

"But why?"

She found a hankie in her pants pocket and blew her nose on it. "For Mona it was the excitement, the razzle-dazzle. Made her feel special, a payoff for standing on sore feet every other day, she told me. And she was just for certain that the Colonel loved her, if you can believe such a thing. Bubblehead. Heck, she thought he was going to divorce his wife so he could marry her. She was my best friend, but she could be dumber than dirt, tell you that."

"You keep dancing around it," Ross said, "but just what was going on? Why is the person in the letter so desperate?"

Jill smiled in a way that made Ross feel pitied.

"We were all alike," she said, "in a way, we were. They picked us out on purpose. We was handpicked for our...our special qualities." She laughed. "Yep, our special qualities. Young, or thereabouts, poor, and more or less attractive, I'd say, and we didn't know anybody with connections. Top of that, we were all easy to tempt. The idea of fun and games with real grown-up men of means with no strings attached—we were dumb enough to think it sounded exciting. A weekend away from our dull jobs? You bet. We were suckered, that was it. We were suckered.

"So off we went, a carload of stupid, silly girls. They were spending money on us, Ross. Lot's of money, at least a lot of money for a bunch of hard-luck gals. And like I said, it was party time. But then...it turned ugly." She stopped talking and stared into thin air.

Ross cleared his throat. "Tell me, Jill. I know what it was, but just...just tell me."

She looked at him and focused on his face. "All right! Yes, they were sleeping with them...with us. Is that what you want to hear? Damn them to hell!" She yelled the words. Then words came softly. "That's what they wanted all along, some young women to have sex with. And we were perfect. We were living lives of drudgery and boredom. We were easy targets. Boy, were we ever."

"How many of you?" he asked.

"Four," she answered. "Four. And didn't we think we were smart. We laughed about it in the ladies' room on the way down to Reno on that first trip. What a bunch of dumb guys, taking us to Reno, paying our way just for a weekend away from their wives. Oh yes, we knew they were all married. That made it safe and them stupid. Us being so smart and all."

"But none of the others stopped like you did?"

She shook her head. "They even got another gal to fill my spot." She laughed a bitter laugh. "Can you believe it?"

"The one that wrote the letter," he said, "the desperation."

"They are desperate, Ross. All of 'em."

He sighed heavily. "But I don't understand. Why—"

"They're trapped!" she yelled. "They are trapped. Get it?" Her blue eyes were blazing at him.

Ross blinked. "Okay," he said, "okay. Tell me."

"Some of it I understand," she said, "and some of it I just don't. I don't."

"Tell me the part you think you understand, then," he said.

"Well Mona, you already know that one. Got herself into thinking a rich, powerful man was going to marry her. The others...well, they were up against it because they're all married."

"Married?" Ross said. "My god, how could they get away with that?"

She shrugged. "Couple of loggers who were gone weeks at a time in the woods. One gal is married to a long-haul trucker, same thing there. Except for Mona and me, they picked real careful. The girls said they didn't want to do it no more, and then the bullying started. *You don't want your husbands to be told about this, now do you? Let's just keep on having fun.* That's how they put it to the ones with an old man. And...and the longer it went on the harder it got to fess up. And the more these guys pressured the girls to go along."

"Jesus," Ross spat out.

"Pretty soon," she went on, "the Reno trips were less and quick trips to the coast for a weekend shack-up were more likely. But there was always money and fancy dinners and gifts, geegaws that the gals would have to hide or get rid of so their husbands wouldn't see them. And there's something else," she said.

"What?"

"In some ways," she said, "they are drawn to these guys. They're desperate, like the letter says, but at the same time caught up in it. You know, attracted to the whole thing. I mean Mona, she was always excited when she was going to get time with the Colonel or going off with…all of them. Ugh, I can't go on." She got up and poured the cold coffee in her cup into the sink.

Ross was still. He sat with his hands folded on the tabletop. He looked at Jill as she stood at the sink and saw skin younger than his and smoother than Maybelle's, the lollipop cheekbones and the blue eyes. She was pretty, and like the fools she had just described, he was in this young woman's apartment having thoughts. He was there for a good a reason; did that give him the right to have thoughts? She was nice to look at, and she was open to him in a way. What could he do with his thoughts? A door slammed across the hall; the old man must be back with the cigarettes.

Ross came out of his stupor when it was obvious that Jill was crying. Her shoulders were rising and falling, and her head was bobbing in rhythm with her sobbing. He slid his chair back but didn't know whether he should sit still or attempt to comfort her. After a moment, he went to her and put his hands on her shoulders. She straightened up but otherwise didn't acknowledge his touch. Her hands reached for her pocket and she again pulled out her handkerchief and blew her nose.

Ross took his hands away. "I'm sorry," he said. "I know this is awful for you. I…I don't know what to do, but these men, whoever they are, have to be stopped. Jill, look at me." She turned from the sink and faced him. Her eyes were wet and red. "You must tell me who these people are."

Her head shook slowly. "I can't," she said. "I promised. There'd be trouble for them."

"Jill, I have to know who they are."

"Not now," she answered. "Give me time." She leaned against him.

He held her gently and tried to balance his own infatuation against his revulsion for her tale of sexual exploitation. Was there a difference between him and those unnamed men? *There must be. I've only had thoughts, I've only imagined. But isn't that likely where they also began?*

He took a step back and peered into her face. The instant of sweet sensuality that he had imagined slid away. She smiled, and he touched his lips to her cheek.

Out on the landing, Ross could hear the woman next door barking at her husband.

25

Ross stood out on the walk in front of the apartment building and breathed in the cooling night air. There had been a brief shower; the smell of damp asphalt met his nose. Fall was coming. He could feel the edge of it and was slightly chilled walking back to his car. In a way, the coolness helped clear his head, but that only made him shudder with regret. He sat behind the wheel and his mind wandered about until he had replayed all he wanted to replay. The starter whined, and the big V8 woke up; Ross pounded the steering wheel once and drove up the hill. The evening news was on the radio. The Soviets had hit the moon with a rocket after three misses. *So*, he thought, *other things have been going on.*

Maybelle was in the kitchen doing something. He called out that he was going to exercise and take a shower. She said something that sounded like a question, but he went down without responding and stripped out of his clothes and stepped into a pair of gym shorts. There was a sound at the top of the stairs. He knew she was standing there, but she didn't say anything or come down and eventually went away. He concentrated on the bench press and worked up in weight until the burn across his chest began to punish him, to maybe purge him of idiocy. At one point the weight and the repetitions became too great, and he could not lift the bar off his chest. He thought of yelling for Maybelle; instead he held the bar steady and waited until he regained enough strength to wrestle the weight up and grunt it back onto the rack above his head. He sat up and toweled the sweat from his face, probed his chest, and winced.

When he entered the bedroom, Maybelle was sitting at the vanity, her face covered with cold cream; the sweet smell of the emollient tickled his nose. She paused in her ritual and looked at his red-faced reflection in the mirror then went back to smearing while he hung up his clothes.

"Thought you said the thing at the Humane Society wouldn't take long," she said. "Where have you been?"

He sat on the bed with his ratty bath towel still wrapped around him. He'd been thinking about that very question. "Showdown board meeting tomorrow, remember. Foundation. Went back to the office to get ready for it," he lied. "I'm ready for them this time."

"Phoned down there once, didn't get an answer." She was wiping the white goo off with facial tissue and looking sideways at him in the mirror.

"Hmm, don't know," he persisted. "Must have been when I was down the hall in the john. I had to go a couple of times, get rid of the coffee I borrowed earlier."

"Uh-huh," she hummed. "So the meeting tomorrow, what are you going to do?"

He stood and took off the towel, saw her examine his na-kedness in the mirror for a moment then look back at her face. "It's my turn, May," he said. "To set this right. Going to mess up the anthill. Did you hear? The Russkies put a rocket on the moon."

"Huh? What's that got to do with anything?" she said. "Who cares?"

"Mostly the people on *that* anthill," he answered. "Got to take care of yourself on the anthill you're dealt, or end up sweeping out."

She scooted around on the vanity seat, her hair held up from her face by two combs. The effect was stark, a pale, glistening face with no mascara or lipstick. "What's that line across your chest?" she asked.

He grunted a laugh and slipped under the covers. "Too much weight on my last lift, couldn't get it up. Had to set it on my chest until I regained my strength."

"Ross, you're going to be okay tomorrow, aren't you?" She was looking at him in the mirror again. "Is it going to be messy?"

"Could be," he said. "Tell you, May, I am not going to be the whipping boy on this anymore. I've got the goods, going to use it to call the shots." He thought of the anonymous letter but decided not to mention it.

Maybelle stood at the foot of the bed in her pink nightie and looked at her husband as he lay with his arms behind his head on the pillow. She started to say something, then didn't, went to her side of the bed and got in next to him. Ross had watched her and was choked with self-reproach. A little more than an hour before, he had been with another woman whom he had wanted. He was sure that he radiated his guilt like a beacon; he had scrubbed himself torturously in the shower to remove any remnant of scent and now lay like a post in the bed, waiting to be accused. *But I didn't do anything. I only thought about it—laughable.*

Before Maybelle turned off her light, she reached over to him, took his hand, and squeezed it. "You'll do fine," she said. "I'll fix you breakfast before you go. Okay?"

He nodded and squeezed her hand back. When her light went out, he lay awake in the dark, breathing shallowly, waiting for justice to erupt beside him. But before five minutes had passed, he heard her breathing deepen and soon a gentle purring snore. After that he ran a hand over his tender chest and tried to erase the memory of holding Jill. He thought of other things, the board meeting, the letter from the unnamed woman, the Russians hitting the moon. It didn't matter; his transgression was still in his head. It only left when he finally fell asleep. Blessedly, he didn't dream.

||||||||||||||||||||||||||||||||||||||||||||||||||||||||||||||||||||||||||||||||||||||

Matters on Ross's anthill got underway at nine o'clock the next morning. It began with Charlie Beamus, Captain of the Lift, as he was now calling himself, grousing about the Soviets hitting the moon with their rocket. He slammed the gate, just missing Ross's rump, and started in.

"Damn Commies, getting there before we do," Beamus said. "Can you believe it? What's things coming to when Na-keet-ah, that fat little prick, when he can beat the U.S. of A. at something? Humiliating."

"Hey," Ross gestured at the rheostat handle, "this thing move?"

Beamus jammed the lever and the car lurched upward. "But don't it frost you?"

"So they plopped a tin can up there," Ross said. "Took four shots to hit it. Anyone upstairs?"

"Yeah, a woman," Beamus nodded.

Germaine was waiting in the corridor, leaning against the wall, looking as if she had eaten ground glass for breakfast. Her torched eyes fended off Ross's smile.

"My key doesn't work," she complained.

"Had the locks changed last week," Ross said. He put his shiny new key into the lock. "Seemed every other person I know had one. No offense, Germaine, just a security thing." He held the door open, and she stomped by.

The others arrived in a clump; their usual banter was reduced to quiet murmuring and a slow milling about until each had taken a place at the table and awkwardly welcomed Germaine McKenzie.

"Glad everyone could make it on short notice." Ross smiled and looked at each face around the table; the only smile in return was Miss Emeline's.

"Let's get on with this," Neville said. "Your show."

Ross observed Neville's slack face and Kribs's scowl. "All right. This get-together is about one thing, the money. Who took it and where it went. And then—"

"I'm warning you, Ross Bagby," Germaine interrupted, "If you dare to—"

"Germaine," Neville raised his chin, "please. Don't know squat until he's put it on the table."

Germaine sank back in her chair and glowered.

"Get on with it," Neville said.

Ross turned his head from side to side. "Look people," he said, "get one thing straight. I'm done being cuffed upside the head on this. I'm not rolling over for anyone's convenience."

"We'll just see about that," Kribs said.

Ross inhaled. "No, Kribs, I'm dead serious. You think I'm not, you'd better hear me out first. The game-playing is over."

Kribs coughed out a grunt and shook his head.

"Hey, scowl all you want. We're going to put this thing to rest today, and I'll tell you now it's not going to be by scraping my backside some more."

"We get the picture," Neville said. "Wendell, put a sock in it. I mean it."

Ross took his time, lifted his briefcase off the floor, pulled a file folder from it, and laid it on the table. He put an open hand on the folder and said, "In here I have documentation that confirms the who, how, and why of the missing ten thousand dollars. I'm going to tell you where that money went."

He opened the folder and began.

When he was done, no one spoke. Germaine had slunk down in her chair and now stared at Ross glassy-eyed

"You can't let him do this," she said, pouting.

"Do what?" Neville's voice was resigned.

"Denigrate Gordon this way," Germaine whined. "I'll be humiliated."

Neville snorted. "Come on, Germaine, Gordon screwed around on you for years. This Mona Johnson was just the next one. Should I say, the *last* one."

"Liar," Germaine complained. "What's that look mean? Well, okay, but we were working things out he...he'd promised." She rose up in her chair. "You're not going to expose me to ridicule. I won't stand for it. Neville, now, Neville, I know things. You know that I know things. Don't force me to—"

"Germaine, quit now." Neville shoved his fingers up under his glasses and massaged his eyes. "Be quiet." He looked around the table. "Guess we're mostly family here. Right?" His face contorted into a dispirited smile. "Way I see it, anyway. Look, Germaine, hate to tell you this, but anything you think you know—which can't be much—I can trump with other bad news. The Colonel, I *made* the Colonel, by the way. Anyway, I bailed his ass out of more shit than you want to know about. Believe me, dear. No," he raised a hand, "no, don't even ask." He sighed. "Now Ross here has the goods. He does. Thing is, what'll we do about it? Nope, Wendell, I want to hear from you, you'll be the first to know. Until then, zip your lip. So, any ideas?"

"Have to see that the money is reinstated," John said. He nodded to Ross.

"Yeah, we've done that before," Neville said. "ALC will write a check."

"I don't want to hear about that," John said. "Please, not another word. Think it has to be cleaner than that. It should come from the Colonel. Germaine has to repay the money."

"Wait a darn minute," Germaine argued. "I'm not in any position to come up with that much money."

"That's beside the point," John said. "Don't care where the money comes from, but Germaine will be repaying it. Understood?"

Neville looked at John, who had his attorney face on, and nodded. "Okay. End of the day today." There was quiet agreement.

"We're done, then?" Neville said and planted his hands to push up from his chair.

"Not yet," Ross said and pulled Myrtle Johnson's letter out and smoothed it with his hand. "As long as we're cleaning things up, we might as well scrub the bottom of the pot." He turned to Neville. "You know, I wasn't going to do this."

Neville returned his gaze with a question in his eyes until it came to him. Then he lowered his eyelids. "Jesus, you got your redress. Let it go."

"Can't," Ross said. "Can't because Mr. Kribs here is a low-life."

"Hell you talking about?" Kribs sat up straight.

"Myrtle Johnson, Mona's mother?" Ross said.

"Yeah," Kribs said, "so?"

"You pulled the plug on the agreement with her," Ross said.

The color rose in Kribs's vein-laced face, and he cast a glance toward Neville. "Strictly business, all it was."

"What the hell did you do, Wendell?" Neville said.

"He went back on your agreement to compensate Myrtle Johnson after Mona's death," Ross said.

"The woman's dead?" asked John. "How…"

"My stars," groaned Miss Emeline, "what is going on?"

"Jesus, Ross," Neville said, "we have to go into that? You gave us the math, Gordon took the money, he was a bastard, let it go."

"Not the only bastard," Ross added.

"I want to hear this," said John. "Go on, Ross."

Ross inhaled. "Mona Johnson committed suicide. Less than a month ago. She was already pregnant when Gordon was injured."

Germaine reared up, started to say something, then slumped back down.

"Goddamn it!" Neville shouted. "Stop this." He looked at Miss Emeline and John. "Somebody has to do the dirty work while you all stay nicey nice. Not one of you would have the stomach for it. Not one of you." He pointed at them and wagged his finger.

John studied Neville's troubled face. "Go on, Ross, tell us."

Neville shoved his chair back and walked into the outer office. They could hear him pacing as Ross told them everything about Mona Johnson's miserable existence. Kribs's face got redder and redder and he sat kneading his hands.

"Then Kribs," Ross continued, "he tells Myrtle Johnson to forget the monthly payments and cuts her off."

"Hell, the girl's dead. Why should we keep paying her kin?" But Kribs spoke with defeat in his voice.

Ross leaned forward and jutted his chin out. "Because, Mr. Kribs, Mona's mother promised me she'd turn everything she has over to the newspaper, radio, and television stations up here and make all of us instant celebrities. And because a deal is a deal, a promise is a promise, Kribs. If you had an honorable bone in your body, you'd understand that. But I can tell by the look on your face that you don't follow what I'm saying."

Kribs started to say something but didn't.

"Is this true, Mr. Kribs?" Miss Emeline asked. When Kribs winced but didn't respond, she said, "Disgraceful, just disgraceful. What should we do, Ross?"

"This is the easy part," Ross said. "ALC reinstates the agreement with Mrs. Johnson and guarantees that it will continue as long as she lives."

"Then that's what will be done," Miss Emeline said. "You'll see to that, Neville?"

Neville was standing in the doorway; he did not protest.

The meeting broke up like a funeral. Neville, Kribs, and Germaine evaporated from the premises leaving no trace save the diminishing residue of Germaine's scent. John made eye contact with Ross in quizzical manner and was gone before more

could be said. Miss Emeline patted Ross fondly and congratu-
lated him for setting things right.

"It's a start," he replied. That was all he could say for the
moment, but in his head he was saying, *Except it isn't over yet.
More bad stuff to come.*

26

Then everyone was gone. In the stillness, Ross sagged into the high-backed chair and leaned his elbows on the desk. The random rumbling of the elevator was the only sound that cut into the quiet as he mulled over what had just occurred; he knew that his performance with the board had aggravated existing animosity. He had won that round, but at the same time the nagging chill of a desperate woman pleading for him to help her hung in his mind like a bad dream. He knew that somehow the Colonel and the beautician and the anonymous women were connected. *Something shameful is going on*, the woman had written. That may be, Ross reasoned, but Colonel McKenzie is dead, Mona Johnson is dead. What more could he do? *Surely it will all go away*, he persisted in his thinking. The men involved would retreat in the face of the deaths, and the anonymous woman and her friends would be free of their contemptible entanglement. *Soon it will be over*, Ross rationalized. The desperate plea for help would no longer apply. Besides, he was suddenly ravenous.

Outside on the street, he noted that the gauntlet of plywood that had covered store windows had largely been replaced with new glass, and the constant rumbling of the raw cleanup, the mechanized shovels and the caravans of dump trucks, was mostly a memory. Graded, empty lots offered silent testimony to structures that had held that ground before. The smell, the acrid sour ash odor that had bullied in and overstayed, wasn't mugging his nostrils this day. Roseburg was on the way back.

―――――――――――――――――――――――――――――――――――

Ross wasn't ready to see Jill again right then; he needed to distance himself. He bypassed the café, walked up the street to the B & M Tavern, and ate part of a slimy corned beef sandwich. He had a beer to wash it down, and replayed the morning's events before walking back to the office.

A second letter was waiting for him among the other mail delivered while he was out. As before, it was addressed to *Ross Bagby, Director, Armbruster Foundation* and marked *Personal*. The handwriting was different, a scrawl in lieu of the neat hand of the first letter. The envelope was plain white, the size used to pay bills with; the message was written on a small sheet of plain notepaper. *Dear Sir,* it began in a loopy hand. *Them being dead, Mona and the Colonel, don't mean anythings changed.* Ross raised his head; it was as if the writer had read his mind. *Cause it hasn't,* the writer went on. *What can you do? Help us please.* No name.

Jill saw Ross when he yanked the door open and came into the café. He caught her eye and motioned for her to come outside. She looked around, said something to Blanche, and came out from behind the counter. He was waiting out on the sidewalk. She blinked in the sunlight and approached him but kept some distance between them and held a hand up to shade her eyes.

"What?" she said.

Ross held out the envelope. "This."

She took it. When she finished reading, she handed it back and stared wide-eyed at him.

"You know who wrote this?" he asked.

She hesitated. "Yes, I think so."

"They want me to do something," he said. "Me. What the hell can I do?"

She waited until a woman with a child walked past. "I don't know," she said. "I suppose you can...oh, I don't know."

"Do you want these women to get out of their mess?" he asked.

She nodded. "Yes."

Ross looked at the letter in his hand. "I can't help if I don't know who these people are—and I mean all of them, men and women." He paused. "Even then I don't know what good I could do."

She looked into his eyes without responding.

"Jill, damn it," he said. "Who are they?"

"Not here," she answered. "Come by my place. I get off at three, and I'll go right home."

Ross was waiting across the street in his car when Jill entered the apartment building. She gave him a little wave, went in, and left her apartment door ajar. He could hear her in the kitchen. When she came out into the living room, she found him standing, hands in his pockets, glowering.

"I put the coffee on," she said.

"Not necessary."

She shrugged. "Oh well, want to sit down?"

He dropped onto the couch and she took the armchair as before. They looked at one another in silence before Ross spoke.

"Okay," he began, "no dilly-dallying. I want to—"

"I made a list," she said. "All the names." She pulled a piece of paper out of the patch pocket of her waitress dress. It was folded into a tight square.

He stood, stepped forward, and held out his hand.

"Wait," she said. "I need to say something first."

He sat back down. "Okay, what?"

She sighed. "I...I planned all of this. The letters and all."

"You did?" he said.

"Yes, to make the nightmare go away for them," she said.

"Told them to write you those letters and I'd see what happened. Needed to know if you were different from them...the other men. See how you'd react to these girl's troubles."

"How I would *react*?" he said.

She lifted a shoulder. "You could've just ignored them."

Ross took in a deep breath and let it out in a grunt. Jill smiled. "Like your wife said, like Maybelle said, about you being gentle-like. And you are. You care about people."

"Bullshit, Jill," he said. "I'm up to my neck in one mess after another. I'm trying to keep my head out of the slime, that's all. Now, who are these people?"

She held out the folded paper, and he stepped over to get it. He lowered himself onto the couch again, held the patch of paper in his hands, and looked over at Jill. He saw the apprehension in her face.

"Last chance," he said. "Last chance to call this off...me seeing who all's involved."

"I know," she said. "But it's got to happen. These gals...they need out."

"I'm no tough guy," Ross said. He held the paper, massaged it a moment then began to unfold it.

"Wait!" Jill said. "One more thing."

"What?"

"Those names? You're going to be...well, you could be unsettled by them, least some of them."

"Unsettled," he said and unfolded the sheet and straightened it. He scanned the names Jill had carefully printed, the women then the men. "Jesus," he said and lowered the paper then raised it again and studied the names. "You're telling me..."

"Yes," she said.

Ross laid the paper beside him on the couch and stared off across the room. After a moment he picked it up again and rattled it in his hand. "I can't believe this," he said.

"I know. But it's true...sorry, I'm really sorry."

He sighed. "Who are these women?" he asked. "Don't recognize their names."

"First one," she began, "she's a secretary out to Armbruster's Lumber, someplace out there. Don't know what department or nothing. Second name, Caroline? She's a teller at U. S. Bank. Next one's Margo. She works for some logging company, in the office. And then, well…Mona."

Ross stood suddenly and walked about in a circle. "Damn," he blurted, "I can't believe this." He held the paper up, gripped in both hands and read the list again.

The sound of the percolator bubbling away in the kitchen could be heard in the sudden quiet. Ross went back to the couch.

"So, what you going to do?" she asked.

He kept looking at the paper in disbelief. "Hell, I don't know."

"But you're going to do something."

He was slumped down, but he nodded. "Yeah, I'll do something."

Ross shoved through the door of the offices of Chapman, Hughes, and Knox and told the receptionist that he needed to see John Knox. When she hesitated, he said—*Now.* She blinked and swiftly left her station. In less than a minute she was back saying he could go right in. John was at his splendid desk. He stood, his face unsmiling.

"Ross," he said. "Something wrong?"

"Have to talk," Ross said and remained standing.

John sat down and tilted back in his chair. "Okay," he said, his face wrinkled in curiosity. "What about? Sit down, would you? Gives me a kink looking up."

Ross sat in the leather chair and set his elbows on the walnut armrests. He took a deep breath. "Something's come up," he said. He felt his chest tighten, and he fought a little to get his breath. "Serious," he added.

"If it's about the Foundation money, I heard from Neville an hour or so ago that Germaine will be sending a check tomorrow."

"No," Ross said. "Not that."

"What then? Spit it out, man."

"Did you know Mona Johnson?" Ross asked straight out.

John sat forward in his chair. "I knew of her, of course, like we all do. Why do you ask?"

"But did you know her? Did you ever meet her, been around her?"

John's face slackened, and his eyes narrowed. "What's going on?"

"Did you, John?" Ross could hardly breathe. "Think carefully now."

"I don't know," John said. "I may have met her once. Ross, what the hell are you driving at?"

Ross pulled the folded paper with the names on it out of his pants pocket and held it up. "This," he said. "And I'm just hoping what's on this piece of paper is a big mistake."

"What's that? Maybelle's grocery list?"

"Don't," Ross said. "This is disturbing."

"Disturbing?" John held a shallow smile on his face. "What you have there?"

Ross slowly unfolded the paper, looked at it, then reached out to place it on John's desk. His father-in-law stared down at it, and the smile faded from his face. After a moment he tapped a forefinger onto the sheet of paper then sagged back in his chair.

"Where'd you get that?" he asked.

"How could you be part of something like that?" Ross said.

"What do you think you know, Ross?"

Ross stood and leaned over John's desk. "I know that four men have exploited several young women for sexual favors. I know that it's been going on for some time and your name is right there on the list!" He jabbed his finger in the air, pointing at the paper.

As he spoke, Ross saw his father-in-law's reaction run from being staggered to appearing contrite, before returning to an expression of self-assuredness. With Ross standing over him, John raised his arms above his head, stretching.

"It was the waitress who told you all this," John said. "Wasn't it? Jill what's-her-name."

"John, for crying out loud, what does that matter?"

"Knew she'd do that at some point." John shook his head.

"So you've been caught," Ross said, "and she's the reason? The hell difference does that make? John, did you do this? *Are* you doing this…with these women?"

John rubbed his hands over his face and sighed. "What if we did? Consensual between adults."

Ross slammed a hand down, causing the phone on the desk to jump. "Don't you throw lawyer talk at me. Try and justify this, this…your behavior. Here." He threw the anonymous letters on the desk. "You think this was all fun and party, look at these."

John hesitated before picking them up. He read them and afterward set the pages down gently. "So what do you want?" he asked.

Ross sat back down and gripped the arms of the chair. "John," he said, "you did this? Why on earth? I'm thinking of these women and the desperation and shame they feel. I…I don't understand. I just don't."

At that moment the receptionist knocked and came into John's office. "Mr. Knox," she said, casting a suspicious glance at Ross, "your next appointment is here."

John waved a hand at her. "I can't see anyone just now," he was nearly shouting. "Reschedule. Just reschedule."

The woman backed out of the office and closed the door.

John rose from his chair and turned to the window. "It all started as a lark," he said, his back to Ross. "A little getaway with some pretty girls to spend a few hours away from the routine and boredom. That's all. But then the temptation to take the next step was too enticing. And the girls, they didn't seem to mind, not really. We all had fun…I thought."

"Bullshit!" Ross said. "That's crap, and you know it. Your power over them, the money, the influence. You backed them into a corner they couldn't get out of. You boxed them in between you and their husbands and…and decent lives. God, John, it's just awful."

John turned from the window. "I know," he said. "I've known all along, even while I was seduced into the excitement and the diversion. Jesus." He slumped back into his chair. "What do I do now?"

"I'll tell what you're going to do, John. You call off these other men," Ross began. "That's first. Or else, John. Or else I'll make their lives an open book. And yours, too. Tell Smythe and Clemson Hardway that prominence has its price. You tell them that, just tell them that. These women's lives have been scarred. Now it's over."

John sat with his elbows propped up on his desk. "All right," he said, sighing. "Okay, it's over. I'll take care of it."

"What I can't tell you," Ross said, "is how you face Anna. And Maybelle."

John looked up. His eyes were red and his face drained. "Oh god," he said and held his face in his hands. "Please, Ross. They can't know."

Another knock came, and the office door opened partially. A portly, bald-headed man Ross knew to be Stanley Chapman, stuck his head in. "Uh, John," he said, "thought I'd let you know that I'm heading out." He cast a quick look at Ross.

John nodded and raised a hand. "Okay, Stan, see you tomorrow."

Chapman remained in the doorway and cleared his throat. "So okay," he said. "Everything going okay?"

John turned in his law partner's direction and mustered a smile. "No, everything's fine. Just finishing up here. See you tomorrow," he repeated.

Chapman raised a hand, said goodbye, and closed the door slowly.

"Your partners in on this?" Ross asked.

"No." John shook his head firmly. "Don't have a clue."

Ross leaned back in the chair, stretched his legs, and blew a big breath out. "John," he said, "my god, it's going to unravel. You know that. What are you—"

"I know, I know. Damn it, Ross. I know."

"Why? That's what I keeping asking myself," Ross said. "Said you were bored. You tired of Anna or what?"

John sat upright and placed both hands, palm down, on the desk. "Enough," he said. "I don't want any more censure from you…please, Ross."

Ross fell silent and watched his father-in-law work his jaw muscles and breathe in short emphatic bursts. For several minutes neither man spoke, each struggling with his own thoughts.

John would look at Ross then close his eyes and turn away; he did that three times before he heaved a sigh and spoke.

"Gordon McKenzie," he began. "The Colonel, damn his soul. Came up with the idea of—god, I can hardly say it—of inviting some gals to run on down to Reno with few a fellas for a fun little weekend. Seemed frivolous at the time, not yet disgraceful, which it was. Smythe, he calls me up and cajoles me with his good-time Charlie don't-be-a-spoilsport pitch. Pretty quick, it was like I'd agreed. Was the same as going to a football game with the guys—no big deal. Boys' night out, a little innocent fun." He shook his head. "Told Anna, my sweet Anna, told her I was going to a law conference. In Reno. Damn!" He turned in his chair then back. "Soon as I told that white lie, something curdled in my gut. Then being with them, these cute young women, was fun. I enjoyed being a Big Daddy for a weekend. Hell, we all did. Their fresh faces, high spirits, and all the time looking to us as… shit…as important men with all the answers. Ludicrous. But the temptation was there to not let that feeling go."

"John," Ross said, "we're all of us tempted. I'm sure as hell no saint on that. Been so close to it my eyebrows got singed. But, boy, do you make me glad I pulled up short."

John's smile was bitter. "Lucky you."

"Did you…John, did you go to bed with…" Ross said and paused.

"Yes," John said. "Did. Sure."

"Were there complications?" Ross asked. "I mean, like with Mona Johnson?"

John looked at him, eyes steady and leaden. "One other time. Girl asked for help that time—pleaded really. Terrified about what her husband would do because she couldn't have gotten pregnant by him. Guess he didn't want kids and always wore protection. We took care of it."

"Anna," Ross said. "What are you going to do?"

John's face had aged in half an hour. His shoulders dropped. "I can't tell her about this," he said. "It would kill her, just kill her. She doesn't deserve this. Give me time, Ross. I need time to sort this out."

"John," Ross said, "she's not going to hear about this from me. Of course, you have at least six other people out there to worry about. Seems like they all have to keep their mouths shut, but all pipes leak over time." Ross shifted his weight in the chair. "And Maybelle, I'm not telling her either, not names anyhow, but I need to tell her the scope of this…because, well, because I have some fence-mending of my own to do with your daughter." The thought of his own fixation sent a chill across his shoulders.

"All right," John said. "Thank you for that. But damn it to hell!" He suddenly picked up the coffee mug on his desk and threw it across the room. It hit the bookcase, bounced off the spine of a law book, and dropped onto the carpet, where the dregs in the cup dribbled out.

"You know," Ross said, "old Neville and Kribs are always so cocksure about snooping out the dirt, about anything that could reflect on good old ALC. They have a clue about this?"

"Nope, we closed the loop, just us four," John said with no satisfaction.

"Would've thought for sure Kribs would be in on this," Ross said. "A real fit."

"Not on your life," John said. "His flapping mouth, no sir. The Colonel was the one who put the kibosh on Kribs." He paused. "Wish he'd done the same to me."

"Yeah."

"You know," John said, "if it wasn't for that truckload of explosives, this whole mess would never have been brought to light."

Ross rose to leave. "Tell those girls that."

27

When Ross exited the U.S. National Bank Building, he discovered that it had sprinkled while he was inside, not much, but it settled the dust and smelled good. It was the second week of October; it hadn't reached sixty degrees. He took a deep breath, shuddered, and went straight home.

Maybelle was curious when Ross coaxed her from the kitchen, sat her down in the living room, and made them both martinis. He straddled the ottoman and sat down in front of her. She asked what he was doing. He looked into her unsuspecting face and spoke to her in a tone that drove the giggle from her throat. He told her many things. He told her how the board meeting had gone and how the enigma of the missing money was to be set right. He told her of Kribs's deplorable treatment of Mona Johnson's mother and how that was to be set right. He said these things with his hands held out as a prayer or maybe a cleaver—the emphasis could be whatever she felt it to be. He spoke with clarity and conviction. Maybelle was puzzled at being captivated by Ross, but she was, by what seemed a transformation. At that moment, the man on the ottoman was someone else, someone who had dropped by—like a new neighbor, or someone she used to know and had always admired.

She held out her glass at one point, and he made her another drink. "You're not you," she said when he handed the glass back. "Should I be frightened of this stranger in my house?" Her voice rose in a tease.

"Still me, or maybe I've decided to be me again," he said. "Or finally."

She sank back more in the chair, a tiny smile forming on her mouth. "All this mess, it's made you more assured or something. Certain—you seem certain," she said. "Think that's it?"

"Don't know." He moved to the couch, looked across at her, and considered how to proceed with what he had yet to disclose.

She emptied her glass in one swallow and set it on the lamp table next to her chair. "Baggy, my man of mystery," she said with a flourish.

"May," he said. "There's something more."

"Ooh, can't wait," she teased.

"This is serious," he said.

"What is it?" she asked, her eyes steady on his face, her smiled erased.

Ross breathed in and let it escape slowly. And very quietly, he began to tell her of four women and four men and their degrading circumstances. He had to. He couldn't keep it to himself, not all of it anyway. He wanted his wife to know the story, to know that he had done right by those women and to then hope he might begin to expunge the guilt over his own ignoble temptations. He spoke not of his father-in-law, nor did he tell her the other names he knew. She accepted his reasoning when he told her he couldn't tell her names, that it was the only way to close out the miserable situation. Maybelle sighed audibly and had tears in her eyes when he had said all he had to say. They sat with their own thoughts for a time. Finally Ross rose, collected the empty martini glasses, and took them into the kitchen.

Maybelle came to him when he was rinsing the glasses in the sink and put her arms around him. He turned around, wiped his hands on his pants, and kissed her; and she kissed him back, really kissed him, like the kisses they left behind in college. He said *My, my,* she sighed a soft laugh, and he led her upstairs.

They undressed one another slowly; laughed at the buttons that wouldn't cooperate and the zippers that balked. They began by laying each piece of clothing on the bed as they disrobed until Maybelle swung her brassiere over her head and let it sail. Ross laughed and threw his boxer shorts over his shoulder, and they were naked, intentionally—not as those neutral persons who strolled around the bedroom with no clothes on, moving by rote and routine.

He was really seeing her in the way he used to, warming and feeling arousal. Of course, she had changed. Her breasts were fuller; there was more flesh on her hips and buttocks and gentle mileage around the eyes—and yet she was still beautiful. But then he could grasp a handful of flab at his waist and pat a little potbelly; only weight lifting had kept his stomach from growing into one of those preggy bellies he saw on other men. That hadn't prevented falling follicles and the ensuing exposed scalp.

"I must still look okay when the light's dim," she teased. "Bring any vials with you?"

"Should have become a man of mystery long time back," he said.

They got into bed from his side and rolled and twisted in an awkward over and under syncopation to get into that familiar position and laughed when they thunked heads. Their laughter calmed to smiling hums, and they lay quiet for a time until their breathing and their contours were in sync. The best part was their hands exploring each other and their kisses. It was like the first times in Minnesota—no, better—but like that. Ross had not entered her with such tender slowness in a long time. Having sex when he knew she was with him, when he knew they were together, that had happened so far back that it was not even a memory. He lay above her, and when she came he rested on his elbows and felt the same oneness that used to be; it was a quiet intensity. Ross followed her soundless shudder, and they lay together glistening and breathing deeply. He kissed her cheek, and when she smiled and nestled against him, her eyes closed, he wondered if he had at last fallen in love with her—again.

He smelled the familiarity of her hair and felt the scar on her buttock from a childhood fall and decided that the oneness of being known only comes with time and the stress marks they had made together. As Maybelle lay beside him, breathing slowly and drifting off, he wondered if this moment would hold until morning, if it were only an aberration or the martinis, after all.

The next morning, Ross awakened early, kissed Maybelle's smiling, drowsy lips, and left for the Foundation office without taking time for breakfast. The phone rang right after he arrived, but there seemed to be no one on the line. He hung up, and a few minutes later the door to the outer office opened. When he went to look, a large-bodied man with a reddish complexion and thinning blondish hair was standing, wide-legged. His eyes were open wide as if he had just been startled.

"You Bagby?" the man asked.

"I am," Ross answered. "How are you, Mr. Hardway?"

"You know me?" the man said, narrowing his eyes.

"I do," Ross said. "Clemson Hardway, G.M. of Douglas Diesel. Neville Armbruster introduced us once. Out at the country club?"

Hardway stood mute for a moment. "Yeah, okay, remember that."

"What can I do for you?" Ross asked, swallowing back a tingling nervousness.

Hardway straightened, and the short-sleeved white shirt he wore tightened across his chest. "Look here," he said, lowering his voice. "You're sticking your nose where it doesn't belong. John Knox called me, gave me a heads-up about your meddling."

"That right? Then he told you this business—with the women—he told you it's over," Ross said. "Has to stop."

The big man spun around in a circle and faced Ross again. "He told me, yeah, he told me. Said something about you blabbing about us...and the women. Well Mister, they damn well enjoy it. Never had it so good. Party time, money—shit they love it."

"No they don't." Ross said. "*You* love it, they deplore it."

"Nah," said Hardway, "and let me tell you, buddy, you keep your nose out of things none of your business. Get my meaning?"

Ross stepped forward, looking up at the bigger man, nerves raging. "No, you listen," he said. "That day at the country club you and your friend Smythe told me to be good to my wife Maybelle or you'd run me out of town. Unless you stop this despicable treatment of those women, you'll be the one ridden out of town. How would your employer react to his general manager being one of the most disgusting men in town? Your wife, she know about this? You have children?"

"Goddamn it," Hardway erupted, his faced growing even more florid, "you just better not..."

"Or Mr. Smythe?" Ross added. "How would his social status change if this lurid affair were known? So stop it—now! And don't contact any of those women. Don't. I'll know if you do. I'll let them know that they are free of you *gentlemen*. Now get the hell out of my office!"

Hardway stumbled back, opened and closed his mouth twice, but didn't say anything. After a moment he yanked the door open and stumbled off down the corridor. Ross immediately called John Knox, who took the call. He sounded like hell to Ross; his voice was but a whisper, and lifeless. He cursed when told of Hardway's visit and promised Ross the matter would be handled this time. Ross said there must be absolutely no contact with the women, got no argument, and asked how his father-in-law was doing. "How the hell do you think?" was the answer just before John hung up.

The café was in a lull between the breakfast rush and coffee break time when Ross came in. He greeted Blanche, who walked past arms loaded with plates of eggs and pancakes. Jill was behind the counter thumbing through her sales slips from breakfast. He caught her eye and motioned that he was going to the back booth. She froze for a moment then nodded. A couple of minutes later she set a cup of coffee on the table and scooted in opposite him. She was anxious but waited while Ross doctored his coffee.

He sipped from his cup and set it down softly. "Hell of a thing," he said. Jill didn't say anything back. "Just a hell of a thing," Ross repeated. "Now look, Jill, I don't want to get involved with them—the women. Okay?"

She nodded and stared at him intently.

His stomach fluttered having her eyes trained on him that way; he couldn't help it. But he shook it off, took another drink of coffee, and cleared his throat. "Has to be that way. No heart-to-heart chats, none of that."

"Okay," she said.

"Has to be," he said again. "I couldn't take it."

"Okay, I understand," she said. "Ross, what is it?"

"It's over," he said, "over and done with."

"Really?" A smile slowly formed. "It's really over, for sure?"

"Yes," he said, matching her smile.

"But," she began then paused to look over her shoulder. "But what…I mean, what can I tell them?"

"There will be no more contact from the men, none," he said. "And for god's sake tell them not to call these guys, or write to them—nothing. See them on the street, walk the other way. It's done. If any of these men tries to get in touch or anything, you let me know, and I'll act on it. But all bets are off if one of these gals makes contact on her own. No stupid stunts or thoughts like Mona of riding off into the sunset with one of these jerks. Won't happen."

"Oh, Ross," Jill said and put her hands over her mouth, "you did it. You really did it. I could kiss you."

He smiled. "And that would be nice, but not good."

"I know," she said and reached out to pat his hand. "How's Maybelle?"

"She's good."

They laughed, then Ross let Jill hug him, and he left the café. It was warm outside and the sounds of the town continuing to rebound filled the air, but he felt and heard none of it. How could he? The celebration in his head was superior to all else.

EPILOGUE

The annual Umpqua Women's Golf Tournament was held beneath clear skies and temperatures in the high sixties. It was more evidence that in the aftermath of the blast Roseburg was made of strong stuff and was picking up the pieces and moving on. Maybelle ran the event with the flawless outcome of a successful military campaign. Ross attended every moment, applauding her, running errands, and basking in her accomplishment. They kept each other in sight much of the time, exchanging silly grins and waving and sharing hugs and kisses when they happened to be in the same place at the same time. He was proud and told her so, again and again.

When the last trophy had been awarded and the final round of applause given to sponsors and the committee, Ross slipped outside and waited for his wife in the cooling evening air. He heard his name and turned to see Neville coming toward him out of the shadows.

"Neville," Ross said. He tried to smile away the flutter in his stomach; it was the first face-to-face between them since the Foundation board showdown.

"My favorite niece did herself proud, I'd say," Neville said.

"She did," Ross agreed. "Very proud of her."

"As you should be, as you should be." Neville fell silent as he lit up a cigarette. "Been wanting to talk to you, Ross."

"No time like the present," Ross said.

Neville looked at the burning ember of his cigarette. "Been biding my time," he said. "We've been in a bad spell all the way around."

"Yes," Ross said, "we have at that."

"Damn explosion, started everything," Neville said.

"It was plenty bad on its own, don't you think?"

Neville drew on his cigarette. "Sure enough. Bad time, no arguing that. What I mean is, and I think you get my drift, the thing with the Colonel, the woman, the money, all that blew up when that damn truck exploded."

"True," Ross said, "but it was there all along. Those things would have come to light eventually, don't you think?"

"Oh sure, oh sure, you're probably right. But it might not have been so messy."

"You mean you'd have controlled the *sleaze* factor?" Ross asked.

Neville chuckled. "I told you too much, I fear. But yes, I've thought on that and I do think I could have handled it all more discreetly, shall I say."

"Maybe. But sleaze under the carpet is still sleaze. Bound to start smelling on its own."

Neville dropped his spent cigarette and put a heel into it. "You don't think much of me, do you? Think I'm a hard-nosed bastard, don't you? Unscrupulous even?"

"I've had those thoughts," Ross said with a smile. "There was a time I was in your cross hairs and you were ready to pull the trigger. I was disposable. Armbruster's first, right?"

"Well, I bluff a lot, Ross. Bluster and bluff."

"Never get me to believe that," Ross said.

"So where's that leave us then, you and me? We're family, got to find a way to get by, don't we?

"Family, but not blood," Ross said.

"Oh now see, you have to forget that now, Ross. We have to start somewhere, don't we?"

"So Maybelle, she give you a good tongue-lashing, did she?" Ross asked.

Neville hesitated then chuckled. "We had words, and your name came up."

"And?"

"Well, Mrs. Bagby, she told me if I didn't mend my ways where you're concerned, I would be out of her life," Neville said. "And I can't have that. I love that girl."

"Mrs. Bagby?" Ross said.

"That's what she called herself, as I recall." Neville laughed. "You need an explosion more often, Ross. Things have sure gotten a hell of a lot better for you since."

"I'll have to find another way," Ross said. "Don't want my town to ever blow up again."

"So I can tell Mazie that you and I are going to come to terms?"

Ross waited a moment. "Tell her we're opening negotiations."

"You forced us to do the right thing," Neville said. "I'm beginning to appreciate that—and you. Maybelle, she did all right after all, bringing you all the way from Omaha."

"North Platte," Ross chided.

"Sorry," Neville said with a smile. "Well, Ross, as Wendell Kribs might say—if he was still with us—enjoy being Foundation *dye-wreck-tore*. Jonah and Emeline did good tapping you to take the job permanent."

They shook hands, and Ross watched Neville walk away and join his wife; Nelda had been standing back waiting. She gave Ross a small wave, and they walked toward the parking lot. Soon he heard the whine of the Cadillac's starter and watched until the big car's taillights blinked once then moved out onto Garden Valley Boulevard.

Just before Halloween, Jonah Armbruster passed away. In spite of his decades of a bigger-than-life presence, there was no grand funeral; that was his wish, along with being cremated. The family drove back into a stand of old growth timber that Jonah had preserved, to a spot that he loved. There was a quiet time of remembrance, and then his ashes were spread near the base of a huge Douglas fir, ancient and hoary.

Late in November of that year, John and Anna Knox moved to Portland, where John joined a law firm. It was all polished over as a unique opportunity to finish his career by practicing in a large city for a few years, something John had always wanted to do. Poor Anna, shocked and teary, brave but clueless, left her beautiful home. Before he moved on, John called his son-in-law; they spoke briefly of the future, and John reflected on leaving Ross behind as the trustee of his transgressions. His fellow transgressors managed to hunker down and keep low profiles. Ross never heard again from the young women, nor did he want to.

Ironically, that same month Germaine McKenzie was appointed to the board of the Douglas Community Hospital, a post the Colonel had held before her. *Let the myth live on*, Ross reasoned. And Jill was gone from the Snappy Service Café, having joined her anonymous boyfriend, Tony, in Alaska. She called Ross the day she left town. They met at the café, had one last cup of coffee together, laughed, and shed a tear or two. Afterward, Ross walked her to her car. The Chevrolet was loaded with all she owned; it sat low on its springs. Ross wondered aloud if the car could make it all the way to Anchorage. Jill said, "Who knows?" then gave him a big hug, a kiss on the cheek and drove out of town.

On a Friday that December, two weeks before Christmas, Maybelle and Ross celebrated their thirteenth wedding anniversary by downing many beers with Monte Coe at the Timber Room. Maybelle instantly liked Monte, and he her; both chided Ross that neither was like the person he had described to them. Ross said he didn't know what the hell they were talking about, and ordered more beer.

A lesser city might have died on the spot and been consumed in its own funeral pyre. Roseburg rose to the occasion.

The Oregonian, August 7, 1960

BIOGRAPHICAL NOTES ON
The Author

George Byron Wright was born in The Dalles, Oregon. Along with his mother and brother, he migrated to three other small Oregon towns as his father pursued the life of a mortician. Living in Baker City, Tillamook and Roseburg endowed him with a lifelong fondness for small places.

Following a lengthy career in the not-for-profit sector, during which time he wrote professionally, publishing books on management and board development, George returned to his love of fiction. In 1996 he began work on what has become his "Oregon Trio", three novels set in the small towns of his youth. Baker City 1948 was published in 2005, followed by Tillamook 1952 in 2006, and now Roseburg 1959, completes this unique body of work.

George lives with his wife and first reader, Betsy, in Portland, Oregon.

503-223-0268 • FAX: 503-223-3083

GEORGEC3PUB@COMCAST.NET • WWW.C3PUBLICATIONS.COM

ORDER MORE COPIES OF THIS BOOK
AND OTHER TITLES FROM C3 PUBLICATIONS

Fiction Titles

Tillamook 1952

On August 24, 1933, Verlin Lundigun is helping fight the fiercest of forest fires when he catches a piece of pitch-fired flaming tree trunk with his face. He lives but later dies from a gunshot. Eighteen years later a nephew is driven to find out why and how his uncle died.

ISBN 0-9632655-3-9, 288 pages, $15.95 + S&H

Baker City 1948

In Baker City, Oregon in 1948, nine-year-old Philip Wade faces adult realities over the violent death of a local schoolteacher and his father's surprising defense of the accused.

ISBN 0-9632655-2-0 200 pages, $13.95 + S&H

Roseburg 1959

A truckload of explosives guts Roseburg, Oregon at 1:14 a.m. on August 7, 1959, and Ross Bagby stands at the edge the conflagration unaware that his so-called life is about to go up in the flames. On all fronts, he is tested against circumstances beyond his control. He has been living a life of acquiescence—now he will discover what he's made of.

ISBN 978-0-9632655-4-8 272 pages, $15.95 + S&H

Nonfiction Titles

Beyond Nominating: A Guide to Gaining and Sustaining Successful Not-For-Profit Boards

This popular manual is a road map to attracting the competent, leadership every not-for-profit organization needs. Includes 25 forms, model documents, worksheets and guidelines. Written by former not-for-profit executive, George B. Wright, who applies his 40 years of experience in the volume.

ISBN 0-9632655-1-2, 87 pages, paper, $25.00+ S&H.

The Not-For-Profit CEO: A Survivor's Manual

Before you recruit another board member, raise another dollar, or prepare your next budget, read this book. Apply the author's six management checkpoints: 1) Managing a Democracy, 2) Search & Deploy, 3) Relate, Relate, Facilitate, 4) Dollars In, Dollars Out, 5) Out and About, and 6) Wide Angle Lens.

ISBN 0-96322655-0-4, 138 pages, paper, $11.95+ S&H.

COPY THIS ORDER FORM

NOTE: Order our books through your local bookstore, on our website using PayPal, or by completing this form and mailing your payment using check or money order.

Qty	Title	Amt
_____	Roseburg 1959 ($15.95)	_____
_____	Tillamook 1952 ($15.95)	_____
_____	Baker City 1948 ($13.95)	_____
_____	Beyond Nominating ($25)	_____
_____	The Not-For-Profit CEO ($11.95)	_____
_____ Total Amount of Order		_____
_____ Shipping & handling (add $4 for 1st book, _____ plus $1 for each add'l book)		_____
_____ TOTAL PAYMENT ENCLOSED		_____

Order now from our website: Send Mail Orders to:
www.C3Publications.com   C3 Publications
503-223-0268   3495 NW Thurman St.
Fax: 223-3083   Portland, OR 97210
georgec3pub@comcast.net

Colophon

The text of this book is set in highly readable Minion Pro, an Adobe Type Foundry OpenType version of the typeface rendered by Robert Slimbach and inspired, according to the foundry, by "classical, old style typefaces of the late Renaissance." Titling, drop caps, and folios are set in Impact Lt Std. Principal tools were the programs of Adobe Creative Suite 2 on a Macintosh computer system.